THE INVISIBLE MAN FROM SALEM

Christoffer Carlsson

Translated by Michael Gallagher

SCRIBE
Melbourne • London

Scribe Publications
18–20 Edward St, Brunswick, Victoria, Australia 3056
2 John St, Clerkenwell, London, WC1N 2ES, United Kingdom

Originally published in Swedish as *Den Osynlige Mannen Från Salem* by Piratförlagets 2013
First published in English by Scribe 2015, by agreement with Pontas Literary & Film Agency
This edition published by Scribe 2016

Typeset in Dante by the publishers
Printed and bound in the UK by CPI Group (UK) Ltd, Croydon CR0 4YY

Scribe Publications is committed to the sustainable use of natural resources and
the use of paper products made responsibly from those resources.

9781925106466 (Australian edition)
9781925228786 (UK edition)
9781925113655 (e-book)

CiP records for this title are available from the British Library and
the National Library of Australia.

scribepublications.com.au
scribepublications.co.uk

To Karl, Martin, and Tobias

I'm hanging around outside your door, just like I used to all those years ago. Only it's not your door, you're not here. Haven't been here for a long time. I know this because I am following you. I'm the only one here. And I'm not even really here. You don't know me. Nobody knows me, not anymore. No one knows who I am.

You can sense that something isn't right, that something is about to happen. You remember the times recorded on these pages, but you choose to push them away. Isn't that right? I know this, because I'm just like you. Those few times the past turns up in your everyday life, you do recognise it. You recognise it but you're not sure what was true and what wasn't because everything gets blurred over time.

I am writing this to tell you that everything you think is true, but not necessarily in the way you think. I'm doing this to tell you all that I know.

I

SWEDEN MUST DIE. The words are daubed on the wall of the tunnel, in thick black capitals. There's music coming from a nearby shop, and outside the tunnel the sun is shining, warm and white, but in here it's cool, quiet. A woman with headphones and a ponytail passes by, jogging. I watch her until she disappears.

From somewhere a child appears, running along holding a balloon. The balloon is bobbing jerkily and excitedly on a string behind him, until it hits something sharp in the roof of the tunnel and bursts. The boy looks scared and starts to cry, perhaps because of the loud noise, but probably not. He turns around like he's looking for someone, but there's no one there.

I'm in Salem, visiting for the first time in ages. It's the end of the summer. I get up from the bench and walk past the child, out of the gloom and into the bright sunshine.

II

When I wake up it's dark, and I just know that something has happened. Out of the corner of my eye I see something flashing. Across the road, the wall of the building opposite is struck by a bright-blue flashing light. I get out of bed and go to the kitchenette, drink a glass of water, and pop a Serax pill on my tongue. I've been dreaming about Viktor and Sam.

With the empty glass in my hand I go over to the balcony and open the door. The wind, warm but damp, makes me shudder, and I can see the world that's waiting down there. An ambulance and two police cars are grouped outside the entrance. Someone is pulling blue-and-white incident tape between two streetlamps. I hear muted voices, the crackling of a police radio, and see the silent flashing of the police cars' blue lights. And beyond that is the hum of a million people, the sound of a big city in temporary slumber.

I go back in and pull on a pair of jeans, button a shirt, and run my fingers through my hair. In the entrance hall I hear a fan spinning somewhere behind a wall, the muted rustle of clothes, a quiet, mumbling voice. Someone pushes the button to call the old lift down, and it starts its descent with a mechanical crunch, making the whole shaft vibrate.

'Can't we shut that bloody lift off?' someone hisses.

The lift masks the sound of my footsteps as I make my way down the staircase that winds itself around the lift-shaft. I stop at the second floor and wait. Below me, on the first floor, something has happened. Not for the first time.

4

A few years back, the large apartment was bought by a charity with the help of a donation from someone who had more money than he needed. The group remodelled the apartment into a hostel for down-and-outs, and named it Chapmansgården. It is visited at least once a week, usually by jaded bureaucrats sent by Social Services, but quite often by the police. The hostel is run by a former social worker, Matilda or Martina — I can't remember her name. She's old, but commands more respect than most police officers.

As I look over the bannister I see that the heavy wooden door of the hostel is open. The lights are on in there. An irritated male voice is being soothed by a softer one, a woman's. The lift passes me on its way to the first floor, hiding me from view as I follow it down. The two police officers standing there freeze when they catch sight of me. They're young — much younger than me. The lift stops on the ground floor, and suddenly it all goes very quiet.

'Watch your step,' says the woman.

'Put the tape up,' he says, and holds out the roll of incident tape, to which she responds with a stare.

'You put it up, and I'll take care of him.'

She has taken her cap off and is holding it in her hand; her hair is up, in a tight ponytail that makes her face look stretched. The man has a square jaw and kind eyes, but I think both officers are quite shaken because they're constantly looking at their watches. On the shoulders of their uniforms are single gold crowns, with no stripes. Constables.

He walks towards the staircase with the roll of tape in his hand. I try to smile. 'Listen, something has happened here,' says the woman. 'I'd like you to stay in the building.'

'I'm not going out.'

'What are you doing down here, then?'

I look at the stairwell window, which is large and looks out at the house over the road that is still soaked in blue light.

'I woke up.'

'You were woken by the flashing lights?'

I nod, unsure what she's thinking. She looks surprised. I detect a sour smell, and only now do I notice how pale she is, that her eyes are bloodshot. She's just been sick.

She tilts her head ever so slightly, almost imperceptibly, and furrows her brow.

'Have we met before?'

'I don't think so.'

'Are you sure?'

'I'm a policeman,' I venture, 'but ... no, I don't think we've met.'

She looks at me for a long time before pulling out her notepad from her breast pocket and flipping through it, then clicking her pen and jotting something down. Behind me, her colleague wrestles clumsily with the tape in a way that gets on my nerves. I look at the door behind the woman. It shows no sign of having been forced.

'I had no information about any police officers living here. What's your name?'

'Leo,' I say. 'Leo Junker. What's happened here?'

'What department are you with, Leo?' she continues, in a tone that reveals she's far from convinced I'm telling the truth.

'IA.'

'IA?'

'Internal Aff—'

'I know what it stands for. May I see your ID?'

'It's in my coat, up there in my flat,' I say, and her gaze moves over my shoulder, as though she is trying to make eye contact with her colleague. 'Do you know who she is?' I chance. 'The body.'

'I ...' she starts. 'So, you know what's happened?'

I'm not really that observant, but it's pretty rare for men to use the hostel. They have other places to go to. Women, on the other hand, don't have that many hostels to choose from, since most places turn away anyone using drugs or involved in prostitution. Women are generally allowed to do one or the other, but not both. The problem is, of course, that most of the women *do* do both. Chapmansgården is an exception, which means that lots of women come here. This place has just one rule when it comes to being allowed in: you mustn't be carrying a weapon. It's a generous attitude.

So the chances are it's a woman, and, judging by the commotion, she's no longer alive.

'May I …?' I say, and take a step towards her.

'We're waiting for Forensics.' I hear her colleague's voice behind me.

'Is Martina there?'

'Who?' says the woman, confused, and looks at her notepad.

'The one who runs the shelter,' I answer. 'We're friends.'

'You mean Matilda?'

'Yes. Exactly.'

I step out of my shoes, pick them up, and walk past her into the hostel.

'Excuse me!' she says sharply, grabbing my arm. 'You stay here.'

'I just want to know how my friend is,' I say.

'You don't even know her name.'

'I know how to move around a crime scene. I just want to know that Matilda is okay.'

'That's irrelevant. You're not coming in.'

'Two minutes.'

The policewoman stares at me for some time before she lets go of my arm and looks at her watch again. Someone is knocking on the door downstairs, forcefully and sharply. She looks for her colleague, who's moved up the stairs and is now out of sight.

'Wait here,' she says, and I nod and smile, doing my best to look sincere.

THE WORLD SEEMS hauntingly quiet inside Chapmansgården. The roof hangs low above my head; the floor is an ugly, rutted parquet. The hostel comprises a large hall, a breakfast room with a kitchen, a toilet and shower, an office, and what I assume is the dormitory, furthest from the entrance. The smell brings to mind what you'd expect to find in an old man's wardrobe. Just inside the door there's a big basket, and beside it a hand-written sign: WARM CLOTHES. A pair of gloves are sticking out from underneath a hooded top; I pull them out.

A little way down on the right, off the large hall, there's a neat, tidy kitchen with a square, wooden table and a couple of chairs. At the table, Matilda, the old bird, with her pointy features and fuzzy silver curls, is sitting opposite a man in police uniform. She seems to be answering questions in a quiet, composed voice. They look up as I go past, and I nod to Matilda.

'You from Violent Crime?' he asks.

'Sure.'

He looks at the gloves in my hand and I look down, and I notice the pronounced shoe-prints that are visible on the floor. It's not a boot, more like a trainer of some sort. I put my own shoe alongside the print, noticing that I have the same-size feet as whoever's just been here.

'Where are the other women?'

'She was the only one here,' says Matilda.

'Do you recognise her?'

'She's been here several times this summer. I think her name's Rebecka.'

'Rebecka with a "ck"?'

'I don't know, but I think it's a "cc".'

'And her surname?'

She shakes her head.

'As I said, I don't even know how she spells her first name.'

I carry on down the hall and into the dorm. The walls are sickly yellow, covered in pictures. A window is ajar, allowing the August night to seep in and making the room unusually cool. There are eight beds, arranged along both sides of the room. The bedclothes don't match: some are floral like the walls of a Seventies apartment; others are in bright colours — blue, orange, and green; still others have ugly, insipid patterns. Each bed is marked with a number, clumsily carved into the wood. In bed 7, second from the far wall, lies a body with its back to me, clothed in bleached jeans and a knitted jumper. Unkempt, dark hair is just visible. I leave my shoes on one of the beds and put the gloves on.

People shoot, stab, hit, kick, chop, drown, and strangle each other, attack each other with acid, and run each other over. The results vary from being as discreet and effective as a surgical intervention to being as messy as a mediaeval execution. This time, life has ended suddenly and neatly, almost unremarkably.

If it wasn't for the little maroon flower adorning her temple, she could be asleep. She's young, between twenty and twenty-five — maybe five years older than that — but a hard life leaves its mark on a person's face. I lean over her to get a better look at the entry wound. It's slightly bigger than the head of a drawing-pin, and the traces of blood and black dust from the weapon speckle her forehead. Someone has stood behind her with a small-calibre pistol.

I look at her pockets. They appear to be empty. Her clothes seem undisturbed; a glimpse of her vest is visible under the knitted jumper, but nothing suggests that her body has been searched, that someone was looking for something. I carefully place my hands on the body and feel along her side, shoulders, and back, hoping to find something that shouldn't be there. As I roll up the knitted sleeve, I notice the results of intravenous drug use, but they look neater than usual — she'd almost turned meticulous shooting-up into a competitive sport.

I hear Matilda's footsteps behind me. She stops in the doorway, as though scared to come in.

'The window,' I ask. 'Is it always open?'

'No, we usually keep it closed. It wasn't open when I arrived.'

'Was she dealing?'

'I think so. She got here about an hour ago and said she needed somewhere to stay. Most of the women usually come a bit later.'

'Did she have anything with her? Clothes, bag?'

'Nothing apart from what she's wearing.'

'Are those her own clothes?'

'I think so.' She sniffs. 'She didn't get them from us, anyway.'

'Did she have any shoes?'

'By the bed.'

They're black Converse sneakers, with white laces way too thick for them. She must have bought those later and replaced the original ones. They're lumpy and split — she's been hiding pills inside them. I hold up one of the shoes and inspect the sole, nondescript and grey, before carefully putting it back. I get my phone out and point it towards her face, take a picture, and for a split second the phone's tiny flash makes her skin painfully white.

'How did she seem when she got here this evening?'

'High and tired, like everyone else who comes here. She said she'd had a bad evening and just wanted to sleep.'

'Where were you when it happened?' I ask.

'I was washing up, with my back to the door, so I didn't see or hear anything. I always do it about this time; it's the only chance I get.'

'How did you discover she was dead?'

'I went in to see if she'd fallen asleep. When I went over to close the window I saw that she ...'

She doesn't finish the sentence.

I walk in a wide arc around the body, over to the window. It's quite high up — it would take a serious jump to reach Chapmansgatan, down on the pavement below. I look again at the body, and in the light from the streetlamp something is glittering in her hand, like a small chain.

'She's got something in her hand,' I say to Matilda, who looks puzzled.

From the hall I hear a voice I recognise. I take a last look at the body before I pick up my shoes and follow Matilda back into the hall, where I meet Gabriel Birck. I haven't seen him in a long time, but he looks the same, with his suntanned face and his dark, close-cropped hair. Birck has the kind of hair that makes you want to change your shampoo, and he's wearing an understated black suit, like he's just been yanked away from a party.

'Leo,' he says, surprised. 'What the hell are you doing here?'

'I … woke up.'

'Aren't you suspended?'

'On leave.'

'Badge, Leo,' he says, tightening his lips to an ashen line. 'If you don't have your badge, you need to get out of here.'

'It's in my wallet, which is in my flat.'

'Go and get it.'

'I was just leaving,' I say, holding up my shoes.

Birck observes me silently with a grey stare, and I put the gloves back and go towards the door and out into the stairwell again. The policewoman looks startled as I walk past her.

'How the hell did he get in here?' is the last thing I hear from inside the hostel.

Instead of going back to my place, I head down the stairs and around the lift on the ground floor, out into the dark, empty courtyard. Only when I feel the cold ground on the soles of my feet do I realise that I've still got my shoes in my hand. I put them on and light a cigarette. Above me, the high walls of the building form a frame around the night sky, and I stand there a while, alternating between smoking and chewing my thumbnail. I walk across the courtyard and unlock a door that takes me back inside, but into a different part of the building. The stairwell here is smaller and older, warmer. I go towards the entrance and out onto Pontonjärgatan.

We live in a time when people feel insecure among strangers. Somewhere close by, there's the sound of heavy, throbbing dance music. Pontonjär's Park is in front of me, silent and full of shadows; some distance away, the noise of screeching brakes is followed by the sound of an engine cutting out. At the crossing, a man and woman stand arguing, and the last thing I see before I head off is how one raises a hand to the other. I think about how they are hurting each other, about the dead woman in bed 7 and the little object that glittered in her hand, about the words I saw on the tunnel wall earlier today — Sweden must die' — and I think that whoever believes that and wrote it might be right.

I TURN ONTO Chapmansgatan again and light another cigarette; I need to keep my hands busy. The mute blue lights drift across the wall and disappear, again and again. More uniformed police are moving around outside the building now, busy cordoning off parts of the road, diverting traffic and pedestrians. The police wave people on forcefully and irritably. Bright white light from large searchlights illuminates the tarmac. A big tent is unloaded from a van, as a precaution in case it starts raining.

Chapmansgården's open window is swinging and bumping gently in the wind. Inside I can see heads sweeping past — Gabriel Birck, a forensic technician, and Matilda. Under the window the pavement is waiting to be inspected; I want to study it more closely, but the commotion in front of the house hides it from my view.

I look at my phone instead. A new day started half an hour ago. I hear the humming noise of a nearby bar, and music coming through its open windows. I put the cigarette out, turning my back on Chapmansgatan.

A LITTLE STRIP of pale tarmac links two of the larger streets on Kungsholmen. I don't know what it's called, but it's short enough that you could kick a ball from one end of the street to the other. In one of the buildings jammed along it there is a wine-red door. Written on it, in faded yellow paint, is a single word: BAR. I open it and see a head of blonde, tousled hair resting on the bar. As the door slams behind me, the head lifts slowly and the wavy hair falls down into a centre parting. Anna looks up, her eyes half-closed.

'Finally,' she mumbles, as she runs her hand through her hair. 'A customer.'

'Are you drunk?'

'Bored.'

'A bit of advertising on the door would get more people in.'

'Peter doesn't want advertising. He just wants to get rid of the place.'

BAR is owned by an uninterested thirty-something entrepreneur, whose father bought the premises in the early Eighties, turned it into a bar, and owned the place until he died. BAR was left to Peter, who, in accordance with his father's wishes, was not allowed to sell it for five years. That was four-and-a-half years ago; so, barring Armageddon, Anna has six months left behind the taps.

BAR is the sort of place you would only find if you were looking for it. Everything in here is made of wood: the counter, the floor, the ceiling, the empty tables, and the chairs that are strewn about the place. The lighting is warm with a yellow hue, making Anna's skin seem browner that it really is. She carefully dog-ears a page in her thick book and then closes it, pulls out a bottle of absinthe from a cupboard, grabs a glass, and pours what I guess is supposed to be a 20-ml measure but is in fact significantly more. It's illegal to sell the stuff, but a lot of what goes on in bars tends to be illegal.

'It's quiet in here.'

'Do you want me to put the music on? I turned it off — it was annoying me.'

I don't know what I want. Instead I sit on one of the bar stools and drink from the glass. Absinthe is the only spirit I can cope with. I only drink occasionally; but when I do, that's what I choose. I found this place early this summer; I'd been on my way home, high, and I stopped to light a cigarette. I needed to lean against the wall to keep still enough. Everything in my vision tugged leftwards the whole time, making it impossible to focus. When I finally did, and saw the word BAR on the wine-red door across the road, I was pretty sure it was a hallucination, but I stumbled over the road anyway and started banging on the door. After a while, Anna opened the door, baseball bat in hand.

I don't know how old she is. She could be twenty. Her parents own a mansion in Uppland, just north of Norrtälje. Fifteen years ago, Anna's father had started an internet business at exactly the right time, and then sold it just before the bubble burst. He invested the money in new companies, which he allowed to expand. It's this sort of manoeuvre that makes people rich nowadays. Anna fluctuates between needy self-interest and enormous contempt in her dealings with him. She's studying psychology, and works part-time at BAR, but I never see her reading textbooks. All she reads is great thick books with ambiguous covers. That's all I know about her. It's almost enough to pass as friendship.

I catch my reflection in the mirror hanging behind the bar. I look like I'm wearing borrowed clothes. I've lost weight. I'm pale for the time of year, which is a tell-tale sign that someone's been keeping a low profile. Anna puts her elbows on the bar and rests her head in her hands, looking at me with a cool gaze.

'You look awful,' she says.

'You're very perceptive.'

'Am I, hell! It's completely bloody obvious.'

I drink some absinthe.

'A woman was shot in my apartment block,' I say, putting the glass down. 'There's something about it that … bothers me.'

'In your block?'

'In a homeless shelter on the first floor. She died.'

'So somebody killed her?'

'If anyone's likely to die an untimely death in this city, it's the addicts and the whores.' I stare at the glass in front of me. 'But more often than not it's an overdose or suicide. The few who do get killed by someone else are nearly always men. This was a woman. It's unusual.' I rub my cheek and hear the scratchy sound. I could do with a shave. 'It looked so … simple. Discreet and clean. That's even more unusual, and that's what bothers me most of all.'

In the courtyard of my building there are a few kids — all one family, I think — who are always racing each other across the yard, from one side to the other, noisily, laughing, so that the sound echoes between the walls. I don't know why I'm thinking about that now, but there's something about that image, the way they look and the way they sound, that means something to me — an image of something that has been lost.

'That's not your department, is it?' Anna says. 'Investigating homicide?'

I shake my head.

'What is your department then?'

'Have I never told you?'

She laughs. Anna's mouth is symmetrical.

'You don't say much when you're here. But,' she adds, 'that's fine with me.'

'I work on internal investigations.'

I drink from the glass, realising I want another smoke.

'You investigate other police?'

'Yes.'

'I thought only sixty-year-old gents got the honour of doing that. What are you, thirty?'

'Thirty-three.'

She looks at the bar, dark and clean, then frowns and grabs a cloth, and sets about making it even cleaner.

'It is unusual,' I say. 'To get thirty-three-year-olds in IA. But it happens.'

'You must be a good cop,' she says. She puts the cloth back, and then leans against the bar.

Anna is wearing a black shirt with the arms rolled up, unbuttoned over her chest. A black piece of jewellery hangs round her neck on a thin chain. I look from the necklace to the glass, and the lighting flickers. There are no windows.

'Not exactly. I have certain faults.'

'Who doesn't?' she says. 'Are you really thirty-three?'

'Yes.'

'I thought you were younger.'

'You're lying.'

She smiles.

'Yeah. Take it as a compliment.'

I glimpse myself in the mirror again, and for a second my reflection dissolves, becomes transparent. I've been out of the game for too long. I'm not really here.

'Why did you become a cop?'

'Why did you become a barmaid?'

She seems to be considering her answer. I'm thinking about the little chain I saw in the dead woman's hand. I wonder what it was. An amulet she needed so she could get to sleep? Perhaps, but unlikely. It looked as though it had been placed there. I get my phone out, open the picture of the woman's face, and stare at it, as if her eyes might open at any moment.

'I suppose everyone has to find something to keep themselves busy until they work out what it is they actually want to do,' she eventually replies.

'Exactly.' I drink from my glass, look at the picture on the phone, show it to Anna. 'You don't recognise her?'

Anna studies the image.

'No. I don't recognise her.'

'Her name might be Rebecca.'

'With a "ck" or a "cc"?'

'Why do you ask?'

'Just wondered.'

16

'Not sure, but right now I think it's double-c.'

She shakes her head.

'I don't recognise her.'

'It was worth a try.'

I LEAVE ANNA as she puts the first of the chairs up on a table. According to the ticking wall-clock, it's now a few minutes to three; but, bearing in mind the state of everything else in BAR, there's no reason to think that the clock is right.

'You can ring me, you know,' she says, as I stand with my hand on the door and turn around.

'I haven't got your number.'

'You'll work it out.' She lifts up a second chair, and the wood-on-wood makes a loud clunking noise. 'Otherwise, I'm sure I'll see you soon.'

The lights pulse again, and I push down on the door handle, leaving BAR. My head is rocking gently, not unpleasantly.

The Stockholm night is raw, in a way that it wasn't earlier. If the clock behind Anna is right, it's going to be dark for hours yet. Suddenly, a shadow flickers in the corner of my eye, making me freeze and turn around. Someone is following me, I'm sure of it, but when I survey the street there's no one there — just a traffic light changing from red to green, a car turning a couple of junctions away, and the hum of a big city expanding in the darkness and devouring lonely souls.

When I get back to Chapmansgatan there are several cars lined up along the incident tape: another police car; cars from the main news agency, from state television, one of the tabloid newspapers; and a shiny silver van, with tinted windows and AUDACIA LTD written in black on the silver paintwork. The street is cordoned off, and people are standing by the barriers, silhouetted by the light from the police car's headlamps. The odd camera flash goes off. Someone hangs up a drape alongside the van, and the flashes accelerate to an intense, dazzling rattle. I catch a glimpse of a stretcher, a hand grasping its handle, but nothing more.

The blue lights are no longer operating. The signals of death have been turned off, and only the photographers' flashes continue; a sigh escapes from those lining the cordon, possibly one of disquiet, but more likely a sigh of disappointment. The drape being held up by two uniformed officers is obscuring everything they've come to see. The two men carrying the body get into the silver van and steer it carefully through the barrier.

I go back into Chapmansgatan 6 via the rear entrance. As I pass the first floor the door is open, and I can hear Gabriel Birck's voice coming from inside. The incident tape is still up; it will be there for days, maybe longer. I'm detached from it, from everything, and I go up to my apartment and get back into bed as if it's been just minutes since I woke up.

STRANGE, how a shudder goes through the room just before morning arrives.

III

What was it like growing up in Salem?

I remember this: the first policeman I ever saw hadn't shaved in a long time. The second hadn't slept for days. The third stood at one of Salem's crossroads, diverting traffic after an accident. He had a cigarette in the corner of his mouth. The fourth policeman I saw pushed his baton between my friend's legs, unprovoked and without warning, while his two colleagues, equally expressionless, stood nearby looking at something else. I was fifteen. I didn't know if what I saw was good or bad. It just was.

I lived there until I was twenty. In Salem, the houses stretched eight, nine, ten storeys up towards the heavens, but never so close to God that He would bother to put out His hand and touch them. In Salem, people seemed to be left to their own devices and we grew up fast, became adults ahead of time, because that was what we had to do.

IT WAS AFTERNOON, and I took the stairs from the eighth to the seventh floor, and called the lift. You could travel to and from the seventh floor, but never higher. No one knew why. That's what I remember about Salem: every morning I took the stairs down one floor, and every afternoon I had to climb the stairs that last bit home. And I remember that I never gave a second thought to why it was like that, or indeed why anything was the way it was. We didn't grow up thinking to question the way of things. We grew up knowing that no one would give us anything if we weren't prepared to take it from them.

On the seventh floor, I waited while the lift rumbled up the shaft. I was sixteen and wasn't on the way to anywhere in particular, just out. Behind the door of one of the flats I could hear heavy, muffled hip-hop, and when I opened the lift door there was a strong smell of cigarette smoke. Out on the street, the sky hung low, white, and cold. The streetlamps came on as I was walking past the youth centre. A fog was on the way. I remember that, too: when the fog came to Salem, it swallowed everything. It washed over us, enveloping the buildings and the trees and the people.

In the distance, through the trees, I could see Salem's high, mushroom-shaped water tower, its dark-grey concrete forming a black silhouette against the cold sky, and I wondered if the cordon was still there. A couple of days earlier someone had fallen from it. I didn't know his name — just that we went to the same school, and that people said he'd written NOTHING TO LOSE on his locker that last day, like a message. The day after his death, when everyone else had gone home and the corridors were empty, I walked up and down along the lockers, looking for the message without success, to the sound of a CD player someone had forgotten to turn off before they threw it in their locker.

The water tower was the kind of place that the adults in Salem would have liked to put under constant police surveillance, had the resources been available. In the daytime, kids went there to play; in the evenings and at night, parties and drug deals took place. The kids stayed on the ground, as did the parties most of the time, but sometimes we'd climb up it. And sometimes, at night, someone would fall — often by accident, sometimes not, and that water tower was tall. No one who fell ever survived.

I made my way through the woods that surrounded the tower, and stood at its base. The ground was compacted gravel, and I looked for traces of people who'd been there before me, but found none. No cans, no condoms, nothing. Maybe someone had cleaned up after the guy had fallen. I wondered where the point of impact could have been.

Somewhere above me I heard a bang, and then a rustling in the treetops, before I noticed something fall, hitting the ground with a thud. I looked up, not knowing what to expect. When nothing else happened, I went over to see whatever it was that had fallen: a bird, black and white, with its beak half open, wings spread and in disarray. In its white feathers I could see dark-red splashes. One of the bird's eyes was sunken, just an orangey-red open wound, as if someone had taken a teaspoon and gouged a bit of its head out. I stood looking at it, lit a cigarette, and managed to take several drags before one of its wings jerked and a leg twitched.

I started looking for something heavy to beat it to death with. When I couldn't find anything, I stared up at the rounded roof of the tower before looking back down at the bird again. It wasn't moving anymore.

I dropped the cigarette, stubbed it out, and walked over to the narrow steps that wound their way up the tower. The ladder shuddered under my feet, and I held on to the rail. The exertion made my arm hurt. Halfway up, I heard another shot.

The water tower had a ledge, and from there a little ladder took you up another couple of metres to a second ledge, right underneath the tower's mushroom-shaped roof. Above me I heard the rustle of clothes rubbing against each other, and I lit a cigarette, loudly. The rustle stopped at the noise of the lighter, and I peered towards the sky, which seemed unnaturally bright and strong.

'Who is it?' I heard a voice say.

'No one,' I said. 'Are you the one shooting?'

'Why do you ask?'

The voice was cautious, but not threatening.

'I just wondered.'

'Come up. You're scaring the birds.'

I tried to see where he was sitting up there, but couldn't. The upper ledge wasn't slatted like the one below; it was solid wood.

'Can you hold my fag?'

I climbed onto the ladder and held the cigarette up over the rim, then felt a hand take it off me. I grabbed one of the joists that stuck out from the ladder and hauled myself up onto the ledge. The thought that if I did fall I wouldn't survive briefly crossed my mind.

It was wide enough up there that you could have your back against the body of the tower, your legs outstretched, and your feet against the fence-like railing, without being seen from below. The railing came up to your thighs. Up here the wind was stronger, and Salem spread out below me — the heavy buildings with their small windows, the low, detached houses with their sloping roofs and warm colours, the sporadic greenery, and the dark-grey, heavy concrete. The landscape looked even weirder from up here than it did at ground level.

I looked at the hand holding the cigarette. He wasn't holding it like a smoker would, but uneasily, with three fingers at the base of the filter.

'It is you shooting,' I said.

'What makes you think that?'

I recognised him. He went to Rönninge High School, but he was in a different class from me. He had short, blond hair and a thin, angular face; he was wearing baggy jeans and red Converses, and a grey hoodie with the hood up. His eyes were deep green and clear. He was holding a heavy, brown air rifle, and next to him was an open box of pellets. He tipped his head back, closing his eyes.

'What are you doing?'

'Shh. You have to listen.'

'To what?'

'The birds.'

'I can't hear anything.'

'You're not listening.'

I pulled on the cigarette and heard nothing but rustling from the trees, and someone aggressively beeping the horn in a car nearby.

'I'm John,' he said eventually.

'Leo,' I replied.

'Sit still.'

He opened his eyes, raised the weapon, and put his eye to the black telescopic sight on the rifle; I followed the line of the barrel, trying to see what he was aiming at. In the trees around us, everything seemed still. John breathed in and held his breath. Instinctively I pressed myself against the wall. The bang was followed by more rustling in one of the trees. I couldn't see it, but a bird fell to the ground.

'Why are you shooting them?'

He put the rifle down.

'I don't know. Because I can? Because I'm good at it?' He looked at my right arm. 'Does it hurt?'

The climb had really made it ache, and I was massaging it. The pain reminded me of Vlad and Fred, two older guys in Salem; they had hard knuckles. They always punched me at exactly the same point, right on the nerve, giving me a dead arm followed by pain as the feeling came back. They'd stopped doing it ages ago, but when I put any strain on the arm it sometimes started aching in a way that made me remember them.

'I walked into a bannister today.'

'Bannister,' John repeated.

'Yes. Do you come here a lot?'

'When I want some peace,' he said. 'You need somewhere to go when you can't go home.'

'Shall I go?'

'I didn't mean it like that.'

I smoked the cigarette right down to the end of the filter and threw it over the railing, my eyes following it down till it disappeared.

'What else are you called, apart from John?'

'Grimberg.'

John Grimberg had a big hold-all next to him, the kind the footballers in Rönninge used to drag around with them. He opened it and put the gun away, then pulled out a bundle of cloth and unwrapped it: a bottle of vodka inside a T-shirt. He screwed the top off and took a swig without wincing. I thought about how high up we were. Below us, Salem was slowly being swallowed by fog.

'People call me "Grim",' he said. 'Well,' he corrected himself, 'people who know me.' He looked at the bottle in his hand. 'There aren't that many.'

'That makes two of us.'

'You're lying.' He looked at the bottle, seemed to be weighing up whether or not to offer it to me. 'I've seen you at school. You're never on your own.'

'You can still be lonely even when you're surrounded by other people.'

John seemed to be contemplating the truthfulness of this until he shrugged his shoulders, more to himself than at me, and took another slug from the bottle. Then he offered it to me. I took it off him and drank some of the clear liquid. It burned, and I spluttered, clearing my throat, which made John laugh.

'Pussy.'

'It's strong.'

'You get used to it.'

He took the bottle from me, drank from it, and looked out over Salem. The fog moved in, enveloping everything.

'Have you got any brothers or sisters?' I asked, for some reason.

'A little sister. You?'

'A big brother.'

At the same height as the ledge, just an arm's length from the rail, a black bird swept quickly past and squawked, then another one, and then a long, long procession of birds that became a blurred, black stripe in front of us. I looked at John's free hand — the one not holding the bottle — but he didn't make any attempt to reach for the rifle.

'Did he hurt your arm?' he asked instead, when the birds had passed. 'Your brother?'

I was thrown by the question.

'No.'

John tipped his head back again and drank some more.

'How old is your sister?' I asked.

'Fifteen. She's starting at Rönninge High this autumn.' With his eyes still closed, he turned his face towards me and sniffed the air, inhaling three, four times. 'You live in the Triad, don't you?'

I nodded. The Triad was what the three identical concrete blocks that were encircled by Säbytorgsvägen and Söderbyvägen were called. The roads looped around, crossing each other and forming an irregular circle around the three buildings.

'In the one on the left, if you're coming from Rönninge. How did you know that?'

'I recognise the smell from the stairwell. I live in the middle one. Those blocks all smell the same.'

'You must have a good sense of smell. And good hearing.'

'Yes.'

Later we walked home, giggling and slurring our words together, back through a foggy Salem, and straight away it felt like a bond between us had been formed, like we shared each other's secrets. A year passes quickly when you live between the high-rise blocks, yet the time that followed felt like an age.

I REMEMBER THIS, that on the outskirts of Salem there were nice detached houses and small row houses with well-kept lawns, and when you went past in the summer you'd smell barbecued meat. The closer you got to the train station, the more the little houses gave way to heavy concrete blocks and tarmac, graffiti. Young and old, small-time criminals, teenagers and hooligans, electro fans and ravers and the kids into hip-hop — this was where we all hung out, and I remember a song I used to hear a lot, a sharp voice that sang about a head like a hole, black as a soul. We sat on benches and drank spirits, and tipped over soft-drink vending machines, and ones with sweets in, and sprayed them with paint. Quite a few others got done for threatening behaviour, assault, and vandalism, but we always got away with it by running into the shadows that we knew so much better than the people who were chasing us. In the adults' eyes, we were all aspiring gangsters. Things had been bad in Salem for a long time, but not this bad. Even Salem Church had been broken into, and they'd had a party inside. I heard about it at school — I hadn't been there myself, but I knew who'd done it, because they were in the parallel class and we did Swedish together. A few weeks later, the church was broken into again, and they hung a Swedish flag the size of a cinema screen with a big black swastika on it. No one could see the point of it — maybe because there wasn't one.

Salem. At school we were taught that it had once been called Slaem, which was a compound of two words meaning *sloes* and *home*. Then, at some time in the seventeenth century, the name was changed; no one really knew why, but the teachers and local historians liked the notion that it had something to do with the biblical Salem, as in Jerusalem. It made Salem sound like a peaceful place, since the word means 'peace' in Hebrew — a place our parents had moved to, long before it got this bad, in search of a happy life.

And in our blocks on the estate we would stand at the windows when we couldn't go out, observing each other at a distance. Once we were out, we kept away from people who could hurt us. We were drawn to those like us, like me and John, who hung around outside the entrances to each other's blocks when we had nowhere to go but didn't want to go home; in the distance you could hear shouting, screaming, and laughter, and car alarms echoing through the night.

IV

The incident tape around Chapmansgatan is flapping in the wind as I go out onto the balcony, with the gentle buzz of Serax around my temples. A little distance away, a woman crosses the street with a boy, perhaps her son, in a wheelchair. The boy is hooked up to tubes and is sitting completely still, as though he were just a shell.

A blue-and-white patrol car is parked outside the building, and two visibly bored police officers move up and down the line demarcated by the tape. My gaze follows them until one of the pair looks up towards me, which makes me scurry back inside like a startled animal.

The night's events have been summarised in a short article in the paper: a woman of around twenty-five has been found dead, shot at a homeless hostel in central Stockholm; the police are working flat-out to sift through the tips that have already come in; a lot of work is still to be done; those who claim to have seen something all report seeing a man in dark clothes running away from the scene. The forensic investigation was reported to be continuing as the article went to press.

THAT LITTLE ARTICLE is enough to send me back to what happened this spring, and what happened this spring might have started happening much earlier; I don't know. What I do know is that I was handpicked by Levin, that sly old fox of a chief superintendent, to serve in the Internal Affairs unit after a spell as a detective sergeant with the city's violent crime squad. The point of this wasn't, in fact, that I should be part of the Internal Affairs investigative team — those who investigate other police officers suspected of crimes. My role was a step beyond that: to monitor the unit itself from within. Levin suspected that the internal investigations, especially those concerning the work of informers and illicit intelligence, were spurious and fabricated. There was a major problem at HQ, and everyone knew it. Levin was the only one who dared to spell out where the problem really lay: in the self-regulation and investigation of the riskiest parts of the organisation's activities, where the police knowingly cooperated with criminals, sometimes provoking criminal acts.

Officially I was just part of the unit's administrative department, but my real task was to wade through the internal investigations' reports, looking for short-cuts, omissions, cover-ups, or downright lies, which investigators had been pressured into by those above them while investigating their own. The ordinary files were red. The specially selected ones — those I was really there to work on — were blue, and it was always Levin himself who put them on my desk. He screened every internal investigation; and when something seemed too straightforward or transparent, he would put it in a blue file and give it to me for further examination and checks.

Often the holes were easy to find. Most of the events were described as 'incidents' — a good choice for downplaying their significance — and the account given followed a set pattern:

The internee's behaviour led to the incident in lift number four. During the lift's passage the patrol deemed the person aggressive and forced him to the floor. This caused injuries to the face (L. cheek, R. eyebrow), diaphragm (bruising from second to fourth rib, L.), and right hand (metacarpal fracture). Soft-tissue injuries sustained by the internee resulted from a heavy fall, after the patrolling officers had calmed him down and helped him to his feet.

The internee in this case, for example, claimed that his injuries were the result of what the police call a 'drum solo': repeated baton strikes to the groin. The addict would not submit, instead protesting his innocence. The case went to trial, where two well-presented police officers testified against a man deep in the clutches of a fifteen-year-long opiate addiction. The police, of course, emerged victorious from the proceedings, the only consequence being that an internal investigation was ordered. This was completed one month later, and concluded that the injuries being a result of the fall could not be ruled out. No medical expert had been consulted on the subject. When I contacted one myself, it was in fact immediately clear that this could indeed be ruled out. Cases like this were a regular occurrence, mainly involving young people in the city centre or out on the estates. Other times it was much more difficult, because the police in question had been more adept, the crime far more advanced, and the events themselves much more complicated and tangled.

I learnt quickly and I was soon good at my job. Everything happened quietly, thanks to the smoke and mirrors Levin so skilfully deployed. I did the groundwork, identified the hole, and handed the file — always blue, always nameless — over to him, and he took over. By early spring, five major internal investigations had been discredited, and the whispers inside the fortress-like HQ had taken off. I was essentially Levin's mole, and the worst kind of police officer. That's when it all started to go downhill.

THE WHOLE THING was later referred to as the Gotland Affair, or, by some, as the Lasker Affair, after Max Lasker, the informer who died. A police officer and two suspects were also victims in the case, but their deaths did not become symbolic like Lasker's did. Lasker was a crafty little rat-like man with moist eyes, dirty nails, and many years of substance abuse behind him. That's not the kind of person you really want as an informer, but Lasker had contacts, information, and money. This made him valuable, made him the vital link between organised crime and Stockholm's addicts. I knew of him from my time in the violent crime squad, and I think he trusted me. He'd got word during the spring that a large consignment of weapons was about to change hands on Gotland. He contacted me via a piece of paper with a mobile number on it, which he had hand-delivered to my letterbox on Chapmansgatan.

By now I had settled in to the job at IA, which essentially consisted of sitting at a desk, reading reports, and making calls to check details. I forwarded Lasker's information to CID on the ground, without going via Levin. I couldn't understand what IA would be able to do with the information, but somehow Levin got to hear about it. A few days later he came into my office — flustered and ill-at-ease — and brought me down to the basement and into one of the toilets. He asked me to keep an eye on the operation. The weapons that were going to change hands on Gotland were destined for Stockholm. They were to be sold-on to two emerging rival gangs operating in the city's southern housing estates.

'It's going to be a major operation,' Levin said. 'There'll be informants there, along with their handlers from inside this building. That means that someone — probably not the chief constable himself, but someone just under him — is going to put one or maybe two IA guys on the case, to cover their backs if the whole thing fucks up.'

This was the latest technique — proactive internal investigations, whereby IA supervised operations, advising right from the start. It all came down to one thing: covering your own back. This probably sounds rather alarming to outsiders, but for those of us on the inside it was a purely practical measure.

'And you want me to keep an eye on IA?'

Levin smiled, without saying anything. I leant against the cold, tiled wall of the toilet cubicle and closed my eyes.

'You know that there are rumours going around, in the building,'

I said, 'that something isn't quite right?'

'What do you take me for?' Levin said, rubbing his great beak of a nose. 'Of course I know. You report to me, and me alone. Anyone else contacting you is an attempt to expose you.'

My task was to observe the IA investigators and only get involved in exceptional circumstances, to save the raid. Levin was the only one who knew I would be on Gotland and about my role on the fringes of the operation.

A few days before the bust I made my way over to Gotland, to a little hamlet outside Visby. I'd never been there before, and I needed to get my bearings. It was May — grey, windy, and cold. Birds hunted along the coast, as though they were fleeing. Perhaps they were. I walked around, memorising footpaths and tracks, smoking cigarettes, and waiting for something to happen. The closer it got to the raid, the more unsettled I became, without really knowing why. My nights were filled with bad dreams about Sam and Viktor, and I would find myself standing in the hotel bathroom, staring at my own reflection.

Down in the harbour, a stone's throw from where the raid was to take place, I was standing, looking at the sky late one evening when I heard a voice behind me. I turned my head to see someone who was dressed to avoid being recognised — baseball cap, big hoodie with the hood up, baggy jeans — waving at me. Lasker.

'What the hell are you doing here?' he said, dragging me into the shadow cast by one of the larger buildings in the harbour.

'Holiday.'

'Get out of here while you can, Junker. I've got a bad feeling about this.'

'What do you mean?'

'Something's gonna go wrong.' He let go of me and started backing away. 'Everything's fucked.'

He disappeared into the darkness, and I stood there smoking, alone. A shiver went through me. Was this an attempt to expose me, as Levin had said? I guessed it was, but I couldn't figure out Lasker's role in the whole thing. He was working for us, after all.

The boat carrying the goods docked two days later. In the meantime I lay low, checked out of the hotel, and stayed at a nearby guesthouse, using a false name. It was important to keep moving. I noted the IA investigators and the firearms unit arriving in Visby, tailed the unmarked cars rolling out of the belly of the Gotland ferry, and made notes of who the officers were, where they were staying, what they got up to. I restricted my notes to a single black notepad, which was always in the inside pocket of my jacket. That gave me a sense of having things under control.

The internal investigators were not going to be present in the harbour itself. They were to be stationed in a nearby apartment, and would receive updates from the officer leading the operation. They would then pass this information on to Stockholm. I wondered who was waiting at the other end of the line, how high up this went, and what would happen if something did go wrong.

The vessel was a small motorboat, unlit, that glided through the night. I was hidden by the building where I'd talked to Lasker a few days earlier. Shadowy figures moved along the quay, and I tried to hear their voices. Members of the firearms unit were waiting at a distance: they were not to intervene until after the goods had changed hands. I was carrying my weapon, although I hadn't wanted to.

I saw the boat pull alongside, and then the shadows flitted by, surrounded by darkness. The harbour was deserted. A large jeep emerged from somewhere in the darkness and rolled quietly towards the boat. When it stopped, a figure climbed out and opened the boot. There was the sound of voices — buyers against sellers.

'Let me see,' said one. 'Open one of them.'

'We haven't got time,' said another voice at his side.

I recognised that voice: it was Max Lasker.

'Quickly.'

'I want to see,' the first voice said. 'Open it.'

'Alright,' said a third.

There was the sound of a box opening, followed by no one saying anything for far, far too long.

'Are you taking the piss?' I heard the first voice say.

The man holding the box lifted the lid and looked down into it. 'What?' He stuck his hand into the box and rifled around inside. 'It ... I ... I don't know what ...'

Somewhere behind them a huge floodlight came on, its yellowy-white light illuminating the harbour and the tall silhouettes. Voices behind the floodlight shouted *'Police'*, and that's how it all started. Everyone, including Lasker, was armed. His movements were fitful and jerky, as though he couldn't control them. The man who had just looked inside one of the boxes was standing with a pistol in his hand, staring up towards the floodlight, and then he ducked out of the way and behind a car, out of my sight. Suddenly the box fell to the floor. It landed with a heavy thud, and I took my pistol from its holster and held my breath.

The firearms crew rushed in with their weapons and shields, looking as though they had come to fight a war. I don't know who, or even which side, fired first, but there was a bang from somewhere. Lasker raised his gun, but was hit in the thigh before he'd had the chance to fire. In the stark light, the smattering drops of blood looked black, and his leg went from under him. His face contorted and he dropped the weapon, grabbing his thigh as he let out a high-pitched squeal.

Someone started the boat again, perhaps trying to leave the harbour. There was a blare of gunshots, and the sound of glass shattering. From the corner of my eye I saw a police officer fall to the ground; I wondered who it was. Their uniforms made them faceless.

Further away, blue lights and sirens were switched on, flashing and wailing. I moved out of the shadows, weapon drawn, not knowing what I was going to do. The man who had taken cover behind the car must have spotted me, because something cold and hard whistled past me, forcing me back into the darkness.

The jeep's driver's door opened, and the man climbed in and started the engine. I saw how the interior lights came on before he closed the door and sped away. I watched as it disappeared from view. My hands were shaking.

The gunfire didn't stop altogether, but its intensity tailed off. A police car chased the jeep, and I wondered just how many police were there, how many were hiding in the shadows. I went over to Lasker, who was lying very still, grasping his thigh. As I rolled him over, I saw that he had also been shot in the head. His mouth was half open, and his blank stare was fixed on a point just above my shoulder.

Several police had managed to get on board the boat and disarm those who'd taken refuge in the cabin. The sound of a shot rang out from somewhere — I didn't know where — and I think I must have panicked, because I fired off a shot towards something moving in the darkness between two stacks of shipping containers.

I had wounded people before, but had never shot anyone. I was overawed: everything went quiet, and all the receptors in my body were sending their signals and impulses to my hand, to my index finger. The finger that had pulled the trigger was stinging and throbbing as though I'd burnt it.

My legs pulled me forward. I rushed towards whatever I had hit, and could just make out two heavy boots. Sensing that everything had gone terribly wrong, I pulled out my phone to light up the scene. That's my strongest recollection now. It was so unnaturally dark there in the harbour. I illuminated the ground in front of me, and saw the blood running in a fat ribbon from his throat, how still he was, and the badge on his shoulder, gleaming blue and gold:
POLICE.

V

John Grimberg and I became friends, and I started calling him 'Grim'. We were quite different characters. I realised early on that he was at times full of contradictions, at least on the outside. He claimed to have difficulty coping in social situations. Despite this, he was able to talk his way out of most scenarios if he found himself backed into a corner. He could either come up with an excuse, or simply express regret and then apologise, seeming perfectly sincere. I was much worse at dealing with those situations, and I never worked out how he did it. And he never seemed to have problems talking to people. I asked him how he could be unsociable, as he said, and yet deal with people so effortlessly.

'It's just like masks, you know,' he said with a quizzical expression. 'When someone's talking to me, I'm not really there.'

I didn't know what he was going on about.

Grim was good-looking, and his chiselled features, thick blond hair, and crooked smile were straight out of a summertime TV advert. I was taller than him, but lanky and not as broad-shouldered. I tried to keep up at school whereas Grim seemed completely uninterested in the whole business. He was a year older than me, having repeated a year because he hadn't got the grades he needed to carry on to high school. In spite of that, he skived off less than I did and was much more clever, but perhaps he'd realised that there were more important things to concentrate on than learning stuff. The only conclusion I could come to was that he simply had nowhere else to go. I was much sloppier than him. Grim didn't really commit to an awful lot, but those few things he did put his mind to he would do properly.

He had a little video camera, and we started making short films together, which we would then edit on the computers at school. They were simple films, often set around the water tower. We filmed them as we drank booze; wrote scripts, directed, and played all the parts ourselves. He found it easy to get into character, as though he could camouflage himself whenever he needed to. I did get better at that after a while, but I was never as good as Grim.

THE SKY OVER SALEM was the colour of ink that had been spilled onto a blank page. We had only known each other a couple of weeks. I was carrying a bag full of beer and I was late, on my way to a party. I hurried round our block, past the block where the Grimbergs lived, looking up at the façade and the small square windows. Some were in darkness; many had their lights on. The lights came on behind one of the windows on the top floor, and shortly afterwards someone opened the window and threw something out. It fell in a wide arc before hitting the ground with a plasticky crash. I looked up to the window; the silhouette had disappeared, but the lights were still on. I carried on, but stopped as I heard the heavy front door of the block open and then slam shut with a boom, and someone came out. He ran over to whatever had been thrown, and picked it up. As he looked up, he caught sight of me, standing there under one of the streetlamps.

'Leo?'

'Everything okay?' I said, taking a couple of steps towards him.

'My Discman.'

Grim was holding it out in front of him. The lid had almost come off its hinges, and the headphones were hanging limp on their wires.

'I think it's bust,' I said.

'Yep.' Grim scratched his blond hair and pushed a button that was presumably supposed to open the lid. Instead the whole lid flew off, pirouetting in the air before falling to the ground. Grim looked upset. 'He will fucking pay for this.'

'Who?'

He pulled the CD out of the smashed player and stuffed it into the back pocket of his baggy jeans. He threw what was left of the device into a bush behind the row of benches running along the front of the block, and noticed the bag in my hand.

'Party?'

'I think so. There's always a party somewhere around here.'

'I suppose,' Grim said, deep in thought, and nodded towards the line of benches. 'Do you want to sit down for a bit?'

'I was actually on my way,' I said, but when I saw how dejected Grim looked, I nodded, pulled out two cans, and gave one to him.

'A bit of music would've been nice,' he said, sniggering as he opened his can.

I opened mine after tapping the top twice with my index finger.

'What are you doing?' Grim said.

'What do you mean?'

'Tapping the can like that. Why?'

'If there's a lot of carbon dioxide near the opening, it froths over.'

'And tapping it is going to help is it?'

'I think so. I don't know.'

'Pointless,' mumbled Grim and drank some of his beer, and I drank some of mine.

It was only then it first occurred to me that the only reason I always tapped the can before opening it was that I'd seen my brother do it.

We sat there talking. After a while we heard music and raucous voices, and on the other side of the road a gang of skinheads went past. One of them had a Swedish flag draped over his shoulders. They were playing Ultima Thule, and seemed to be hoping for a reaction, that someone might confront them. It had been like this for a while; there were even some at Rönninge High School. Several fights had occurred around Salem. A twenty-year-old guy from Macedonia had had his teeth knocked out a few weeks earlier.

I'd stopped thinking about the party I was supposed to be going to. Grim was easy to be around, maybe because we talked about simple things: music, school, films we'd seen, and rumours we'd heard about older guys from Salem who'd graduated from high school. Some already had kids. Some were working full time; others were out travelling. Others still were studying. A few were in young offenders' institutions. And one, then, had recently had his teeth knocked out.

'Do you know anyone who's been in prison?' I asked.

'Apart from my dad, no.'

'What was he in for?'

'Drunk driving and assault.' Grim sniggered again, but it was a hollow laugh. 'He was driving once, drunk, and he nearly ran this guy over. The guy had walked out into the road without looking. Dad stopped the car and started shouting at him. It turned into a row, and my dad ended up smacking him in the face. The guy hit his head on the floor and was knocked out, got concussion.'

'Do you get prison for that?'

'If you're unlucky. But he only got six months.'

Grim drank some more beer, and took a packet of fags from his pocket and offered me one. He didn't smoke himself, but if he ever came across any cigarettes he would save them, just so he could treat me. I took one and lit it, and sat there for a while thinking about what I would have done if my dad had been in prison. I immediately felt restless — felt the need to get moving, to go to that party.

'Here comes Julia,' Grim said and nodded towards someone walking in our direction in the darkness.

'Who?'

'My sister.'

She had her dark hair up in a ponytail, and was wearing a white dress under a denim jacket that hung open. A wire ran from the jacket pocket, split in two at her chin, and carried on up to two white earphones. A necklace dangled round her neck. Her legs — black, because of her black tights — were long and thin. Unlike Grim, who had a slightly strange look about him, Julia Grimberg didn't look like she was going to have any difficulties when she started at Rönninge High that autumn. She was browner than her brother, but had the same thin face and prominent cheekbones, and she smiled as she noticed him.

'Where have you been?' he asked.

Julia pulled out the earphones, and I could hear the music and someone singing. She took the CD player out of her jacket pocket and turned it off.

'Out.'

'But where?'

She shrugged, looking at me.

'Hi.'

She stretched out her hand, which surprised me. Julia behaved more like a parent than a little sister. She smiled. Her front teeth were big, almost rectangular like a child's, yet her eyes conveyed that cool distance and scepticism that you only see in adults. I still remember that now, how childlike and grown-up at the same time Julia Grimberg was, and how she could flip from one to the other in the blink of an eye.

When I held her hand in mine, it was small and warm, yet strong.

'Julia.'

I took a swig of beer.

'Leo.'

'Is there another beer in that bag?'

'Yes,' I said and looked hesitantly at Grim, who was gazing at something else and didn't seem to be listening.

Julia sat next to me on the bench, with her legs crossed. She had heavy black boots with the laces undone, and she smelt fruity, like shampoo. On the road in front of the Triad, someone walked past wearing a long black trench coat and headphones round his neck. I watched him until he turned off the road and disappeared from view.

'Why don't we go somewhere?' said Julia.

'Leo's on the way to a party.'

'I reckon it's a bit late for that,' I lied, and lit another cigarette. 'It's probably dying down by now.'

'We could go back to yours, couldn't we?' said Grim.

MY PARENTS WERE AWAY for the weekend, and my brother was out somewhere. That's the only reason I went along with it. Our flat comprised four rooms and a little kitchen, and although I only rarely brought friends back, this wasn't the first time. It was, however, the first time I experienced the place through someone else's senses. I saw the ugly rug in the hall, and noticed the smell of cigarette smoke coming from the arms of the clothes hanging on the hooks inside the door. I heard the hum of the ventilation system, and saw the photo of my grandparents and how wonkily it was hanging above the living-room sofa. The tap in the kitchen sink was dripping, as it always did. Like most things that never change, I'd got so used to it that I no longer noticed it, but that evening it seemed more intrusive and noticeable than usual. My dad drove a forklift truck in a big warehouse in Haninge. He'd been a boxer when he was young, and claimed that was why he'd never studied. He could do physical work, which was better than using your head. He preferred to leave his head in peace, and to concentrate on other things. I liked that way of thinking. My mum worked in reception at a hotel in Södertälje. They were born the same year, met in a pub on Södermalm when they were nineteen, and split when they were twenty-two because they weren't ready for commitment. They met up again when they were twenty-five, and had my brother when they were twenty-seven. There was something romantic about it all, their splitting up, looking for someone else, only to realise that the person they were looking for had been there all along. He worked days, she often did the night shift, and the flat didn't get cleaned that often.

'What's that noise?' Grim asked.

'The kitchen tap. Can't turn it off.'

He stepped out of his boots and looked around.

'Which is your door?'

'The one nearest the front door, on the left.'

My room contained a bed and a bookcase half-filled with CDs, films, and some book a relative had once given me. Opposite the bed was the desk, where I never spent any time. Clothes and shoes were strewn across the floor, and the walls were plastered with posters for *Reservoir Dogs* and *White Men Can't Jump*.

'Lovely,' said Grim, without going in.

The three high-rises in the Triad were identical. Their flat was probably exactly the same as ours, possibly a mirror image. I opened another beer and sat down in an armchair in the living room. I had two left, and I put them on the coffee table for Grim and Julia. Grim went to the toilet, and Julia turned on the stereo on the shelf behind me and went looking for a record in my parents' LP rack. When she didn't find one, she put the radio on.

'You can put one of mine on instead,' I said when she sat down on the sofa opposite me. 'If you find anything you like.'

'I don't want to go in your room. It feels private,' she replied.

'It's fine, I don't mind.'

'Yeah, but still.'

When Grim came back from the toilet, he took a seat in the armchair next to mine and we drank beer until we all started laughing at the DJ and mimicked his slow, soporific voice. I put the telly on instead and we watched MTV. When the beer ran out,

I went down and got a bottle of spirits from the basement and we drank that, mixed with pop. Julia fell asleep on the sofa after a while. I looked at her as often as I dared to without making Grim suspicious. Her mouth was half open, and her eyes lightly closed. Then she moved, fumbling the bobble out of her hair. I think she did it in her sleep, without waking up.

'Do you normally drink together?' I asked.

'Better that she does it with me than with someone else.'

I laughed, drunk.

'Sounds a bit over-protective.'

'Maybe.'

'Doesn't that get on her nerves?'

'I don't fucking know,' he snarled, waving his hand.

I looked down at my glass. It was nearly empty.

'By the way,' said Grim, 'do you need any money?'

'Why do you ask?'

'I know where there is some.'

'How do you know that?'

He tapped his nose lightly.

'I know that smell.'

'Money doesn't have a smell,' I said.

'Everything has a smell,' Grim said, standing up; he went out to the kitchen and stood in front of the cupboards above the sink and the stove.

Above the kitchen cupboards were the more expensive wine glasses, a few vases, an old tin jug, and a heavy pestle and mortar that had belonged to my granddad. Grim stood and stared at them as he sniffed the air in front of him.

'That one,' he said, pointing to the vases.

'Which one?'

'The floral one, second from the left.'

'It's empty. Look at the dust on it'

'Wanna bet?'

'How much?' I said.

'Half of whatever's in there.'

'What do I get if you're wrong?'

He hesitated.

'My rifle.'

'I don't want your rifle.'

'Then I'll sell it, and give you the money.'

I laughed at his cockiness, pulled a chair over, and clambered awkwardly onto it. I lifted my hand up and pushed it down into the vase, feeling the rustle of notes against my fingers. When I showed them to Grim, he didn't look at all surprised.

'How much is there?'

I climbed down from the chair and counted the notes.

'One thousand six hundred.'

He stretched out his hand.

'Half of it's mine.'

I could see that he was expecting to get it. We'd made a bet. It was money that my parents were saving for something. It wasn't much, but it was all we had.

'I can't give it to you.'

Grim's expression darkened.

'We made a bet.'

'But it's … it's my parents'. I can't.'

'But we had a bet. You can't break it.'

I stared at him for some time, imagining my mother's face, how hurt she would be. I gave him a five-hundred note and three one-hundreds.

'Almost enough for a new Discman,' he said, folded the notes, and stuffed them in his back pocket.

I have started hallucinating. It's the sleep deprivation. Sometimes I manage to sleep but sometimes I go days without any sleep at all. The person I ended up becoming, was that the best I could have managed? Maybe it was either that or take an overdose or something. That would've been preferable, I now realise. I wish I'd done that. Maybe that's what I should do? Am I just too weak? Too weak.

I have left your old door, I'm lying low. I'm travelling as I write this, I'm on the move. As a child I didn't like it, but now I do. Keep moving and you don't get caught. I've learnt that. Keep moving and you don't get seen, just a blurry shadow in photos. If you were in the same carriage as me, would you notice me? Would you know it was me? I don't think so. You don't remember. You remember nothing.

I'm writing this because you have to remember, although it's not as I planned it. I'm too broken, too ambivalent. Too shaky. Might be the methadone. I'm travelling through leaves falling from the trees. On a street corner near the station I catch a glimpse of the lowlifes and I think to myself: we were like them, once. Still are?

I should have written to you a long time ago.

VI

The officer I'd hit in the neck among the shadows of Visby harbour died. He, Max Lasker, and a gang member from each side were the victims of the bungled raid. I know all of their names. I've seen so many pictures of their faces since then that I could draw them from memory. The boxes of weapons contained old copies of *Aftonbladet* and *Expressen,* orange plastic cars, swords and chainmail in grey and black, boy and girl dolls in blue and pink, and lots of Lego. The police were not responsible for the switch. Nobody seemed to know who had duped whom.

When the scandal broke in the press, everyone went looking for a scapegoat. The police's methods were exposed as risky and illegal, and everyone in the organisation hid behind someone else — except me, who had no one to hide behind. I was deemed to have had some kind of breakdown, and was kept under strict observation in Visby before being loaded onto a boat to the mainland under the supervision of two guards. One was called Tom, and when I asked him for a cigarette he looked at me as though I'd asked to have a go on his Taser. I went to the toilet and locked myself in, and spent most of the crossing in there with my head in my hands, not knowing what might happen next. The boat rocked constantly, making me so seasick that I vomited, causing the two guards to smash down the door. They thought I'd tried to kill myself. I was dragged off the boat and into an unmarked police car that took me to Sankt Göran's hospital in Stockholm. I heard someone, perhaps a colleague, whisper in my ear that I wasn't to talk to anyone.

I got my own room. There were no curtains on the window, because they were worried that patients could use them to hang themselves. On a table next to me there was a plastic glass and matching plastic jug. The ceiling was white, like fresh snow.

Levin came to see me later that same afternoon, and looked regretful. He pulled a chair over to the bedside, put one leg over the other, and leant forward.

'How are things, Leo?'

'They've pumped me full of pills.'

'Do they make you feel better?'

'Good as new.'

He laughed.

'Good. That's good.'

'What happened?'

'I was going to ask you the same thing.'

'There were no weapons,' I mumbled. 'Just toys and newspapers. I don't know which side started shooting, but once it started, it just carried on.' I hesitated and looked at Levin.

'I was down in the harbour the night before.'

'Okay?'

'Lasker was there.'

Levin didn't react.

'He told me to get out of there,' I went on. 'That something was wrong.'

'What did you say?'

'Nothing.' My lips were dry, and I licked them with the tip of my tongue. 'I thought he'd just got scared. But he probably knew something was going to go wrong.'

'Or not. Lasker was a paranoid bastard — you know that yourself. He might well have said the same thing even if everything had gone according to plan.'

'That's what I've been wondering. What was it that was supposed to happen?'

'You're wondering if someone set you up?'

'Did they?'

'No.'

I looked at Levin and tried not to blink. When that failed, I looked the other way.

'Why weren't there any weapons?'

'No idea.'

'Someone must know.'

'Someone must. Someone always does. But I don't know who that might be.'

I didn't believe him, but I didn't know why. Something wasn't right. Everything went quiet. He looked at his watch and poured some water from the jug, then drank it, before filling the cup again and giving it to me. I shook my head.

'You need to drink water.'

'I'm not thirsty.'

Levin pulled a notepad from his jacket pocket and wrote something, then pushed it over to me.

I think the room is bugged

I looked at him.

'Now you tell me?'

good they're getting your version

'Who are they?'

Levin didn't react. I leant back again, and sighed. The room tilted, and I felt drawn towards the window, but I was too tired to move.

They were worried that I might talk, I think, even though I'd been told not to. Exactly who 'they' were remained a mystery. They were police — that much I did understand. In the circumstances, controlling the flow of information was vital. They wanted control over what I said and to whom.

Levin wrote something else on his pad, then laid it on my chest. I picked it up and held it out, straining to focus.

I can't save you now, Leo

THEY NEEDED A SCAPEGOAT, and they got one. Officially, according to the version given to the media, I was put on sick leave until the end of the year, after which I would be redeployed, if indeed I wanted to remain in the force. Both the media and the organisation itself were happy with that, since unofficially I was suspended. Everyone knew it. The blame for the botched raid was pinned on me, the new boy at IA. It was the simplest, most watertight, thing for them to do. Since the police's role in the whole affair was to be investigated by Internal Affairs, where I was already, I had no one to turn to. I was put on sick leave, with Serax for the acute anxiety, and Temazepam to help me sleep and to deal with my nervous tension, as the doctor put it. I tried to call Levin, but he didn't answer. I don't think he dared have anything to do with me. That was late spring, and I was discharged; summer came along and swished past, in a series of foggy days and long nights.

Either the tablets were making me paranoid, or they were making me realise what had actually happened. I wasn't sure which it was; I'm still not. I began to suspect that I had been sent to Gotland not to check up on the internal investigators, but rather for just this reason. I was useful for them; they could get out of the spotlight, hidden behind one another, leaving me alone out there if something went wrong.

OUTDOORS. I'M OUTDOORS, and I've stopped by a shop window on Kungsholmen that has a display of summer cottages. I look at the images, the little red wooden houses with the white detailing. In some of the pictures there's even a Swedish flag hanging from the roof. I imagine glasses being raised by people as they toast, smiling and laughing; I imagine children with floral wreaths in their hair. Everything is as it always has been, as though time has stood still. I imagine glasses on the table round the back of the cottage, as empty as words. How a shredded, red-splattered shirt lies on the lawn, out of the sight of passers-by. I am captivated by the pictures, and it's a while before I realise that the cottages are for sale and that I'm standing outside an estate agent's. I grind my teeth and stand hunched against the windowpane, my forehead just a hair's breadth from the glass. Clouds rush overhead, as though they were chasing someone.

MY PHONE RINGS. I'm in the stairwell in front of the lift — I came in the back way after studying the cordoned-off scene around Chapmansgatan 6. I stand there with my phone ringing; the call is from a withheld number.

'Hello?'

It's Gabriel Birck. He wants to talk to me about what happened yesterday. What happened yesterday, that's the phrase he uses.

'I thought you had people to do the legwork for you,' I say, calling the lift.

'I always make at least one call myself.'

He sounds professional and strict. As though he's either forgotten or doesn't mind the fact that I'd broken in to and rummaged around his crime scene less than twelve hours earlier. This makes me uneasy.

'Okay,' I say.

'Is this a bad time?'

'I ... no.'

I'm standing by my front door, looking at the lock. There are scratches around it — scratches that I don't recognise. I take a step back and look at the floor near the door. Reveals nothing. I rub my finger over the scratches, wonder if they're new, and carefully push down the door handle. It's locked. I need a Serax. I go inside and over to the kitchen worktop, fill a glass with water, and get a pill out.

'Leo?'

'Eh?'

'Did you hear what I said?'

'No, sorry, I … never mind.' I pop the pill on my tongue, drink a gulp of water. 'Go on.'

'I need to record this conversation. Is that okay?'

I shrug, despite the fact that he can't see me.

'Hello?'

'I suppose so.'

Birck pushes the button on his phone and I hear the quiet but distinctive squeak. The tape is rolling.

'Can you tell me what you did yesterday?'

'I was at home. No, I went to Salem in the afternoon.'

'What were you doing in Salem?'

'Visiting my parents. Then I came home.'

'What time did you get home?'

'I don't know. Five, maybe six.'

'And what did you do at home?'

'Nothing.'

'Everyone is always doing something.'

'I wasn't doing anything. Watched telly, ate, had a shower, fell asleep about eleven. Nothing.'

'When did you wake up?'

'I can't remember. But it was the blue lights that woke me up.'

'They woke you up?'

Birck sounds surprised.

'I'm a light sleeper these days,' I mumble.

'I thought you had medicine for all that?'

'Doesn't really help,' is all I manage, distracted, because something in the flat has caught my attention, but I can't work out what.

I go to the bathroom door and push it open slightly. Everything looks untouched. I step in, seeing my confused face in the mirror, my hand holding the phone.

The light. It's on. Did I leave it on?

'Eh?' I say, fairly sure that Birck said something.

'What did you do when you woke up?' he repeats, clearly irritated and impatient.

'Got dressed, and went to see what had happened.'

'Which means?'

'I went down to Chapmansgården.'

I open the bathroom cabinet with my free hand, and study the contents: toiletries and powerful medicines; a little box containing a ring that I used to wear every day and which at that time was my most prized possession. I close the cabinet.

'And?' says Birck. 'What else?'

I tell him about how I got into Chapmansgården after talking to the two police officers; how I went past Matilda as she sat talking to a third cop. Birck listens, asks follow-up questions, more urgent than before. I realise I'm close to something important, and stop talking.

'Did you examine the body?'

'Not exactly.'

'This is a formal interview,' Birck says. 'Conduct yourself accordingly.'

'I didn't examine it.'

'Did you touch it?'

'No, I just looked at her.' That's pretty much true. 'Why?'

'Her hand,' Birck goes on, as though he hadn't heard me. 'Did you see if she had anything in her hand?'

I hesitate, and sit down on the edge of the bed.

'I don't remember.'

'You're lying. Was there anything in her hand?'

'Yes.'

'Did you touch it?'

'Eh?'

'I'm asking whether you touched what was in her hand.'

'No.'

'Are you quite sure about that?'

I wonder what he's thinking.

'Yes,' I say. 'I am sure. Why?'

'Thank you.' He breathes out. 'That's everything.'

When Birck hangs up, I just sit there with the phone in my hand. My head's spinning; I'm trying to untangle everything, without any success. Deductive reasoning has never been my strongest suit; I'm too slow, not logical enough, too irrational. I scan the flat instead, looking for signs that someone has been here. I'm certain that there must be some, waiting there right in front of me. I just can't see them. Or else I'm just paranoid. I look up at the bathroom light again. It might have been on when I went out. I feel the Serax flood out and start buzzing at my temples. Nothing happens, and I open the balcony door, smoke a cigarette.

A surname. I need her surname. If I get that, I'll be one step further on. When I call the switchboard on Kungsholmsgatan, I'm put through to Birck's office and the call is then forwarded to his mobile. He's the type of cop who answers by just saying his surname.

'It's me, Leo.'

'Well? I haven't had my lunch yet, Leo, I haven't got ti—'

'Rebecca,' I say. 'Her name was Rebecca, with two Cs, I think.'

'Yes, Salomonsson. Rebecca,' Birck says, puzzled. 'Don't you think we know that?'

'Good,' I say. 'Thanks. I just wanted to give you all the information I have.'

I think he realises that I've tricked him, but he doesn't say so. Rebecca Salomonsson. Standing at the bathroom mirror, razor in hand, I'm surprised to see my eyes looking clear and alert, as though the fog has lifted and they've caught sight of something to focus on.

WHEN I WAS NEW to the force I had to do long nights on the beat, on the streets around Medborgarplatsen. To keep myself awake, I used to use prescription caffeine tablets that a colleague and I had confiscated from a rave out in Nacka. I smoked cigarettes while no one was looking and sent texts to Tess, my girlfriend at the time. She had the reddest hair I've ever seen, and worked in the cloakroom at Blue Moon Bar. My partner on the beat was a man from Norrland who everyone called Tosca, because he'd once attempted to become an opera singer. He was gentle and kind to everyone, yet thick-set and sturdy. He voted for the Centre Party and he always claimed that I thought like a conservative voter, which I may have done. We didn't have an awful lot to talk about, but when Tess and I split up he was the first person to know. I guess that's only natural when two men spend hours and hours in a car together, just waiting for something useful to do.

But when I started on those patrols, one of the first things I learnt was the importance of contacts — junkies, whores, moles inside the organised gangs, teenagers kicking around the concrete estates, old soaks sitting on the steps outside the methadone clinic every morning. A couple of well-chosen individuals can give you more useful information on a case than three hundred others. The challenge is identifying them, and if there's one thing I'm good at, it's that: judging whether someone is useful or not. It's not a trait that makes you well liked, but it's what I've got.

I went on from there to the armed-response unit, as a sergeant with the city police, where serious violent crimes would end up on my desk. It was at the city police that I met Charles Levin, who was a superintendent at the time. I was there for several years, during which time I worked closely with Levin, who taught me more about police work than anyone else. He watched me go from work-a-day cop to skilled investigator. By then I'd met Sam, and Levin watched our relationship grow and then die.

Levin's apartment is on Köpmansgatan in Gamla Stan. When I get there, a chill rain is falling hard, and fallen leaves are swirling about in the wind. Autumn is almost here; I can taste it on my tongue. Across the front of the building, near the entrance, someone has written I KNOW I LOST in white capitals, each letter the size of a man's face. I examine the letters, attempting to decipher their meaning, trying to imagine someone writing them. Around me is the smell of damp clothes and the constant swarm of tourists streaming along lanes too narrow to accommodate them. I take the lift up and knock on the door.

'Leo,' Levin says as he opens the door, clearly taken aback. He studies my face. 'When did you last shave?'

'An hour ago.'

'I thought so.' He steps to one side and lets me past him into the hall. 'This must be important.'

'Thanks. Yes.'

Levin has a rare eye for detail. It's the key to his success. According to him, it comes from childhood and his early interest in train sets and models. Miniature aeroplanes, buildings, landscapes, and flagships were the young Charles Levin's major interest. The difference between a mediocre model and a great one was all in the detail. Now they are all displayed in a large glass-fronted cabinet covering most of one wall in the bright living room. They are arranged in chronological order, like an alternative life story.

It's quiet up here. Through the window I can see the buildings rising up, but at a comfortable distance. The city isn't as suffocating here. That's what money can buy you in Stockholm: peace and quiet. Distance.

'Coffee?' he says as I sit down in a comfortable armchair with its back to the cabinet.

'And absinthe, if you've got any.'

'Absinthe?'

'Yes.'

'I'm afraid not,' he says frostily.

'Well, water then?'

'I think we can manage that.'

Levin is tall and thin, with a shaved head, and a pair of small, round glasses perched on the end of his nose. He's wearing black jeans, a white vest, and an unbuttoned shirt. He's been abroad. The holiday brochures for Argentina are still on the table. After his wife died from cancer, Levin started travelling, because Elsa loved it but they'd never been able to do it together. Levin's job got in the way. She used to go away on her own instead, and showed him the photos when she got home. Now it's Levin taking pictures of his own trips. When he gets back he visits the grave, sits there showing the pictures and describing them, just as she once did for him.

Levin comes back to the living room with two cups of black coffee and a glass of water.

'The owner before me was a policeman,' he says. 'Did you know that?'

'No.'

'He was the good kind of cop. Led the national murder unit at one time. He moved here after he got divorced.'

I take a Serax from my inside pocket and pop it on my tongue, then swallow it with a gulp of water.

'Three a day,' I say as Levin's eyes follow the trajectory of my hand.

'Because you still need them?'

'Because they check that I'm taking them.'

'You could chuck them.'

'I suppose so.'

We take the first sip of coffee without looking at each other, as though it were some kind of ceremony. It isn't; I'm just trying to work out what I'm going to say. Since the Gotland affair we've had very little contact, and what contact we have had has been cool, apprehensive. He knows something I don't, that much I'm sure of.

'How's life, Leo?'

'I manage.'

'And Sam?'

'We don't talk anymore. It was just that once, when I'd just come home from hospital after Gotland; she wondered how I was doing.'

He nodded slowly, like a psychologist might.

'Well, Leo.' He lifts the coffee cup and slurps. 'I understand you have something on your mind.'

'That's right.'

'Is this about the Gotland affair? I haven't heard anything new.'

'It's not about that.'

This surprises him. He leans back in the armchair, and puts one leg over the other.

'Go on.'

'A woman died in my block last night. Shot at point-blank range in the temple. The perpetrator is a ghost, by all accounts.'

Levin is aware of the incident, I can tell, but it takes a moment for him to make the connection with where I live.

'Right underneath your place,' he says slowly. 'Wasn't it?'

'Eight, nine metres under.' I clear my throat. 'Her name was Rebecca Salomonsson. There's something about her death that bothers me.'

'Rebecca Salomonsson,' Levin repeats.

'Probably about twenty-five, druggie, possibly on the game.'

'It's unusual for women to get killed,' Levin muses as he drinks some more coffee. 'And for them to be shot.'

'Even more unusual is the fact that nearly twenty-four hours have passed and there is still no suspect. No motive either, as far as I know. And no idea what actually happened, except that he entered Chapmansgården through the front door and left through the window. He had size forty-three shoes and knows how to handle small-calibre weapons.'

'Sometimes it takes a while for the right witness to come forward, or to do the right forensic tests. It's early days yet.'

'She had something in her hand, some sort of jewellery — could have been a necklace.'

'And?'

'I think it's important.'

'Has the necklace gone to the lab?'

'Yes.'

'Well, there you are.' Levin looks puzzled. 'We'll have the results in a few days.'

I look down at my hands.

'I want to be part of the investigation,' I say quietly, so quietly that it comes out as a whisper.

'Since you live in the building, you already are. As a potential witness.'

I look up at him. I think I'm looking pleadingly, but I can't be sure. There's a burning sensation behind my eyes.

'You know what I mean. I need to do something. I need ... I can't just sit around my fucking flat smoking cigarettes and necking pills. I need to be doing something.'

Levin says nothing for a long time, and avoids making eye contact.

'What exactly are you asking me for, Leo?'

'I want to go back on active duty.'

'That's not in my remit.'

'Not much of what you've been getting up to is actually in your remit.'

'What do you mean?' he asks, calmly, and drinks some more coffee.

I hesitate, hoping to provoke him instead. 'You know that I'm a good detective. No one knows what really happened in Visby. No one knows who duped them. It was chaos. If you had been there, you'd understand. It wasn't my fault.'

'But you're the one who lost it,' he says, suddenly cold. 'You're the one who shot Waltersson.'

'And it was the force who sold me down the river,' I say, only now realising that I've stood up, that I'm now standing over Levin as he sits in his armchair looking strangely tiny. My voice shakes. 'You owe me this.'

'I don't think we should be talking about guilt, Leo. You are never going to win that argument.'

I realise that I'm sinking back down into the armchair again, involuntarily.

'I just want ... something's not right with Salomonsson.'

Levin thoughtfully scratches his bald head, where his sunburnt scalp has started flaking.

'Who is the detective in charge?'

'Birck.'

'So Pettersén's calling the shots.'

Olaf Pettersén is the only Swedish–Norwegian prosecutor in the place. He also happens to be the only person who Gabriel Birck can bear to take orders from.

'If you seriously think something's not right here,' Levin begins, 'then do what you're good at. But,' he adds, 'so far you haven't said anything that points to something being amiss, aside from it being an unusual event. And unusual events occur all the time.'

'I can't do what I'm good at without formal permission.'

'Have I been overestimating you?' Levin picks up one of the holiday brochures, and tears off part of the first page. He pulls a pen from the back pocket of his jeans, scribbles something on the scrap of paper, and offers it to me. 'Use your imagination. And ring this number when you need help.'

I inspect the note.

'Whose number is it?'

'Someone I know very well,' is all Levin says.

VII

I spent a lot of time on my own. I don't know why it turned out like that; my friends were around, but for some reason I didn't really spend much time with them outside school.

Vlad and Fred used to hit me. It started when I was ten, and went on for a couple of years. At first I didn't hit back, and when I did they were so incensed that the beatings just got worse. So I stopped fighting back. That was best for everyone. Vlad was the worst. Fred could sometimes look at me with something approaching empathy; I wouldn't really know what to call it. But Vlad never did. He seemed to genuinely hate me.

I never told anyone. I was ashamed. It always happened outdoors, with few or no potential witnesses around; despite my determined efforts to avoid certain places, they always seemed to find me, as though they could track me, follow my scent. They stole my cap, my money. Then they would normally hit me in the stomach or on the arm — never on the face, where it would show. I told my parents that I'd lost the cap, that I'd spent the money on sweets, that I'd fallen awkwardly at school and had strained my stomach muscles, that I'd been arm-wrestling a classmate and strained something. I didn't understand why it was happening, or why they were picking on me, but I assumed that I must have done something wrong, that it was just the way life was.

One day in early spring, when I was thirteen or fourteen, I'd finished school early but forgotten a book in my locker. My mum made me go back and get it. As I was walking from the bus stop up to Rönninge Middle School, I heard someone make a noise. It was a stifled sort of sound, like someone breathing through pain.

The school stood like a giant among the small houses and the trees that were just getting their leaves back, and I looked around, wondering where the noise had come from. The back of the school was just a stone's throw further on, the goods entrance. Daily deliveries arrived there at the loading bay. After nightfall you would sometimes hear heavy music coming from a ghetto-blaster, mumbling voices and sudden laughter, beer cans opening and lighters clicking away. If you got close enough, you could catch the sweet smell of hash smoke.

This was something else.

On the loading bay, with their backs to me, were two guys I didn't recognise. They didn't look like pupils at the school — more like high-school students. I stood behind one of the trees so they couldn't see me, but ensuring I still had a good view of them. The two guys had trapped someone between them; they were standing close together, each with one hand on the brick wall. Whoever it was had nowhere to go.

'You little cunt.'

One of them hit him, and I heard the choking sound of someone who'd lost all the air in his lungs, and saw his torso fall forward between them. That's when I saw Vlad's face, red and contorted, gasping for air.

'One more,' the other one said.

The first guy pushed him up against the wall and piled into his stomach, making him fall forwards again. I carried on watching them, although I didn't really need to in order to understand what was going on. Vlad might have snogged or maybe even shagged someone he shouldn't have, or borrowed money he couldn't repay, although I doubted it. Everyone had seen this sort of thing before. It happened because it could happen; people treated each other like this because they could. Because they were bored. Because no one cared.

'Wallet,' the one who had hit Vlad said, holding out his hand.

'What are you playing at?' said the other one.

The first guy turned his head and looked around, making me take a step back behind the tree.

'We might as well take it,' he said. 'This dick's not about to report us is he? He never has, so why would he do it this time?'

'We've never taken his stuff before.'

'He's never been this cheeky before.'

'Cunts,' Vlad managed to force out.

'And he's asking for it. He deserves to have it nicked.'

I heard them pulling at his clothes. Once they'd taken the wallet, one of them kneed Vlad in the stomach while the other one looked around sheepishly. Vlad collapsed on the loading bay, and the two of them jumped smoothly to the ground, walking away with calm, deliberate strides.

Next time he and Fred started on me, Vlad went completely white when I confronted him about it. I can't remember what I said — maybe something about him being a pussy.

Fred gave Vlad a look of complete surprise; in turn, Vlad just stared at me, blinked once, and started chasing me around the outskirts of Salem.

THIS WAS YEARS AGO, but as Grim and I got off the bus and started walking up towards the school's goods entrance it all came back to me. Vlad and Fred had turned eighteen and had both moved away from Salem. That happened to lots of them. They just disappeared.

I tried to remember whether they'd got hold of me, the time I'd confronted Vlad and they'd started chasing me. That time merged with so many others. Maybe I got away that time; maybe not.

'You look thoughtful,' Grim said, walking alongside me.

'I just remembered something.'

'Something bad?'

'Why do you ask?'

He lowered his gaze and gave a quick nod.

'Your fists are clenched.'

I didn't look at them, straining to relax them instead.

'No they're not.'

He looked at my hands again, which were now exaggeratedly relaxed and floppy. We went over to the loading bay, and jumped up onto it. I leant against the bit of wall that Vlad had once been pinned against. We were waiting for Julia, who still had a while left at the middle school. I wondered how it was possible that I'd never seen her before. She'd started the year after me; we must have seen each other in the corridor. Julia Grimberg was the sort of person I should have noticed. Grim sat there swinging his legs. A click came from the big roller shutter to our left, and with a little creak it started to open. When it reached my thigh level it stopped, and out came Julia, in her light jeans and a black T-shirt with THE SMASHING PUMPKINS printed on it in soft yellow characters.

'You can just go round, you know,' Grim said. 'You don't have to sneak out this way.'

'There's a supervisor just round the corner. She would have seen me.'

Julia sat down with Grim on the loading bay, and I sat next to her. I don't think Grim thought it was weird, but I wasn't sure. Her denim rubbed against mine. Grim pulled a big notebook out of his bag and flipped through to a blank page. As he was doing so, I saw that most of the pages were full of stuff that wasn't schoolwork: sketches and little cartoons; some had so much scribbled text that I couldn't decipher what they said.

'What's this note about?'

'I don't know,' Julia said. 'Something about me going away.'

'Are you going away?' I asked.

'No, we're going on a class team-building trip. If you can't go, you need a note from your parents.'

'Can't you ask them for one then?'

She shook her head.

'Today's the last day to hand the note in, and I forgot. Anyway, they would never agree to it.'

'Why not?'

Julia looked at Grim, who didn't say anything. He'd written a short note in handwriting that wasn't his own. The only thing left was the signature. He flipped through to an earlier, full page in the notebook. It was covered with this one pattern, three columns of what must have been a signature. A scrap of paper was glued to the page — what I later realised was the original. He studied it for a second, before flipping back through and, with a couple of deft hand movements, copying the signature. He ripped the page out and showed it to Julia.

'Will that do?'

It was an exact copy of the original.

'Perfect,' Julia said.

He folded the page across the middle and gave it to her.

'They noticed that we were forging them,' she said, looking at me. 'They even had a meeting about it in our class, so if you're going to get away with it now, it has to be really well done.'

'Seriously?'

'Seriously.' She got up and folded the note again and stuffed it into her back pocket. 'I've got to go — lesson's about to start.'

'See you at home,' said Grim.

'See you round,' I said, attempting a smile.

'Yeah, see you round,' Julia said, before disappearing back through the door.

HE SHOT BIRDS with an air rifle, smelled his way to cash, and could forge his parents' signatures. And he was called Grim. He was more like a cartoon character or someone from a film. But he wasn't. He was completely ordinary and real.

'Someone has to pay the bills and sign things,' he said once we were on the bus back to Rönninge High. 'That's how it is in all families, including yours, I assume. It's really not that strange.' He shrugged his shoulders. 'In my family it's me, because no one else remembers to do it.'

It had started when their mum forgot to sign a form from the welfare office. Grim had found it lying on the coffee table. Their dad was off sick at the time, and the form was about the family's financial support. Next to it lay another form, from Social Services, which was also missing a signature. Grim dug out a form with his mum's signature on it, and practised it a couple of times on a notepad before carefully reproducing it on the two forms and posting them off. After that, similar things had happened a few times, and Grim told Julia, who told their dad.

'He was furious, of course. It was sort of illegal, really. I don't know. But before long I knew more about their finances than they did. Dad can't be bothered with it, and Mum's ill. The medication makes it hard for her to keep on top of things. I do it — I mean take care of the bills and stuff — for Julia's sake really, so that she can ... I don't know. So she doesn't need to worry.'

The bus driver had the radio on, and the silence between me and Grim meant I could hear the song playing up front.

'What kind of ill?'

'What do you mean?'

'You said your mum was ill.'

'Hadn't I said that before?'

'I don't think so.'

He sighed and stared out the window.

'After Julia was born, she got depressed. Psychotic even, for a while. They said it was down to the birth. She was ... she tried ...' Grim hesitated, for a long time. 'I was angry when she came along, when Julia was born. At least that's what I've been told; I'd only just turned two at the time. I got angry that she was getting all the attention. But one day, when the psychosis had started, I was sitting on the floor at home somewhere, and Julia was screaming. They say you don't have memories from that early, but I'm certain that I do because it's all so vivid. I came into the living room and it looked like she had been sitting there breastfeeding Julia. Suddenly she just put her down on the floor, or dropped her, or let her go; I don't actually know, and I don't really want to. Either way, she just left her lying there. Dad was at work, so I picked her up, and we sat on the sofa until she stopped crying. It took ages — at least that's what it felt like. I remember being so scared. When she'd finally stopped, Mum turned her head and said, "I can take her again now."' Grim shook his head. 'I didn't want to give Julia to her. It's fucked up; I could hardly talk, I was that small. Yet I had a sense that something was wrong. Eventually my mum got up and took her from me and carried on feeding her. But I stayed there the whole time, worried that something might happen. I don't think Dad ever found out.'

He seemed unsure of where to go from there.

'Later, years later, I still didn't know whether she'd been dropped or not, so I started worrying that she might have been injured somehow. I started looking for signs of it.'

'Signs of what? How?'

'Well, if she had been dropped it could have caused brain damage, I thought. And I knew that certain types of brain damage aren't discovered for years, if at all. So I started looking for speech impediments, amnesia, whether she had any trouble learning.'

Grim told me that he was never ill as a child. He was born healthy and stayed healthy, managed to avoid all the normal childhood illnesses. Julia, on the other hand, got chickenpox, whooping cough, croup, the lot. She was always ill, and when she started school she was almost malnourished, so much so that the school nurse — old Beate, who smoked Yellow Blend and had felt all the boys' balls, including mine and Grim's, to check that all the junior-school boys in Salem had two and not one or three — had expressed concern.

'I took that sort of thing to be a sign of it.' He laughed. 'Crazy, considering Julia's the healthiest of all of us now. It was never really a problem, I suppose. Anyway, Mum's never got rid of the depression altogether. She has better days and worse days, but never good days, so it's hard for her to manage money and stuff. And Dad can't be bothered.'

And by the way, old Beate was now dead, Grim added. His dad had told him, because Beate happened to be the mother of one of his colleagues.

'Right,' I said, not really wanting to change the subject from Julia, although Grim obviously didn't want to talk about it anymore.

I looked out the bus window, and the world swished past: green trees, grey skies, faded yellow houses.

LATER THAT EVENING, the phone rang. We had three in our flat: one in my brother's room, one in my parents' bedroom, and a cordless one, which was never where you thought it would be. Wherever you looked, it was always somewhere else; Dad swore that that phone would send him round the bend one day.

There were phones ringing all over the place, and I didn't answer. I sat flipping through old yearbooks from Rönninge Middle School, looking for Julia Grimberg. I still hadn't found her, but it was a big school with lots of classes. Someone answered the phone, and, shortly after, there was a knock on my door.

'Leo, it's for you.'

'Who is it?'

'Someone called Julia.'

I stood up, opened the door, and took the phone off Mum. I closed the door without saying anything, shut the open yearbook and put it on top of the others, then pushed them out of the way.

'Hello?'

'Hi, it's Julia.'

'Hi.'

'What are you doing?'

'Nothing much.'

Beyond Julia's voice I could hear nothing but silence. I wondered if Grim was there, or if she was on her own.

'Good,' she said.

'What … has something happened?'

'No, not at all.'

Has something happened? Who says that? I wanted to punch myself in the face.

'I just wanted to,' she went on, 'I don't know. I saw your number in John's room.'

'Do you ring all the numbers in his room?'

She laughed.

'This is the first time.'

I lay down on the bed and closed my eyes. We chatted for a while without really saying anything. I wondered why she'd rung, but was too scared to ask.

'Are you watching telly?' she asked.

'No.'

'Back to the Future is on 3. Have you seen it?'

I hadn't. I switched the telly on, but put it on mute. Michael J Fox was busy avoiding a girl who fancied him.

'That's his mum,' Julia said. 'He's gone back to the future to make sure that she and his dad get together, so that he gets born. The only trouble is that his mum has fallen for him, her own son. But you know, she doesn't know that he is.'

We watched the film together. Julia laughed every now and then. It was a nice laugh; it reminded me of Grim's.

'Where would you go, if you could travel through time?' she asked.

'Hmm, I don't know, never thought about it.'

'Would you go forwards or back?'

'Back. No, forward. No, back.' I heard how Julia laughed. 'I don't know, this is really hard. Do I only get one trip?'

'Yes.'

'Sounds like a shit time machine, if you can only go once.'

'But if you can do as many trips as you like, it's pointless.'

'Dinosaurs,' I said.

She laughed again.

'Eh?'

'They say they were wiped out by a big meteorite. But I don't know. I'd like to see if that was true.'

'What fun, Leo. You can go wherever you want, see whatever you want, anything at all, and you choose to go and see some dinosaurs. Anyway, you might die yourself. Could you even breathe back then? I mean, that long ago, wasn't the air all poisonous and dangerous?'

'I'd take some oxygen, to be on the safe side.'

'And what would you do?' she asked. 'Just stand there watching them? Stroke them?'

'You're taking the piss.'

'Only slightly.'

'Where would you go then?'

'Forwards, definitely.'

'Why?'

'Just to see what everything's like. So you don't have to worry. Then again,' she continued, 'maybe you'd go back to your own time and just relax, because you think everything's going to be okay anyway, if everything does look good in the future, I mean. And then perhaps you end up not doing the things that make the future what it is. You get me?'

'I, er … I think so.'

I had no idea what she was on about.

'It might be really important that you don't know how things end up. So maybe I would go back. But then, if everything is fucked

68

in the future, if you did go forwards, then you have a chance to sort it out, don't you, as long as you know what needs sorting.' She hesitated. 'I'd like to know what's going to happen to Mum and Dad. And John. And me.'

'Do you worry about the future?'

'Everyone does, don't they?' She went quiet for a moment, and I could hear her breathing. 'I think Dad's back.'

'Aren't you allowed to talk on the phone?'

'Yeah, but I don't want him to hear. My room's right next to their bedroom.'

It went quiet, again, but it felt calming and warm. Then we carried on talking, about what we were doing that summer, about music and films, and about school. She asked if I'd heard of *The Saint*.

'The Val Kilmer film?'

'Yes?'

'It's out at the cinema, isn't it?'

'Yes. I wanted to go and see it, but no one I know wants to go. Do you want to see it?'

'With you?' I asked, and opened my eyes.

'If you want to, I mean.' She sounded unsure. 'You don't have to. It's just so boring going on your own.'

'No, I just … sure.'

'Don't tell John.'

AS I REMEMBER IT, I used to think about them a lot, the Grimberg family. What their life was like and what had actually gone wrong. What you could see from outside, the family's outward appearance, was nothing unusual for Salem; several people I knew had the same sort of background. I think there was some violence, or at least there had been at some point. Julia always ended up in between her mum and dad while Grim did his best to stay out of the way. For us, that was always the way. At school, at home, during our free time: someone got away; someone else got caught in the firing line.

What made Grim different was that he was so overprotective when it came to Julia. There seemed to be a lot going on that I couldn't grasp, despite my best efforts. Maybe I still can't.

'Sometimes, when I'm on my own, I feel like I'm disappearing,' Grim used to say, and even though I never really understood what he meant by that, that's how I feel about them now. I have to hold on to them, Grim and Julia, fix them in specific scenes so that they won't disappear.

My youth, my childhood ... With the passage of time, that whole period slips further out of focus, and Grim and Julia look increasingly like the mystery that they may well have been all along.

IT ALL FELT FORBIDDEN. During the fairly short time Grim and I had known each other, we had become close. At least that's how I felt; you could never tell with him. Despite that, we had never spoken on the phone. After that first call with Julia, I spent at least an hour a day on my bed talking to her on the phone. There was an intimacy between us that made me shake inside. I felt alive in a way I'd never felt before, as though my feelings were eyes that had always been blindfolded. Julia Grimberg turned everything on its head and made it feel bigger, infinite.

'What are you wearing?' she asked on the phone, the night before the cinema.

I laughed.

'Why do you ask?'

'I want to know.'

'Why?'

'I just want to know.'

I was silent while I checked that my door was closed.

'Boxers.'

'They're called underpants.'

'Underpants is such an ugly word.'

'But that's what they're called.'

'What about you?'

'Eh?'

'What are you wearing?'

'Knickers. Is that an ugly word?'

'No.'

'I like boys' underwear,' she said, and it sounded like she was stretching, before I heard her breathe out.

'Are you a virgin?'

The question just tumbled out, surprising me. I wanted to take it back.

'No,' she replied. 'Are you?'

'No,' I lied, pretty certain that she didn't believe me.

'How old were you?' she asked.

'Fifteen. You?'

'Fourteen.'

I heard her gasping for air.

'What are you doing?' I asked.

'What do you think?' she whispered.

Her breathing became really heavy. The sound was spellbinding. I strained to hear every nuance of what was happening at the other end of the line.

'Touch yourself,' she said quietly, with a thickness to her voice that I'd never heard before.

'Okay,' I said, despite the fact that I was already doing so.

'How does it feel?'

What do you say to that?

'Good,' I attempted.

'Imagine it's my hand.'

I was on the verge of exploding. Suddenly she was gasping, as though she'd been winded again and again, before she slowly seemed to be recovering.

'I bit my lip,' she giggled. 'I think I bit through it.'

Everything was spinning. I'd never experienced anything like it.

VIII

The dealer is a little sparrow of a man, with his close-set eyes, a sharp beak of a nose, and jerky movements. His slicked-back hair exposes his forehead, big and pale. He wears a long black trench coat that flaps behind him. On the back of each hand are two diamond tattoos. I hold up my mobile in front of him.

'Do you recognise her?'

'Is she dead?'

'Do you recognise her?'

He smiles weakly, revealing crooked teeth.

'You're still suspended, right? I don't need to tell you shit.'

'I'm back on duty.'

'Show me your badge then.'

I look around. We're standing on a corner near the Maria Magdalena Church on Södermalm. I can smell freshly baked bread from one of the nearby bakeries; Hornsgatan hums away in the distance. It's a beautiful day. I take a step closer to him.

'How much money do you owe me?'

The smile disappears and he looks up at me.

'I don't know.'

'It's a lot.'

'You'll get it back.'

'Give me this, and we're quits.'

Felix used to be an informer. When we put a stop to the arrangement a few years back, he had nothing left and had to flee the country for a while. When he came back, I gave him the chance to start again, and he did start again, and just like before he snorted all the money. There's probably a price on his head, and it's a miracle that he's still alive, but cockroaches like Felix do have a tendency to survive.

'Straight up?' he asks.

'Straight up.'

Felix's eyes roam across the phone's screen.

'She must be important, eh?'

I push Felix into the shadow cast by the church's bell tower.

'Do you know her name?'

Felix plays with his tongue in the corner of his mouth, as if scratching an itch.

'Rebecca.'

'Rebecca what?'

'Simonsson, I think. No, Salomonsson?' He looks at me. 'It's Salomonsson. Rebecca Salomonsson. It's her from Chapmansgården, isn't it? I saw it in the paper.'

'How do you know her?'

'She sold.'

'What?'

'What do you think?'

'People sell all sorts,' I say.

He nods, approvingly.

'True. But Rebecca stuck to drugs and sex.'

'And where do you come in?'

He looks down, as though he's weighing something up. Felix's forehead has started to moisten.

'I know this is going to look bad, but Christ, I promise, Junker, I didn't do it.'

'Tell me.'

He looks around and leans in towards me, his small eyes wide and glossy.

'I was the one supplying her with the junk.'

'And why does that look bad?'

'I'm not fucking you around, so don't fuck me around,' he says sharply, before apparently composing himself a bit. 'You know what I mean. This sort of thing happens for two reasons. Either she owes someone money, and that someone would of course be me, or else she's seen something she wasn't supposed to. The most likely is the former. So,' he says, and takes a cigarette from the inside pocket of his trench coat, 'it looks pretty fucking bad.'

I look at Felix's shoes as he lights the cigarette. They're small Converses, several sizes smaller than mine. And several sizes smaller than the shoe that left a print on the floor in Chapmansgården. He could have had other shoes on, but I doubt it.

'You want one?' he asks and offers me a cigarette.

'I've got my own. Tell me what you know about her.'

Felix pulls the smoke in, and breathes out through his nose. His eyes are constantly assessing the surroundings, hoping to make sure he isn't being seen anywhere near me.

'She wasn't from here. I think she was from Nyköping or Eskilstuna or somewhere, a smaller city anyway. She'd been here a couple of years. Typical dosser, just like the rest of them. She moved here to work or study, but pretty quickly she fell in with the wrong crowd. The guy she started seeing was a completely wasted Yugoslav junkie from Norsborg. He dragged her down into the shit, before he died of an overdose. That's when she came to me.'

'Is that when she started selling?'

He takes a drag.

'That's right.'

'What was she selling?'

'Whatever I gave her. But the only thing she was doing herself was heroin.'

'And what did you give her?'

'You know me.' Felix is smiling. 'Everything. You can't specialise

74

in just one thing; it doesn't work like that anymore. You need to be able to get hold of everything. Heroin, morphine, amphetamine, coke, bennies, Marios, all that shit.'

'What are Marios?'

'You know Super Mario, the Nintendo character?'

'Yes.'

He looks at me as though that is an explanation.

'The game is full of mushrooms? You're losing it, Junker. You've been off the streets for too long.'

'Yet it still only took me less than an afternoon to find you.' I light a cigarette, and my smoke mixes with his. 'Did she have problems with anyone?'

'We all have problems with each other.'

'You know what I mean.'

Felix smokes some more of his cigarette, and plays with his tongue in the corner of his mouth.

'Not that I know of, no. She did what she was supposed to. She was almost never late paying me. I couldn't tell you whether she's had dealings with others. Since she wasn't from round here, she didn't have many friends.'

'Where did she live?'

'Nowhere, everywhere.'

'Where was she most recently?'

'She hasn't had a fixed address recently. That's why she was sleeping at Chapmansgården.'

'She had no possessions with her at Chapmansgården, but she must have at least had a bag of stuff?'

'Fucked if I know; I suppose she must have?' He flings his arms out and coughs, before taking another strained drag. 'She would often get the southbound Red Line, even after her bloke in Norsborg did himself in. Maybe she knew someone there, stayed with someone.'

'Do you have the names of her friends?'

'No.'

'What was her boyfriend's name?'

'Miroslav something.'

'Miroslav Djukic?'

Felix nods again, excitedly and jerkily.

'Yes, that's it.'

Felix hesitates for a moment, before cocking his head to one side and smiling broadly, as though he's just realised something. It's a strange gesture to make, but the pattern of his movements is completely unpredictable, as if he's forgotten which expressions go with which words.

'Can I go now?'

I wave my hand wearily.

'You know who you need to talk to, right?' he says, walking away, his coat flapping behind him as he walks into the sunshine and takes a look around.

'No.'

'Course you do.'

'No.'

But I do. Felix disappears round the corner and I'm left alone with the cigarette in my hand.

I need to talk to Sam.

SAM IS NOW TOGETHER with the owner of Pierced, the most famous piercing studio south of Mälaren. His name is Rickard, but he calls himself Ricky. Besides countless piercings, he's had Sam tattoo Carl Orff's 'O Fortuna' on his back, in the original Latin. This is a man who, perhaps for obvious reasons, I have never really been able to take seriously, even though I've only heard stuff and have never actually met him.

Sam and I met at a party in a flat on Nytorgsgatan. I'd just started working under Levin at the city police, and I was there to catch up with old friends who I no longer had anything in common with.

It seemed pointless, yet I felt duty-bound to do it. Sam was there for the same reason. It was summer, and her skin was tanned. Her hair was streaked with highlights in a range of lighter shades. A fat pencil bound it into a loose bun on her neck, and locks of her curly hair were hanging loose. Her shoulders were covered in tattoos — sharp black lines, icy blue and steely grey. She was standing on her own with a milky-white cocktail in her hand and a look on her face that, more than anything, showed her intense desire to be somewhere else entirely.

Later that evening, she came over to me in the kitchen, where I was mixing myself a drink, and we started talking because the alcohol had got her in a better mood. She was easy to talk to, once she'd dropped her guard and let me into her world. She was attentive, and could listen without losing concentration, without being passive or withdrawn.

She is, to this day, the best conversation partner I have ever had. Sam has the ability to get the best out of me. Unfortunately, she also brings out the worst in me.

'I own a tattoo parlour,' she said. 'It's over on Kocksgatan.'

'Kocksgatan,' I repeated and finished off my drink.

'I have to go there now.'

'Now? Are you going to work now?'

It was way past midnight.

'I forgot my house keys,' she slurred. 'I've got my work keys and my house keys on different key rings.'

'How … impractical.'

I was also slurring, involuntarily.

That night we had sex in the tattoo parlour, standing against her big brown sofa meant for waiting customers. Trousers round ankles, me with one hand against her chest, the other gripping her hip tightly. Her hair in my face, the smell of hairspray and ink, her nails on my skin, the realisation that this was something I hadn't felt for a long time.

Two weeks later, we became an item. It was Sam that asked me, and I laughed because I found the question itself so youthfully innocent. Soon we were sharing everything, apart from a flat. We spent very few nights apart. As often as possible, we would stay in and watch a film or bad TV series. We went out for dinner, we went to the cinema, we took long walks along Söder Mälarstrand. We had sex in the morning, at lunch, and in the evening. In bed, in the shower, on the floor, on the kitchen table, in Sam's tattoo parlour again, in the toilets at Sergel Cinema, in the Katarina lift, in the middle of the night against the fence along Monteliusvägen, with all of Stockholm laid out beneath us. The months whizzed past and we exchanged keys, and soon I moved in with her on Södermalm, renting out my flat on Chapmansgatan.

It was about a week after we met that Sam found out I was a policeman. I didn't tell her, because I was afraid she would back off. In fact, she'd suspected it right from the start, she told me later. I should have known. I'd claimed to be a salesman — couldn't think of anything better to say. Afterwards it felt pretty silly.

Sam lived on the fringes of the underworld. Dangerous men appreciate good tattoos, and Sam knows what she's doing. The tattoo artist is like the local hairdresser, who knows a lot about the world her customers inhabit, simply through her job. And Sam had nothing against it, nor did she have any desire to get more involved. We perched on each other's outer limits, and I think that's why we were drawn to each other.

Then she got pregnant. We weren't sure at first, but we decided to keep the baby. We bought a ring each, not for an engagement but to have a tangible mutual bond until the baby arrived. That was the beginning of the happiest seven months of my life. We were expecting a boy; we were going to call him Viktor, after Sam's granddad. One night we were in a car on the way home from a party. Sam was driving, and I was sitting next to her, radio on, and I remember someone singing about asking the world to dance.

It was winter, and it turned out that the driver of the car in front of us had such high levels of alcohol in his blood that he really should have been unconscious. Then something happened, and Sam gasped and wrenched the wheel. I still don't know what it was, can't remember. The road was slippery, and there were patches of ice everywhere. The world turned upside down as the car flipped over. Everything went black until I opened my eyes and saw a clear, starry sky. I was lying on my back on a stretcher, and my head was pounding. Every breath brought sharp pains to my torso, as though someone were pushing nails through me. I had four broken ribs. Next time I came round, I was lying under a bright white light at Södermalm Hospital. When I asked about Sam, they told me she was still in theatre. She was going to be okay; it was Viktor they were trying to save.

They couldn't. Sam had lost a lot of blood, and Viktor had sustained serious internal injuries. I was alone when they told me. Sam was still in a recovery room, coming round from the anaesthetic. I remember how bright the light was, how cool it was in the room, how there was a little wooden flag on the table next to me.

The man in front of us, the one who had lost control of his car, was convicted of reckless driving. He was given a six-month suspended sentence. I never told anyone, but late one night about a year later, I looked him up, knocked on his door, and when he opened it I hit him with a knuckle-duster. He offered no resistance.

Viktor's death caused an irreparable crack in our relationship. We stuck it out for a year. But then, as things got worse and life itself seemed to become painful, rows began to erupt — eyeball to eyeball, flying crockery versus flying crockery, back to back in the dark. Spectacular rows about nothing, yet simultaneously about everything that mattered. We tried to paper over the cracks by having sex, which just made things even worse.

Sam and I were one another's first refuge, the first person we would turn to when something went wrong, and she knows the darkest corners of my soul. And I know her. I know she's scared of the dark. The walls of her studio are plastered with posters for *Fight Club*, *The Godfather*, and *Pusher*, but her favourite film is actually *Some Like it Hot*. I know that she has a tattoo on the inside of her thigh, two doves, which sit so high that one of the dove's wingtips strokes her groin. I know that Sam's mother was abused by Sam's father.

But while Viktor's ghost tore away at us, we buried ourselves in our jobs. Whereas this had worked pretty well in the past, perhaps because Sam and I had kept our relationship secret from so many, it now merely created new points of conflict. She rubbed shoulders with the underworld. She got to hear things. When word got out that she was seeing a cop, she didn't just get fewer customers; she got threats from several of them. Sam was outwardly calm, but I could tell that she was shaken. As was I, feeling that it was my fault.

'You should give it up,' I said. 'Try something else.'

'Why should I give up my job? Why not you?'

'It's easier for you.'

'It isn't easier at all,' she hissed. 'You don't love being a cop. I love what I do.'

'You love tattooing serious criminals?' I screamed back. 'Noble work, Sam.'

'You have to twist everything I say,' she said, her voice breaking with a mixture of rage and bitter disappointment.

And so it went on, day after week after month.

'You're not going to split up, surely?' one of Sam's friends asked over coffee.

'Not today,' Sam answered.

WE SPLIT UP two weeks after I'd given her a little necklace with black cubes on it, in an attempt at reconciliation. Around her neck it looked a lot like someone had her in a snare, but she liked it. I moved back to Kungsholmen and Chapmansgatan, and a year later I was involved in what was to become the Gotland affair.

She rang me after seeing the explosion of media coverage; she wanted to know how I was coping with it all. I didn't want to talk just then, but I did call back later. It turned out to be a call full of silence and unspoken words. Maybe that was why, a few days later, I called her again. This time I was high. Sam put the phone down, and I didn't ring back — at least not for a few days. Then I called again. I don't know why; I think I just wanted to hear her voice. It reminded me of how everything had once been so straightforward, so promising. I'd turned thirty without anything dramatic happening, but perhaps now the consequences of being an adult had arrived. I still dream about Viktor.

'SAM,' SHE ANSWERS sharply when I call.

I don't know what to say. So I say nothing, and I'm ashamed of myself.

'Hello?' she says wearily. 'Leo, you have to stop calling me. Are you high?'

'No.'

'I'm going to hang up now.'

'No, wait.'

'What, Leo? What do you want?'

Someone moves in the background — a naked man, in bed, trying to get his girlfriend to stop talking to the man who may still love her. At least that's what I convince myself I am hearing.

'I miss you,' I say quietly.

She says nothing, and it cuts me up inside.

'Don't say that,' she says.

'But I do.'

'No.'

'How do you know that?'

'Stop calling here, Leo.'

'I'm not high. I've stopped.'

She scoffs.

'You haven't.'

'I have.'

'What do you want?'

'I told you. I miss you.'

'I'm not going to say it back.'

We breathe out, and we do so simultaneously. I wonder what that means.

'I need to see you,' I say.

'What for?'

'I need your help.'

'With what?'

I hesitate.

'Did you hear about the woman who got shot at Chapmansgården?'

'Yes.'

'Something doesn't add up. I think you can help me.'

'Are you serious?'

'Deadly serious.'

'Tomorrow, around twelve maybe?' she says, hesitantly. 'I've got a customer at ten, and I won't have time before then.'

'Thanks. Good.'

'Good,' she says.

I wonder what she's thinking.

'Are you happy?' I eventually ask.

Sam puts the phone down, and this time I don't call back.

IT'S NOW LATE EVENING. I'm surrounded by darkness. From my balcony, I can see the building where BAR is located, and I think of Anna, who wanted me to call her. Maybe I should. It might be good for me. Then I think that I ought to go to Salem again, and the thought of it makes me feel terrible. I hear a report about the investigation on the radio. Rebecca Salomonsson's parents in Eskilstuna have been informed of her death. I wonder how they took that news. Losing one another hurts. It's cold out on the balcony, and I smoke one last cigarette. My phone vibrates in my pocket as I walk back in: an anonymous text.

i see you, Leo

I flop onto the sofa, and reply:

who is this?

I hear you're looking for a murderer

tell me who you are, I send.

I pop a Serax from the blister pack lying on the coffee table, swallow it, and take a deep breath.

guess, comes the reply.

is this a joke? I ask.

no

A car starts up, down on the street. I go out onto the balcony and I see it pull away, the city's lights reflected in its dark, glossy paintwork, the back lights glowing red, the inside dimly lit by the light from a mobile phone.

I am twelve. My dad calls me his only friend, everyone else is against him. Beverly Hills 90210 *is on the telly. Dad says that I'm like Dylan. I don't see it myself but it feels good. He's got his arm around me. It's just the two of us at home. Afterwards we get into the car. We're not heading anywhere in particular, just driving. We listen to music and the sun is shining. It's spring. After a while a policeman on the side of the road waves us in. Dad has to blow into a mouthpiece. Then we have to leave the car and get a lift home in the police car. Dad persuades the police to drop us off a bit early, so that we can walk the last bit. I don't know why.*

Mum doesn't shout. She doesn't say anything. She never does. The following spring, Dad agrees to admit himself to a clinic for six months of rehab. He comes home after three days and says that he's fine, that he's okay now. We don't talk to each other anymore because I don't believe him and he knows it. I tell him so once. He throws a chair at me. I run into my room and lock the door. Dad's outside and wants to come in and talk. When I don't open up he gets angry. I put the stereo on and turn it up so I can't hear his voice. Dad bangs on the door with his fists. He bangs so hard that it makes a hole in the cheap plywood. The splinters cut his hands up badly and he gets a taxi to the hospital for some stitches.

What were you doing while I was in the car with Dad? Where were you? Were you alone? I do this a lot nowadays, choose an early memory and think about it, about those early years, before we met. When we were strangers.

IX

When morning arrives, I'm sitting there in the flat, sleepless and red-eyed. The early-morning radio is playing some kind of insane jazz to resurrect any corpses that may have forgotten about the radio before collapsing. It's heavy and angry and it never seems to end, just rising and falling in hasty snippets. Sam. I'm going to meet Sam. Her voice has stayed in my head since our conversation yesterday. I'd almost forgotten how it sounded — how husky yet smooth it is.

I look at my phone.

I hear you're looking for a murderer

Someone wants to make themselves known. I'm supposed to know that someone's watching me.

The psychologist I've been seeing for a while is well known; his face often crops up in the media. I don't know how I ended up here; I just know I'm not the one paying for it. To begin with, I went to a psychologist who specialised in treating police officers recovering from trauma, but after a while I was referred to another. This one has tanned skin, silver-flecked stubble, and a square jaw. He often talks about his upcoming projects: appearing in a television series about mental health, talks in high schools, the book about his childhood that he's planning to write. And then: 'How are you?'

'Good. I suppose.'

'Summer's nearly over.'

'Yes.'

'Autumn's on its way.'

'I suppose so,' I say, looking down at my phone, flipping between the picture of Rebecca Salomonsson's motionless face and the anonymous texts.

'Are you waiting for something?'

'Eh?'

He looks at my phone.

'Could you put that away?'

'No.'

He smiles and carefully stretches out his arms, leans back. He does everything at my pace. He claims that's how we move forward. The truth is that I haven't said anything significant for at least a month. At first he was interested in me, probably because he knew about my background, but his interest soon cooled off. During our meetings I smoke and drink water. I lie when he asks why I'm there, what I think my problems are. Sometimes I shout at him; sometimes I cry; mostly I don't say anything. The hour often passes in silence. Sometimes I'll sit there for the whole session; other times, I'll just get up and leave the room without a word.

This time, I leave the psychologist's room after forty-five minutes.

THERE'S SOMETHING ABOUT this city. Something about the way the besuited barista smiles at the well-dressed, but no one else; something about the sharp elbows on the underground. Something in the way we never make eye contact, about how we're never going to see each other. Everyone's waiting for God to invent something new, something to make it all easier to bear.

Most things in Stockholm used to be something else. Everything can be re-used, renewed. Nothing has any real substance. Buildings that used to be apartments have been turned into shops, and vice versa. The restaurant a short distance from police HQ on Kungsholmsgatan used to be a hairdresser's. A goth-shop on Ringvägen is located in a former strip club. A strip club on Birger Jarlsgatan used to be an antique shop.

I stand on Södermalm and watch as the lunchtime rush chokes Götgatan until all the traffic is at a standstill. Clumps of pedestrians wait on the pavements by every red light. I'm wearing shades, because I always wear shades before and after visiting my psychologist. I head off to the small streets east of Götgatan, and take a Serax when I see the s TATTOO sign. Sam's studio used to be a 1950s convenience store.

The original door has been replaced with a black Plexiglas pane behind thick bars. It's closed but unlocked. Inside, in the chair, sits a young man with vomit-green hair and piercings in his face, topless, leaning forward with his eyes closed, as though he's asleep. Sam isn't there.

But then she appears from a little alcove in the wall furthest from the entrance. She's holding a bottle of red ink, and I involuntarily take a deep breath, raising my hand to knock on the door.

With one hand on the door handle and the other resting on the doorframe, Sam is standing there in front of me, her expression suddenly darker, her jaw muscles straining.

Behind her, the green-haired young man lifts his head and looks inquisitively at us.

'Hi,' she says.

'Hi.'

'Are you going to keep those on?'

'Eh?' But then I remember, and I take my shades off. 'No, I've been to see my psychologist.'

'Right,' she says, apparently confused, and looks down at the little strip of concrete floor that separates us. She lets go of the door. 'I'm with a customer. You'll have to wait.'

'That's fine, I'm not in a hurry.'

Inside s TATTOO there is a strong smell of sterilising fluid and ink. I sit down on the large dark-brown leather sofa. It's worn and frayed. The sofa is in the corner of the studio by the hole in the wall where Sam stores her supply of ink, needles, bandages, antiseptic soap, book-keeping ring-binders, and everything else. As well as film posters, the walls of s TATTOO are adorned with photos on the theme of body parts. Backs, shoulders, necks, faces, hands, stomachs, chests, and thighs — all of them tattooed by Sam.

She's wearing a pair of dark jeans and a white shirt. A snake's tail is just visible, winding its way along her forearm and continuing on under the shirtsleeve onto her upper arm. She puts on a new pair of disposable gloves, and carries on filling in the youngster's back tattoo — a creature from the underworld with the face of a bull and the wings of a dragon, in black, red, and yellow. The electric needle looks and sounds like a dentist's drill, and Sam controls the speed with a foot-pedal.

The young man's face goes from pale to bright red and back to pale again; he's holding on to the chair as if he'd go flying off if he let go.

'I think we're going to need another sitting,' Sam says calmly. 'The only thing I've got left to do is to fill in the other wing.'

'Hmm.' His face is white, his eyes wide open, his lips dry. 'That's okay.' He looks embarrassed.

He leaves s TATTOO, and Sam is standing there with her back to me. It looks like she's watching him, but I doubt it. She takes a deep breath and turns around, walks past me into the storeroom, and comes back with two cans of pop. She sits on the sofa, as far away from me as she possibly can. She opens her can and takes a swig, and I'm struck by the fact that Sam looks even better now than she did a year ago.

'I need your help,' I say.

'I've noticed.' She looks at the clock on the wall. 'I've got ten minutes.'

I pull my phone out and go to the picture.

'Do you recognise her?'

Sam looks at the picture, then looks at me.

'You are unbelievable. How the hell can you just flash a dead woman in my face without any warning?'

'Sorry.' I take a deep breath. 'I just … sorry. Can you have a look and see if you recognise her?'

Sam puts her hand out. When I pass her the phone, my fingers touch hers.

'You're blushing,' I say.

'I'm hot. And upset by this.'

She studies the picture, resolute, blinks slowly with her lips drawn to a thin line, and frowns. It's hard to look at a picture of a dead person. She hands back the phone as though she wants nothing to do with it. Our fingers touch again.

'Rebecca,' she says. 'Isn't it?'

I move closer to her. In her face I see glimpses of the past: I remember what Sam looks like when she laughs. When she cries. When she's asleep. I remember that her face looks peaceful then, like a child's.

'How do you know her name?'

'I met her once, a few months back, at a party. She was there trying to sell. But I didn't get her name then; I didn't find that out till yesterday.'

'Who told you?'

'You know I can't tell you that. Even you just sitting here is risky.'

Threats had started coming in when it became known that Sam Falk was seeing a cop, and there were fewer customers. But that also meant that others came instead — those who'd previously gone elsewhere. Once it had all blown over, Sam's finances were more or less back where they had been in the first place. Then we split up, and I don't know what's happened since then, other than that she still hears things.

'She died in my block, Sam,' I say, looking at her.

'I know.'

'She went out with Miroslav Djukic. Does that name sound familiar?'

Sam raises an eyebrow.

'They were together? I thought he was dead.'

'He is. But you know who he was?'

'Not much more than that. A dosser from Norsborg.'

'Felix thought she might have been staying with one of his friends.'

'I don't know people like that anymore.'

I nod along, although I know that's not true.

'Can you tell me anything else about her? Anything at all?'

Sam bites her bottom lip. This has always had the effect of distracting me, and when she notices my stare she stops abruptly.

'Do you know where she lived?' I ask.

'No, just that she didn't live at Chapmansgården.'

'And how do you know that?'

'A couple of months ago I had a customer who would sometimes spend the night there, when her boyfriend got violent. She told me that no one can live there; it's not that sort of place. You can sleep, get fed and a change of clothes, but it's not exactly a place you'd call home.'

I scratch my cheek. I do that when I'm thinking. At least that's what Sam once told me.

'Something doesn't add up — I just can't work out what it is.'

I tell her what I know about Rebecca Salomonsson, and how illogical her death seems, how efficient the perpetrator has been.

'And according to Felix,' Sam says when I finish, 'there was no one who wanted to do her any harm?'

'Not as far as he knew. He covered himself, naturally, by explaining that he doesn't know everything.'

'Has it occurred to ...?' Sam stops herself.

She bites her bottom lip again. I look down.

'What?' I ask.

'This might not be about her.'

'What do you mean?'

90

'This might not be about a person; this might actually be about a place.'

'You mean Chapmansgården?'

'There are loads of little hidden-away places in this town, indoors and out. Alleyways, parks, junkie neighbourhoods, basements. People like Rebecca Salomonsson have a tendency to be in those sorts of places. If it was about her, why not just get rid of her in one of them? Why Chapmansgården, where the risk of being caught is so much greater?'

'Maybe they were in a hurry,' I say. 'Maybe they were chasing her?'

'Do you just get into bed if you're being chased?'

I shake my head.

'Especially not if you're in such an open place, like Chapmansgården,' I add. 'Anyone can walk straight in.'

Maybe the question is not why she died. The question might be why she died at Chapmansgården. Or perhaps why did *someone* die at Chapmansgården. Something stirs, in a dark corner of my chest. I know this feeling: the problem isn't solved, the question hasn't been answered, but the process has moved on. It's a theory for consideration, something to work on. Work, that's the word on my mind. It feels good.

The door to s TATTOO swings open, and a middle-aged woman walks in and looks around.

'I've got a fortieth-birthday present,' she says, hesitantly.

'A Chinese dragon, if I remember rightly?' says Sam.

'Uh-huh.'

'Maybe we could start with something a bit smaller.'

The woman smiles, seems grateful.

'Just a sec,' Sam says and turns to me again. 'No news about Gotland?'

'Why do you ask?'

'Just wondering.'

'Sometime in the middle of July I gave up trying to find out what happened. No one knows why those boxes were full of toys. No one knows what actually happened. The jeep that disappeared — no clues. As far as I know, I mean. If they weren't trying to stitch me up, that is.'

Sam raises her eyebrows.

'Why would they want to do that?'

'No idea.'

'Doesn't sound very plausible.'

'I know.'

'And what about you?' she asks.

'What do you mean?'

'How are you?'

'I'm going back to work after the New Year.'

'That's a while away.'

'Yes.'

She seems empathetic, but there's something more in her eyes. She suddenly looks vulnerable.

'Have you met someone?'

'No,' I say, 'but I could if I wanted to.'

I'm not trying to hurt her, but when I see the pangs of guilt in her eyes I can't help feeling that she deserves it.

'I understand,' she says.

'Are you happy?' I ask. 'With him?'

'Yes, I am.' She gets up from the sofa. 'Go now. I have to work.'

I'm having trouble figuring out what she's thinking. Then someone calls my phone, from a withheld number. I think about the text messages, wonder if it's the sender contacting me, and I answer the call, still sitting on the sofa.

'This is Leo.'

'I need you at the station as soon as possible.'

Birck. Shit. Sam looks puzzled, turns to look at the clock on the wall. She has crossed her arms underneath her small breasts, pulling her shirt taut over them.

'I'm on leave.'

'You're suspended. But a number of things have turned up, and we need to interview you again.'

'What sort of things?'

'You know how we work, Leo. We can talk about that here.'

I look at the clock.

'I can be there in half an hour.'

'We look forward to it,' Birck says, and the sarcasm lingers on the line long after the call has ended.

'Call me,' is the last thing I say to Sam. 'If you hear anything else,' I add when I notice her confusion, and she nods, blushing.

X

The film was showing at the Rigoletto. I would rather have gone to Haninge or Södertälje, but, according to her, the Rigoletto was the only cinema worth seeing films at, as well as the one with the biggest auditorium. As we sat in front of the screen, I could see what she meant. It was as big and as wide as a tennis court.

When we met up outside I didn't know how to act, or what to say. Julia smiled when she saw me, and I swallowed, several times, and when she put her arm around me and gave me a long hug, I felt her lips touch my earlobe.

Julia wanted popcorn and I paid, even though she wanted to pay herself. She held the box in her lap and I ate some of it, just reaching over the chair and taking some. Even a simple thing like that felt intimate.

It's moments like this that I'll remember forever, I thought to myself. Our teachers and our parents never tired of telling us how certain things felt life-changing now, but would seem silly and exaggerated in a few years' time, but they had missed something. They'd forgotten what it was like to be sixteen. They didn't understand us. That went for everything: we no longer spoke the same language. Everyone was scared of our generation. We were like foreigners to them.

I thought about the film that Grim and I had made a day or so before, how distracted I'd been, and how I'd struggled not to smile the whole time.

'You're too happy,' Grim said, looking up from behind the little camera. 'You're not supposed to be happy in this scene. You need to be oppressed, yeah? Just like I was.'

'I get it,' I said, but however hard I tried, the scene still turned out badly.

Because I was happy. I was neither quiet nor withdrawn, yet I always felt like I was. Dad said that was normal, but I didn't know what he meant. Now I didn't feel like that anymore. Suddenly I felt invincible.

Julia was looking at me for ages. Then she opened her mouth to say something, but stopped herself as the lights dimmed and the heavy red curtains opened, and I remembered nothing from the first half of the film: all I could think of was what Julia had been about to say but I didn't dare ask about.

AT SOME POINT during *The Saint*, Julia put her hand on my thigh. It was there long enough to send a jolt through me, but she suddenly whipped it away, and went stiff in the seat next to me. She leant over, and I felt her breath in my ear.

'Sorry. I meant to put it on your hand.'

I put my hand out in the darkness, and she carefully placed her palm on the back of my hand. Now that we were touching, it was even more difficult to think, impossible to watch the film. After a while she started stroking my hand carefully with her fingertips, as though she were exploring it — the downy hairs, the veins, and the knuckles. I didn't know what to do, so I took a deep breath and hoped that she wouldn't notice. My heart was threatening to strangle me, as though it were now in my throat and about to pop out of my mouth and into my lap.

AFTERWARDS WE WALKED THROUGH a warm Stockholm towards Central Station. She put her hand in mine.

'I like you,' I said after a while.

'How long have you liked me?'

Not the reaction I was expecting.

'Erm, yeah, I don't know, a while?'

'A while,' she mimicked, laughing. 'I'm not going to say it back.'

'Why not?' My heart beat harder again. 'Don't you li—'

'It's not easy for me to say stuff like that.'

On the train home, I kissed her. She tasted salty on her lips, from the popcorn, and sweet inside, from the fizzy drink. It was me that kissed her, not the other way around, and I was ready for her to give me a slap just for trying. Julia Grimberg seemed like that kind of girl. Instead, her mouth met mine, and I soon felt her hand on my thigh again. This time it didn't move away, and I wanted to touch her hair but I didn't dare to move my arm, worried it might spoil the moment. The train stopped, and people got on. They sniggered, and I thought it was at us. I didn't care.

We separated in front of the Triad, where the three blocks towered high and white above us.

I looked at her. She seemed deep in thought.

'I'll give you a hundred kronor if you tell me what you're thinking,' I said.

She laughed.

'It would cost you more than that!' she said, and let go of my hand. 'See you soon.'

GRIM WAS WALKING ACROSS the playground towards me. I wasn't ashamed, but I realised that I was going to have to lie to him. Julia was more important to him than anything else, and my kissing her wouldn't make him happy. I pictured his face if I were to tell him that we'd held hands.

'What did you do this weekend?' he asked.

'Nothing much. Went to the football.'

'Football? Do you like football?'

'No. It was for my dad's sake. We got the train in to Södermalm together.'

There was the lie. Perhaps it should have been hard, but it wasn't. It was easy. I thought of Julia's face. I hadn't seen her since we said goodbye on Friday, and I hadn't heard her voice either. That made me feel miserable.

'What about you?' I mumbled, without looking at him.

'This.' He held something out towards me and I took it off him. 'My first.'

I caught his stare and saw the glint in his eye.

'What do you think?'

He'd given me his ID card. I looked at it, turned it upside down and back-to-front. It was nothing more than that.

'Is this a joke?'

'What do you think that is?' He beamed, broadly and proudly.

'An ID card.'

'That's right.' He leant over towards me. 'Look at the year.'

He put his index finger next to it.

Then I understood.

'You were born in seventy-nine,' I said. 'Right? This says seventy-eight.'

'Compare it with this one.' He sounded excited. 'See any difference?'

He pulled out an ID card identical to the one I was holding. Same style, same information, same photo of Grim staring at the camera with a blank expression, the blond hair short and the lips pursed.

'The year,' I said. 'This one says seventy-eight; the other one says seventy-nine.'

'Apart from that? Any difference?'

'No.'

'Perfect.'

'Have you shown anyone else?'

He shook his head. 'I wanted to show you first.'

I looked up from the ID card and our eyes met; I could see how proud he was, and I realised I didn't know what to do next. I couldn't lie to him about Julia, but I couldn't tell him the truth either.

'I started with Tipp-Ex on an old card, on the surface itself,' he said. 'About six months ago. I put a tiny drop over the nine. And if you just glanced at it quickly, you didn't see that it actually said seventy-nine. But if you ran your finger over, it just felt like a tiny crumb had stuck to it. I thought about how I could make it better, and tried other stuff, until I found a way to redo the whole card.'

I rubbed my fingers over the card, and felt the ridges in the hard plastic.

'It's not completely smooth,' I said.

'You have to cut the plastic really carefully to get it like that. That's what took longest. That, and finding thick-enough plastic. It's the same stuff as they use.'

I must have looked blank.

'The Post Office. The ones who do the real thing.' He took both the cards off me, and stuffed them back in his pocket. 'I think I can make money from this.'

'Probably,' I said, thinking of all the people we knew who would like nothing more than to get into clubs with age limits, where brain-dead bouncers who'd failed to become cops stood on the door and ran the world.

'Do you want one?'

'Me? Er, sure.'

'Give me your ID. I just need it for a week or so.'

I held it out and he took it, studying it so closely that the card almost touched his nose.

'It'll be the first time I've done someone other than myself,' he mumbled, turning the card over. 'I wonder if it will be as good.'

'Grim, I ...'

'What?'

They were alike; not at first glance, but it was still there, in their expressions.

'Nothing.' I looked down at my shoes. 'Doesn't matter.'

We agreed a price for the card. It was lower than I expected, but I still had no idea where I was going to get the money from.

The money he'd sniffed out at my place — I could use that. I hadn't touched it.

Break was over. I left Grim, and walked over towards the nondescript entrance.

SHE WAS WAITING for me behind the water tower. When I got there it was dark and black; squawking birds circled the tower, as though encouraging someone to fall. I had my hands in the pockets of my hoodie and I took them out, hoping that my palms would get less sweaty.

She was wearing jeans, a red vest with narrow shoulder straps, and black Converses, and was holding a thick black cardigan in her hands. I wondered if she might be cold, but when she came over I felt the temperature rise and I could hear a muffled hum — something in the tower, maybe a generator or a motor of some sort, making the spot where she was standing unnaturally warm.

'You're early,' she said.

'So are you.'

When Julia put her arms around me she stood on tiptoes, and then pressed her slim body against mine, her small breasts soft against my ribs, her hands around my neck, and her hair in my face.

'It's very warm here,' she said quietly, with her lips to my ear.

'You could have stood somewhere else.'

'I didn't want to, in case you couldn't find me.'

She let go, and we stood there looking at each other.

'Grim's got my ID card,' I said, because you have to say something.

'I know. He showed it to me,' Julia giggled. 'You look funny in that picture. Sort of young.'

After a while we climbed up the tower, and sat down on the

ledge. Julia's hand was resting in mine, and it felt very small.

'I always get a bit thoughtful, or whatever you call it, when I'm sitting up here,' she said.

'How come?'

She nodded towards one of the many buildings below us.

'I knew someone who lived in one of those blocks over there, the one with the red roof. It just always makes me, well, just thoughtful, really.'

Julia told me that they'd gone to the same pre-school and were the same age and had the same shoes. That's how it had started; the little boy was getting teased for having the same shoes as one of the girls. Julia had helped him out by explaining to the others that he didn't actually have girls' shoes; it was she who had boys' shoes. Julia was a peaceful child — the calm before the storm, you know, she once said to me, and laughed — and the boy was, too, so they would often play the same games and go to the playground together. They became friends, and started at the same school, started listening to music together. They eventually drifted apart, as you do when you start a new school and end up in different classes, but they stayed friends.

'But,' Julia said, 'there was always something strange about him. When we were about eleven or twelve, I started to realise that he was keeping something from me. At first I was sure he fancied me, that it was that. But it wasn't — our relationship was never like that. We were more like brother and sister, you know?'

Julia had even told him about her family, which she hadn't told anyone else apart from Social Services, and that was more or less under duress.

'Isn't that strange?' she said. 'That he never said anything?'

'Yeah,' I said.

They drifted further apart, despite going to the same school. When they met in the dark-grey corridors, they would only say hello.

Another summer floated past, as they always did in Salem, warm and eventful. Julia saw him at the recreation ground during the end-of-term ceremony that June. And then, after the summer, he was just gone. Disappeared. A week or so of the new term went past before it dawned on her. She hadn't seen him, started worrying for some reason she couldn't describe, and called his parents. They weren't living there anymore, and Julia had no idea where they'd gone.

'I haven't seen him since,' Julia said. 'And I don't know why, but it's hard when people disappear. It's hard to deal with; even though you weren't that close before they disappeared, it's still like something is ... well, missing.'

'What was his name?' I asked.

'I don't think you'd know him.'

'Tell me anyway, what was his name?'

'Tim,' said Julia. 'Tim Nordin.'

The name was like an invisible punch in the gut. I was winded.

'No, you're right. I don't know who that is.'

SUMMER HAD COME ROUND again, the kind of summer that paralyses a whole town. Along with my dad, I'd helped my brother move out. He'd turned eighteen and worked in a carpaint shop, making rust buckets look like new, every day from eight till four. I'd agreed to help him move after being offered money; but once we'd finished, taking it didn't feel right. It felt great doing something together. We didn't do it very often then. When we were kids we'd go on outings in the summer, to zoos and amusement parks. We drove go-karts and played football on a field outside Salem. I hadn't been to the field in ages. Maybe I could take Grim there now. He'd like it.

During the move, we were down in the cellar, rummaging through boxes. And in one of the boxes we found a framed newspaper cutting from 1973; the picture showed the remains of an old petrol station outside Fruängen. In the background you could see fallen power lines. MOTORING MADNESS ENDS IN DISASTER was the headline. Dad liked telling that story — how this was before he got back together with Mum, how he used to gamble heavily on the horses. Once, he won a big bet at the Solvalla races and bought a white Volvo P1800 with the winnings, 'the type of car Simon Templar drives in *The Saint*'. He loved to thrash the hell out of it on the roads around Fruängen. At the crossing by the petrol station, he lost control of the car, drove onto the forecourt, and knocked two pumps over, smashing into one of the roof's supporting pillars in the process. The roof collapsed behind him as he carried on towards the power lines, and the last thing Dad remembered was sparks above the bonnet. The power went out in the neighbourhood, and at the time of writing it was unclear whether the 'madman' (the doctor's word, not the reporter's) would survive. Dad was in hospital for two months, and he received a letter claiming damages for several hundred thousand kronor. I'm pretty sure he thought it was worth it.

During the move, Dad told us the story. We had heard it before, but this time we both let him tell it again. It was reassuring to hear something from the past, like some sort of echo from childhood.

'It feels strange,' Dad said, sitting there behind the wheel, on the way back to the Triad. 'Now Micke's gone, and it'll soon be your turn.'

'It'll be a while yet, Dad.'

'I know.' He hesitated. 'You haven't thought about getting a job?'

'What do you mean?'

'A summer job somewhere? Isn't it about time? A lot of people your age do.'

'It's too late now.'

'Yes, it might be, but have you even thought about it?'

I hadn't. Just the very thought of working bored the shit out of me.

'Yes,' I said. 'I've thought about it. But I don't know where it would be.'

'You have to take what you can get, at your age.'

I listened to the radio: a news bulletin was just finishing, followed by a song, and Dad turned up the volume. When the song finished, he looked at me with a faint smile.

'Your mum and I used to dance to that.'

'Course you did.'

'We did! It's ABBA.' He was quiet for a moment.

'He liked it here, didn't he? At ours?'

'What do you mean?'

'Micke.'

'Ah-ha. Yes. Yes, he did.'

Dad looked at me and smiled.

'Thanks.'

We drove on. Dad cleared his throat. He always did when he needed to say something important.

'The money in the vase,' he said. 'I don't care why you took it, and if you've already spent it I don't want it back. But don't ever do it again. Don't take what isn't yours. It's wrong, cheap, and wicked. If you need money, borrow it from us. Or, even better, get a job.'

I didn't know what to say, so I said nothing.

GRIM HAD FINISHED my false ID card. I could now claim to have been born in seventy-eight, instead of eighty. It was flawless. That didn't surprise me, for some reason. I kept it in my bedside drawer. One afternoon at the beginning of June, I met up with Grim outside the Triad. He was walking home from town, the headphones from his new Discman on his ears. He raised his arm and smiled when he saw me, and started taking his headphones off.

'You look pleased,' I said.

'I am pleased.'

'How come?'

'I've got hold of some money.' He winked. 'I'm going to the water tower — you coming?'

'No,' I said, without thinking.

He raised an eyebrow.

'Why not?'

'I've got … I'm busy.' I started walking towards town, and his eyes followed me. 'I'll come later. In a bit.'

He seemed disappointed, but nodded once, turned around, and carried on.

'Leo.'

I turned around again.

'Yes.'

Grim's satisfied look had disappeared, and now he had a dejected, cold expression.

'I'm going away for a month after midsummer.'

'What?'

'I, er, I stole the money from the school's travel kitty. It wasn't the first time, but this time Social Services got called in, and they're sending me away.'

'You're joking.'

He shook his head.

'It was a lot of money. I needed it to do the cards and stuff.'

'Why didn't you say?'

He shrugged, didn't answer. He just looked at the ground.

'Where are they sending you?'

'The summer camp in Jumkil. They think that'll be best. I was going to run away, you know, stay away for a while so they wouldn't find me, but that would just make it worse.'

'Probably.'

He seemed unsure.

'You'll keep … could you keep an eye on Julia while I'm away? So she doesn't … just keep an eye out, while I can't.'

'Course,' I managed.

He looked at me for ages, before he nodded and waved his hand.
'Go on. See you round.'
'Yes. We'll have loads of time before you go. I'll be there in a bit.'
'Sure.'

It was going to be a long summer.

JUMKIL'S SUMMER CAMP was outside the town itself, attached to one of the toughest young offenders' institutions around. I'd heard of the institution, because my brother's friend had been sent there after trying to steal a car. It was the sort of place where feral youngsters were supposed to be treated and then released on the right side of the law, but in fact it achieved the opposite. The neighbouring summer camp's reputation wasn't much better, and Julia was worried what it might do to Grim.

'He'll be fine,' I said, lying next to her underneath the water tower.

Her hand sought mine, and found it. It was the Monday after midsummer, which I'd spent with the family in Blåsut, where Granddad lived. Arthur Junker had joked about Alzheimer's for years; but when it took hold of him, the joke was over and he became miserable and introverted. He called my mum 'Sara', which was my grandmother's name. At certain points during the dinner, he didn't seem to recognise me or my brother. After the meal, I went to a party near Salem Church with Grim. He didn't want to socialise; I think he came along for my sake. During the party, he sat in the corner looking anxious, as though he didn't know how to behave. And now he'd gone, to Jumkil.

'Do you remember after the cinema,' I said, 'when you said it was hard for you to say you liked someone?'

'Yeah.'

'Why is that?'

Julia lifted herself up slightly, propping herself up with her elbows.

'I just haven't had good experiences with boys, that's all.'

'Like what?'

'It usually just … I've only been with a few, like three. But it's always ended with me getting hurt and John getting furious.' She sank down again, looked up at the sky. 'About a year ago I was at a party and I drank a lot. I fancied one of the guys; he was in the first year at Rönninge then. I ended up passing out, I can't remember how exactly. But when I woke up I was lying on a bed, on top of the covers, with no knickers on. It didn't hurt, so I hadn't been … I hadn't been used that way. But I found out afterwards that it was him, the guy I fancied, who'd interfered with me. Apparently someone had come in to get something from that room; they'd put their booze in there so it wouldn't get nicked. It was just chance that someone came in, but he got scared and left. That's the sort of experience I have of guys. I know you're not like that at all, you know? You mustn't think I think that about you; I don't, it's just so hard to sort of … start again.'

'Did you tell Grim?'

'His name is John. And no, not in a million years — are you mental? John would've killed him.'

THAT EVENING, her parents were out, and she took me home for the first time. Their flat was exactly the same as ours — just a mirror image. Inside the door, a faint sour smell came from the bag of rubbish propped against the wall. Julia, visibly embarrassed, went and threw it into the rubbish chute.

She showed me straight to her room, so I only got a glimpse of the rest of the flat. It was tidier than I was expecting. I recognised some of Grim's clothes hanging on the rail by the door. The kitchen looked simple, like ours except without a dishwasher. We'd bought our own, and I guessed that the Grimbergs either didn't mind washing up or couldn't afford one. One of the doors had a hole the size of a fist through it, as though someone had thrown a rock at it or punched it hard. That was Grim's door.

Julia closed the door behind us and we stood there in her room. She didn't seem to know what to do with her hands. Eventually, she lifted them up to the jewellery hanging around her neck and touched the chain. One wall was covered by a bookcase; a narrow bed ran along the one opposite. The shelves were full of books and films. There was a mirror on the desk, and a vanity bag with make-up spilling out of it. The walls were decorated with paintings and photographs.

'Do you like them?' she asked.

'The photos?'

'Yes.'

They were mainly portraits of people about our age, but I didn't recognise them. A couple featured tower blocks, but taken from below and at such an angle that large parts of the image were filled with sky.

'Yes,' I said.

She nodded, let go of the necklace, smiled, took a few steps, and pushed herself against me.

'This is the first time a boy's been in my room.'

'This is the first time I've been in a girl's room.'

She kissed me, and the nerves spread through my chest. My heart beat harder, until I could hear it in my ears.

'Shall we watch a film?' she asked.

I'D LIED TO HER and I didn't know whether it mattered. It was only sex, but I'd never done it before. Julia's skin was pale and unnaturally smooth, as though she'd never been exposed to anything. As I touched it, a wave of warmth went through me and I felt the hairs on my arms stand up. She was fully clothed and straddling me; I could just see the telly over her shoulder, how the film scenes flipped past in the murky room.

'Take your clothes off,' she said.

'Everything?'

'Everything.'

I'd never been naked in front of anyone before. I was embarrassed, standing there in front of her. She must have noticed, because she pulled me towards her and stroked my arms and shoulders.

'You are beautiful,' she whispered and something in her touch made me relax.

'So are you. But ...'

'What?'

'I lied to you before.'

She went stiff. 'About what?'

'About not being a virgin.'

'And?'

'What?'

'All boys lie about that. I'm not exactly surprised. Do you mean you'd rather lose it with someone else?'

'No,' I said. 'No. Were you lying, too?'

'No.'

In the darkness in front of the film, something inside me quivered.

'I haven't got a condom. Have you?'

'Relax. I'm on the pill.'

I wondered if Grim knew that, and realised there were lots of things I didn't know about; I realised how little I knew.

XI

I am at the station for the first time since the beginning of July. For some reason, I'm surprised to see that nothing much has changed. I'm led down the corridor by a stern constable I don't recognise. In one of the rooms we walk past, a lonely radio is playing pop music, and a printer splutters into action, starts spitting out paper. I gaze out the window, thinking about how great the distance between me and everyone else seems to be.

'Gabriel will be along shortly,' the officer mumbles, opening the door to one of the interview rooms. 'Can I get you anything?'

'Coffee.'

The constable disappears and I'm left alone in the room, which is small and square, just a table and two chairs. I'm not actually alone; a hidden camera is pointing at me, recording my every move. A bookcase full of binders stands against one wall. It doesn't belong there. Maybe they're doing something in one of the other rooms. The other walls are cool and silent. The lighting is softer than I remember, almost comfortable. If I strain, I can hear the radio. I look at the texts on my phone. The constable returns with a light-blue coffee cup. I drink a mouthful; it's that taste that really makes me want to come back.

I hear footsteps, and Birck steps through the doorway, without looking at me. He's carrying a folder under one arm that he places on the table, just as his phone starts ringing.

'Birck.' Short silence. 'Right? 'How did you get this number?'

Birck glances at me, for the first time. 'I have no comment to make.' He clears his throat, and goes back to the door and closes it. 'No, I can't answer that. No comment. Thank you.'

He hangs up, and the female voice on the other end is abruptly silenced.

'A good friend?' I venture.

'*Expressen.*'

'Annika Ljungmark?'

'Yes.' He pulls out a chair and sits down, looks for something in his jacket pocket without finding it. 'She was after you, wasn't she?' he says, still looking for something. 'After Gotland?'

'Yes. What did she want?'

'She wanted to confirm a tip-off.'

'About what?'

He takes the dictaphone out of his trouser pocket. He places it between us, runs his fingers through his dark hair, leaves the folder shut.

'Right, Leo.' He looks up; our eyes meet. 'We have some further questions about Rebecca Salomonsson.'

'I had worked that out. What was the tip-off?'

'Right now, I need to ask you the questions. Please conduct yourself appropriately.'

'I'm doing my best.'

He gives me an icy look before wearily stating the date and time for the tape, and then says his name and mine, and the case number of the Rebecca Salomonsson investigation.

'Leo, could you put the phone away?'

I put my phone in my pocket, and drink some of the coffee. Birck looks more tense than usual.

'Could you please describe exactly what you did when you went into Chapmansgården?'

I do so, in short, simple sentences, expressing myself in a way that makes it hard to misunderstand what I'm saying. I want to get out of here as soon as possible. Once again, I describe how I got into Chapmansgården, how I saw Matilda sitting talking to a cop, how I went up to the body.

'According to Matilda, you touched her,' Birck interrupts. 'I have a statement from her saying that you touched the body.'

'I see. That is true. But I was wearing gloves.'

This takes him by surprise.

'Your own gloves?'

'No, I found them in a basket by the door.'

'What were you doing, when you touched the body?'

'Nothing really. The usual.'

'The usual, as in …?'

'What is this about?' I ask. 'What are you after? If you just come out and say it, it will be easier for me to— '

'Answer my questions, Leo.'

I think I'm rolling my eyes, because Birck bites his lip.

'Looking for any marks,' I say. 'Checking her pockets.'

'Why did you do that?'

'To steal things to flog down in Hammarby harbour.'

'For fuck's sake, Leo!'

'I don't know. To see if there were any … I was bored, all right? And it bothered me, the fact that someone had died right underneath me.'

Birck seems to accept this, maybe because it's actually true.

'You didn't say this yesterday.'

'What?'

'When I spoke to you yesterday, you never said that you'd touched the body. Why did you lie?'

'I … don't know. You didn't ask. It's just detail.'

He puts the palms of his hands flat on the tabletop.

'I did ask. It's quite a crucial fucking detail. An unauthorised person has been and rifled around the crime scene before we got there. Do you know what a slick defence lawyer can do in court with a little detail like that?'

'There was nothing in her pockets,' I say. 'But she had something in her hand.'

'How do you know that?'

'Because I saw it. It looked like a necklace or something.'

'And you touched it.'

'No,' I say, and my expression is so open that Birck doesn't manage to find a lie there, try as he might. 'No, I didn't. I only noticed it just as you arrived.'

'So you didn't touch it,' Birck says. 'Have I understood correctly?'

I nod. Birck points wearily at the dictaphone.

'Yes,' I say and lean forward. 'You have understood correctly what I said — that I did not touch her hand or whatever she was holding in it.'

Birck opens the folder lying between us; in place of the first page is a plastic wallet, A4 size. In one corner is something small and silver. A sticker with messy notes, a description of the contents along with the case number, is stuck on the outside of the wallet.

'If you never touched it,' he says, so slowly that it winds me up, 'how come the fingerprint analysis came back with three different prints, one of which is 95 per cent certain to be yours?'

He lifts the wallet and puts it down in front of me. I look at the necklace inside, and an invisible blow strikes me in the stomach, making the world rock back and forth.

'Is this what Rebecca had in her hand?' I say, without looking up from the necklace.

'Yes.'

'Okay.'

I've seen this necklace before, touched it. Once I even had it in my mouth.

'Is everything okay?' Birck smiles. 'You seem a bit shaken.'

'No, I … I've just … I've been wondering what it looked like. You said there were three matches. Who are the other two?'

'You need to answer my question, Leo.'

'I'll answer your question if you answer mine.'

'This isn't a game!'

Birck stands up with such force that the chair clatters across the bare floor. He looks back and forth, first at me, then the dictaphone, then at me again; he seems to be contemplating turning it off, so that what happens next isn't caught on the tape.

'Annika Ljungmark, from *Expressen*,' he says, 'has somehow been tipped off that one of the suspects in the case is a police officer. A police officer with an — how shall we put this? — infamous past. If you don't cut the crap and tell me exactly what you've done, the tip will be confirmed and you'll never get back on duty. And if you do, by some miracle, get back on duty, I'll make sure it's at the back of beyond in some shithole like Mjölby or Säter.' He sits down again. 'How the hell do you want to fucking play this?'

I pretend to be contemplating it, but in fact I'm still just staring at the necklace. It's one of those cheap necklaces; there'll be thousands like it around, but only one has my prints on it.

It's hers.

It must be hers. I can't tell Birck. I can't.

'Okay,' I say. 'I touched it. I saw that she had something in her hand, and I just wanted to see what it was. I looked at it and put it back.'

'Didn't you have gloves on?'

'I had to take them off,' I say, to keep the lie going. 'I had to take them off; I'd just picked them out of the basket, and they were too big and far too thick. I couldn't open her hand with them on, so I took them off.'

Birck stares at me, trying to work out whether or not I'm telling the truth.

'We'll be doing more tests, Leo. If you're lying, we'll notice.'

'I haven't lied,' I lie, and attempt a smile.

'You do know what this means?'

Because I've led Birck to believe that the print on the necklace is fresh, I am, from this point on, a potential suspect. It puts me at the scene of the crime. I could have been the one who went into Chapmansgården, put a gun to her temple, and pulled the trigger, escaping through the open window.

'Who are the other two?' I ask.

'Don't you worry about that.'

'Come on,' I attempt. 'I live in the bloody building.'

'Exactly. That's why we're sitting here.'

'No, we're sitting here because someone has shot a woman. I live in the building; perhaps I can help. Come on. I didn't fucking shoot her — for a start, I've got no motive, and even if I did have a motive, I'm not that daft that I'd shoot her on my own doorstep.'

Birck stares at me long enough for me to start convincing myself that I am managing to persuade him. He stops the tape-recorder, sticks it back in his pocket, and looks at me again. The change in his expression is remarkable. He looks almost compassionate, and since this is Gabriel Birck, that surprises me.

'One set were her own. The other gave no matches. But both yours and the third party were incomplete and inconclusive.'

'She had no possessions,' I say. 'As far as I could see.'

'We found them this morning. Or rather, a dog did. He and his owner were out on their morning walk round Kungsholmen. Her bag was lying in a bush in Kronoberg Park. Everything was there except her phone, money, and whatever drugs she might have had.'

'She was robbed, then,' I say. 'On the night she was murdered?'

'Maybe.' Birck shrugs. 'No one saw anything.'

'So she may have been robbed and then made her way to Chapmansgården to sleep?'

'What would you have done in her position, homeless and with no possessions? Besides, she was probably so high that she didn't know her own name. She wasn't about to go to the police. Stranger things have happened than people in that situation going to bed. The question is whether anyone followed her — a pimp or a punter. As it stands, nothing points to that. And listen,' he adds, 'I'm only telling you this because I believe you. If anyone asks, you are still my main suspect.'

I wonder if he does actually believe me. Perhaps, but he suspects I know more than I'm letting on; I can sense that, and cops — and above all, cops like Gabriel Birck — are sly creatures. They are taught how to play people; they learn little tricks that make it seem like they mean well. He might have just said this in the hope that I'm going to tell him more.

Or maybe he actually believes me. I don't know.

'Okay,' I say, staring down at the desk.

He keeps looking at me; I keep avoiding eye contact. It's so quiet I can hear my own pulse.

'Good,' Birck says flatly. 'Get out of here.'

I'M OUTSIDE, standing under the overcast sky. I take several deep breaths. My head's spinning, and I feel sick; it's hard to breathe. It's been so long since I thought about her. She's been there sometimes, like a ghost. Some nights.

Julia Grimberg's necklace was in Rebecca Salomonsson's hand. They couldn't have known each other. It must have been put there by whoever killed her.

AND, AS IF I'm being watched, my phone buzzes.

not going to have a guess? writes the anonymous sender.

guess what? I write, looking over my shoulder, looking around for anyone who might be sticking out from the crowd.

guess who i am, comes the reply.

are you the one who killed her?

no it wasn't me

do you know who did it?
maybe
who was it?
I can see you, Leo

XII

I light a cigarette, standing near the underground station, and write: *what am i doing right now*

Cars roll past; people walk by. My phone soon buzzes again.

you're smoking on the street

It could be anyone. The apartment windows that make up Kungsholmsgatan's façades are dark — no lights on. You can't tell whether there's anyone standing there. The smells of exhausts and deep fat fryers surround me; the air feels thick, like just before rain. I look at the text on my phone and realise that I'm scared, for the first time in ages.

who killed her? I repeat, and stare at the phone, aware that I'm holding my breath. Nothing happens; no message arrives.

I take out the little note with the number that Levin had written down during our conversation yesterday — the number I was to ring if I wasn't getting anywhere. I stare at the people walking past me, thinking that one of them is the anonymous texter, and that he or she wants to harm me; that somebody is going to appear and rush at me with a knife in their hand. I need to sit down. I need a strong drink, alone.

I wonder who I'm calling. The only thing Levin revealed was that the number belonged to someone he knows well. I turn around, and look at the hulk of the police headquarters behind me. I pop a Serax on my tongue and click my neck, feel the pill bouncing down my throat before it disappears inside me; I realise that the number probably belongs to someone at HQ. Two boys are standing on the pavement: one has dark skin and fuzzy hair; the other one has pale skin, and a posture that gives the impression he's embarrassed about something. The dark-skinned boy is playing guitar, and the other is staring at the road, singing about finding love in a hopeless place, again and again in a light, clear voice while people pass by without stopping.

'Alice here,' someone answers in my ear.

'Hi, it, I ... where have I called?'

'Who is this?'

'My name is Leo Junker. Charles Levin gave me your number.'

'He mentioned you.'

'Are you at HQ?' I ask.

'That's right.'

'And this is a secure line?'

'This is a secure line.'

She sounds measured but distant, as though she's doing something else at the same time, something that has most of her attention.

'Who are you?' I ask.

'Alice. I work for Charles.'

'You're his secretary, right?'

'That's right.'

'I think I need your help.'

'Go on.'

'John Grimberg. I need to meet someone called John Grimberg. I have no idea where he is, or even if he's alive.'

'Okay,' she says, sceptical. That's the first and only emotion she reveals.

'I haven't seen him in over fifteen years,' I say, for some reason feeling the need to explain myself.

'Born?'

'Seventy-nine. But check seventy-eight, too, just to make sure.'

'He was born in two different years?' she asks, puzzled.

'I don't know,' I say. 'Seventy-eight may be false.'

'Born in Stockholm?'

'Greater Stockholm — Salem.'

I hear the tapping of keys in the background. I head down underground now, step onto the escalator, and try to work out if anyone's following me.

'I have a John Grimberg, born seventy-nine; first address is Salem,' I hear Alice say. 'Long criminal record; first offence was ninety-seven. Mother born fifty-six, died ninety-nine; father born fifty-four, died three weeks ago.'

'Only three weeks?'

'That's what it says here.'

'Do you have an address? For John, I mean.'

'No. I, oh … wait.' She sounds confused, and judging by her sudden interest, it's quite unusual for something to confuse Alice. 'The last entry I have is an address in Hagsätra. From ten years ago.'

She gives me the address, and I try to memorise it.

'You mean he's dead?'

'No, and he hasn't left the country either. At least not as far as I can see. He is on the Whereabouts Unknown register, though.'

'Whereabouts Unknown register?'

'I can't see any more than that, just that Revenue and Customs have recorded him there. I can contact them and ask for more details, but even if it's given priority it will still take a few hours.'

The Whereabouts Unknown register — made up of individuals who, for one reason or another, the authorities have not been able to contact. People with shady pasts, but also people who just don't want to be found. Those with secret identities, those who've been given new identities, have their old details entered into the register. The same goes for people who've been missing from the electoral roll for two years or more. The register is never updated, so even if you're impossibly old, your details remain on file there. The only updates occur when the person is certified dead, if it is discovered that the person has left the country, if they have somehow started using their original identity again, or if they reappear on the electoral roll. It doesn't take much for one of those last three to happen — just paying by card somewhere, crossing the border, or talking to an estate agent about a property. John Grimberg hasn't done any of those things, since he's still on the register. As though he's just disappeared.

'I assume that this is important,' Alice says now, and I am down on the platform, watching a blue-and-silver train pulling out from the mouth of the tunnel.

'Yes,' I say. 'It is. It's about his sister.'

'Julia,' I hear her read on the screen. 'Julia Grimberg?'

'That's right.'

'Died in August ninety-seven.'

I swallow hard, and when I blink, the necklace flashes before my eyes.

'That's right.'

THE SUN IS SHINING over Hagsätra, and a group of kids are standing on the square, kicking a ball around. They are tanned, and speak to each other in a language I don't understand. Grim's last known address is here, right by the square. The light-coloured tower blocks and their small windows remind me of Salem. The door to the lobby is open, and I climb the stairs to the second floor, then knock on the first of three doors. No answer. The other two doors are open, and I introduce myself as a friend of John Grimberg's, but neither of them has ever heard of him. They got their flats through the council lists. I wonder which of the three he lived in, get the urge to ask if I can come in and have a look — mainly to get an idea how he might have lived — but I think better of it. It wouldn't be of any use. I thank them for their help, and leave.

I call Felix, who doesn't answer. After that, I spend the rest of the afternoon trying to find any trace of John Grimberg via the contacts

I usually use, but none of them have any useful information. I even go to the tax office on Södermalm and sit down at one of their terminals, to check the public records, but there's nothing there. It's as though Grim erased his own existence ten years ago.

I start to doubt myself. No one knows better than I do that there can be a heavy price paid for withholding information during an investigation, and by late evening I'm standing in my flat, ready to call Gabriel Birck and tell him everything, when the phone starts vibrating in my hand. It's Sam.

On Chapmansgatan, the incident tape is still in place. I look at it flapping in the wind, and see passers-by still stopping and trying to picture what has happened. There are cars parked along the street. I think there is someone sitting in one of them, but I can't be sure.

'Hello?'

'It's Sam.'

'Hi, Sam.'

'I, er ... am I interrupting something?'

'No. No, don't worry.'

'I just thought ... after you were here earlier ...'

'Yes?' I say, and push the phone harder to my ear. 'Yes, thanks for making time.'

'A customer came in later. I think you know who he is — they call him Viggo.'

I know who he is. He's one of Felix's dealers. He was one of the people I met today, after I left Hagsätra. He confirmed that he'd heard a rumour about someone robbing a whore near Kronoberg Park, but he hadn't made the connection with the rumour about Rebecca Salomonsson's death.

'I met him today,' I tell her. 'No help.'

'He told me. Because he knows that you and I ... well, he mentioned that you'd met, and that you'd asked about someone called Grim.'

'John Grimberg,' I say, and my whole body goes stiff. 'That's right.'

'You didn't tell me that, when we met. You never mentioned his name, that it was him you were looking for.'

I recognise that tone in her voice only too well: Sam sounds hurt.

'At that point I wasn't,' I say, apologetically. 'That emerged later.'

'I think ... I don't know who John Grimberg is, but "Grim" rang a bell.'

On the street below, someone starts a car. I go over to the window again, apprehensive. The inside of the car is illuminated by the light from a mobile phone. I can just about make out a silhouette in there, but nothing more.

'Where are you right now?' I ask.

'Why?'

'We have to meet.'

'Leo, I don't think that's a good idea, we can't ...'

'It's not about that.'

'What is it about then?'

I take a deep breath and wonder who's sitting in the car down on the street. Wonder if I'm paranoid, and how this might sound:

'I think this phone is being tapped.'

XIII

Evening. I walk through the streets of Kungsholmen, heading for BAR. It's a stupid place to meet Sam, but it's the only neutral ground I can think of. On the way, I make countless attempts to establish whether or not I'm being followed; I take several diversions, but it's difficult. The neighbourhood is full of small streets and alleys that become deep and impenetrable. It seems to me there are nooks and crannies in this town that, if you were ever to enter, you would never get back out of. Beyond the neon signs and the streetlamps, an unnaturally thick darkness awaits — the kind of darkness that almost materialises, that you can taste on your tongue if you open your mouth.

The car that had been waiting on the street is gone. I haven't seen it since I started walking. My phone is silent. Rebecca Salomonsson is dead, with Julia's necklace in her hand, with my prints on it. Someone put it there — and I need to find Grim. We haven't seen each other for fifteen years; that's almost half my life. Almost half of his. But he might be able to give me an answer. There might be witnesses who can make Birck understand that it wasn't me, that I had nothing to do with her death. The problem with witnesses is that they're unreliable. They're like indicators, like indirect clues as to what has actually happened. No police officer trusts other people, and if any other evidence points to me, I'm in trouble.

His mother died early, while he was still young. I didn't know that; I wonder how it happened. Maybe suicide. Probably suicide.

And the father. I try to recall what Alice said on the phone. Three weeks, she said. His father died three weeks ago. Wherever and whoever he is now, he's an orphan.

I'm thinking about Rebecca Salomonsson — what she had wanted to be when she grew up, how she never got to experience how life panned out. Everything had probably been going downhill for some time, and her future was probably not that bright. For women like her, it rarely is, and I think to myself that it might have been for the best that it ended as it did, her life. That thought, that it might be just as well that it ended as it did, is quite abhorrent, but often it is simply the truth.

ANNA IS STANDING at one end of the bar, pouring a drink from a black bottle of Jim Beam. She looks up as I'm standing in the doorway, smiles weakly, and drinks from her glass.

'I thought you were going to call,' she says.

'I haven't …' I walk over to the bar, acutely aware of the sound that my shoes make on the floor. 'Are you alone?'

'We get ten customers a week, who stay for an hour each.' She drains her glass. 'I'm almost always alone here.'

'I'm here more than that.'

'You don't count.' She puts the glass away. 'What are you having?'

'Nothing. A coffee.'

This surprises her. Her blonde hair is up in a loose knot, and strands of stray hair fall across her face, down her neck to her collarbone, which is just visible through the wide neck of her shirt. *She's a bit like Sam*, I think to myself.

'Someone's coming here in a bit,' I explain. 'Someone who thinks I've stopped altogether.'

'I understand,' she says, turning her back to me and setting to work on the ancient coffee machine. 'I'm guessing it's a she?'

'Yes.'

'If you have to meet someone who thinks you're on the wagon,' she continues, 'is a bar really the best place?'

'Is everything okay?' I ask, tentatively.

'Yes. Everything is okay.'

'I didn't know of anywhere else where it's ...' I say, but don't know where to go from there.

'Where it's ...?' Without turning around, she starts the coffee machine, which splutters and hisses.

'Where it's safe.'

'Are you not safe anywhere else?'

'I don't think so.'

'You sound paranoid.'

'I know,' I say, and I notice that I'm fiddling with my phone, so I stop.

'What makes you think you're safe here?'

Enough coffee to fill a mug has dripped through into the jug, and she passes it to me and turns around. Anna's expression is hard to read. She might be hurt, but she looks almost scared.

'I just think so.'

'What's her name?'

'Who?'

'The one who's on her way here.'

'Sam.'

'Sam, as in ...?'

'As in Sam.' I hesitate. 'We were together once.'

'What happened?'

'An accident.'

Anna walks over to the counter, pours herself another glass, and comes back. When she notices my gaze fixed on the glass in her hand, she becomes embarrassed.

'I'm happy not drinking, if it makes it easier for you.'

I shake my head.

'Drink away.'

The door to BAR opens again, and Sam's face peers round it. It's started raining outside; the pattering sound rushes into the quiet premises, and it's dripping onto Sam's coat. Her hair is lank, sticking to her forehead and her cheeks. She walks up to the bar and takes off her coat while studying the coffee cup in my hand, as though trying to decipher what it means. Then she orders a beer.

'I recognise you,' Anna says. 'Tattoos.'

'That's right.'

Sam gets her beer and checks something on her phone before looking around.

'Interesting place to meet.'

'It is special.' I glance at Anna, who takes a couple of steps back and seems to be trying to make herself invisible by counting the contents of the till. Apart from a handful of lonely notes and coins, it's empty. 'John Grimberg,' I say, looking at Sam, and, as is so often the case when our eyes meet, everything else becomes fuzzy and dim. The only thing I see is Sam.

'Yes.' She drinks some beer. A little ribbon of foam sticks to her lip, and she wipes it away with the back of her hand. 'Well, I think it was him.'

'Think?'

'It was years ago now, when we were exp—. When we were together. I didn't say anything at the time.'

'Why not?'

'Because it didn't seem like the sort of thing you tell someone who is a cop.'

That stings. Even though I was expecting it, it still stings.

'I was your partner.'

'Anyway,' she goes on, 'it was autumn, I think. Someone called just as I was leaving the parlour one evening, refused to say who he was. As you know, I don't usually accept customers who won't give their name, and besides it was late, but this person offered me a lot of money. I was going to get half before the work was done, as soon as they came through the door, and the other half afterwards.'

'How much money?'

'Fifty thousand.'

'Jesus.'

'I know.' Sam takes another swig. 'So I asked what it was about, and the only thing he would say was that he wanted a tattoo removed. That's really a medical procedure, so I recommended a clinic instead, but he wasn't interested. He'd heard that I'd done it before, which was true. That was before the rules were changed. I insisted that what I could do was more painful than, and not as safe as, going to a professional clinic, but he said that wasn't an option. I think he even laughed at the suggestion. So he asked me to stay put, and hung up. An hour later, there was someone at the door — a very, very blond man. I remember thinking that he must dye his hair, because his eyebrows were much darker. I thought it was the guy I'd spoken to. He introduced himself as Dejan, but I doubt that was his real name. He said he was there to get rid of a tattoo. "Was it you I spoke to on the phone?" I asked, and he just shook his head and walked past me, into the studio. Behind him was another person, who I hadn't noticed. It was dark, of course, and it's hard to see just to the right outside the door there, because of the angle. This other person,' she says, looking down, 'it was him I'd spoken to. He was quite tall and was also blond, but not shockingly so like Dejan. He had a handsome face, angular, but well formed and tanned. Nicely dressed in a dark trench coat, looked like an advertising executive just back from holiday. But there was something about the look in his eyes that was very different. It was … empty. Hollow.' She takes another swig of her beer. 'There was nothing there, no identity, neither warmth nor coolness, no feelings whatsoever, nothing.'

'What colour were his eyes?'

'Blue. But,' she adds, 'I think they were contacts.'

'Why do you think that?'

'I wear contacts myself, Leo, so I know what eyes look like after a whole day with them in.'

'Did he introduce himself?'

'As Grim. "You can call me Grim." That's all he said. I was nervous, and you know I try and joke about things when I'm nervous, so I said something about the Brothers Grimm, asked him whether he was the cheerful one or the grumpy one, but that just made him ask if we were going to get started. And he stuck his hand — he was wearing thin gloves, too — he stuck his hand inside the trench coat and pulled out a wad of notes. "Twenty-five thousand," he said, "clean enough to take to the bank." I'd never seen that much cash before, not in a wedge, you know, so I could only nod and put it away in the office. "I've heard you're good," he said. "My usual expert has experienced some difficulties, which unfortunately means I need to find a new one." If there's one thing I know about, it's my job. So I said, "Yes, I'm good, but good at giving people tattoos, not removing them." That made him lean in, towards me, and I know this sounds weird, but I'm pretty sure that he was sniffing me.' Sam blushes.

'It was very uncomfortable. I don't know what he got out of it, but he looked over at Dejan, gave him a quick nod, and said, "Let's do this." So I sat Dejan down in my chair and he showed me the tattoo. A black, two-headed eagle, big as a fist, and level with his heart. It's a well-known motif, but this time it was apparently something to do with his homeland.'

'Albania.'

'That's it.'

'Dejan Friedrichs,' I say. 'Could that have been his name?'

'I never heard his surname.'

Dejan Friedrichs. I was after him once, for an arson attack on a pub on Sveavägen. The owner had declined the offer of protection from one of the cartels, and the price of independence turned out to be a licence for someone to set fire to the premises. I never interviewed Dejan, and I don't think he could ever be tied to the attack, but I had a feeling that it was him. He earned a living as an assassin for Silver, who ran parts of the Stockholm underworld at the time.

'It sounds like him,' I say, and sip my coffee.

I wonder why he introduced himself as Grim. He should have been using another name by then. Maybe he still used it informally?

From the corner of my eye, I notice that Anna is doing her best to appear not to be listening. Sam makes me think more clearly, makes me more focused. I feel awake and alert in her presence. That's the way it's always been, as though the pieces fall into place.

'So Grim sat on the sofa and fiddled with his phone, and I started work on the tattoo, anaesthetising, cleaning, and so on, but I was pretty sure that the result wasn't going to be great, definitely not worth fifty thousand. So when I was about halfway through I suggested to Grim that I take the first twenty-five thousand and that would be plenty, but he said we had a deal, and deals are not to be broken.'

'Did they seem to know each other well? Him and Dejan?'

She shakes her head.

'I got the impression that Dejan was a client. Grim was on the phone pretty much the whole time. When you're sitting in the studio, working intensively — I was incredibly tired, don't forget — when you're sitting there just working, it's like you're in a world of your own, and although I wasn't listening, I just suddenly heard his voice right behind me. It sounded as though he was sorting out all kinds of stuff at the same time. I think he was trying to help the guy leave the country. Money was mentioned, too, in those calls. Something had run into difficulties, and Grim sounded annoyed, hung up and rang someone else, told them it was going to cost more than he'd thought. That sort of thing. It sounded hectic, like he had a deadline to make, and I was getting quite worried because Dejan's tattoo wasn't professionally done. It was an amateur job, probably done in the clink, and it was uneven in the skin. I had to scrape, scrape like fuck. I wouldn't have wanted to be there when the anaesthetic wore off. The guy looked completely flogged, but Grim didn't seem to be bothered. Oh yeah, I remember him taking a pill while I was busy with Dejan. It wasn't exactly the kind of packet you get at the chemist's. I remember that.'

She looks at me as though this means something.

'Okay,' I say.

'Anyway, I was finished; it was about half-two in the morning, and I'd taken care of the wound and all that. It was so deep that I could see his chest muscles, can you imagine? Mental. I gave both of them instructions about how to take care of the wound. I supplied them with things that might help him through the first few days. Grim gave me the remaining twenty-five, and thanked me for a successful collaboration. Just as he was leaving, he leant over to me and said something, something I didn't know what to make of.'

'Which was?'

Sam clears her throat, drinks some more beer. Her eyes flit between me and her feet.

'He whispered that I smelt like an old friend.'

She goes quiet for a moment, and Anna has finished counting the till and is now dusting off the bottles covering the wall behind her, one at a time.

'I took it to mean that he trusted me,' Sam went on. 'As if I were one of his friends. Do you see?'

'Yes.'

That wasn't what Grim meant. For a second, I'm back in Salem. I'm sixteen, watching my friend fake his mum's handwriting; he's standing in the playground at Rönninge High, holding up his first home-made ID card. Coming back from the young offenders' summer camp, able to copy bankcards without it registering in the ATM — that must have been how it started. For over ten years, he's only been recorded in the Whereabouts Unknown register … He's not dead, but he doesn't exist either.

Suddenly I fall into a heap in front of Sam, and she grabs my arm, holds me up.

'Leo,' she says, looking worried. 'Are you okay?'

'It's been a long day,' I mumble, and turn to Anna, ask her for a glass of water.

Forty-eight hours have passed since Rebecca Salomonsson was found dead. Those critical first few days are about to run out. The perpetrator is about to dissolve, disappear. At that moment, I receive another text from the unknown number.

I think you should watch the news

XIV

SEVENTEEN-YEAR-OLD STABBED AT CAMP, SERIOUSLY INJURED.

Julia stood in front of the telly in my room with the remote in her hand, and read the headline on teletext. She'd just called my name. I was in the bathroom when she did so, and I wrapped the towel around me and came out, and stood next to her. The sun was shining outside. It was my parents' last day at work, and it was the first time I'd had a shower with someone.

'It's that camp,' Julia said, surprisingly composed. 'Outside Jumkil. It's the camp he's at.'

She searched, perhaps subconsciously, for my hand as she read. Once she'd found it and I felt her grip, I realised it was deliberate.

At a summer camp for boys between fifteen and twenty, a seventeen-year-old boy had been stabbed. Both police and ambulance had attended. The boy had been taken to Uppsala University Hospital and was being treated in intensive care. His condition was serious, but stable.

Something knotted itself deep in my stomach, and I struggled to breathe. 'Oh my God,' I heard my voice say.

'Call them,' she said and got the phone. 'Call them. Here's the number.'

'Wouldn't it be better if y—'

'I can't. I don't dare. If he was okay, we should have heard something. He should have been in touch.'

I dialled the number. The engaged tone bounced back. I rang again, and got the same tone.

132

'Ring again.'

Julia stared at the telly with a neutral expression. At the fifth attempt, I heard the ringing tone. Someone — a man — answered and, as calmly as I could manage, I said that we had seen the news on teletext and we wanted to make sure that our friend was okay. When I said his name, the man confirmed that Grim wasn't injured, but that he'd been very upset by the incident, since it was his friend.

'It was his friend who got stabbed?' I said. 'Who?'

'No, no,' the man said, 'John is friends with the boy who held the knife.' He went quiet. 'I shouldn't have told you that,' he added. 'Don't spread it. Everything here is just upside down right now.'

THE CAMP WASN'T SUSPENDED because of the incident. They said it was important for everyone to work through what had happened together. That same day, Julia and her parents went to Jumkil to see Grim. The following day, Julia and I went, after Julia had asked if he wanted to see me. He didn't really want to, but he did it for my sake. I needed to see him, needed to check that he actually was all right. And I missed him.

According to Julia, Grim seemed shaken. He hadn't said much when they'd seen him, but the psychologist who was now working full time at the camp had explained that Grim was still in shock. Barely forty-eight hours had passed.

'John never says that much,' Julia said on the bus on the way there. 'But, I don't know, something is different. I'm hoping it's just the shock.'

I searched for her hand, but this time she moved it away, looked out the window. Light summer rain was falling. The townscape was slowly making way for greenery, which grew ever thicker the closer we got to Jumkil. Julia was fiddling with her necklace.

JUMKIL YOUNG OFFENDERS' INSTITUTE was a square, light-grey building, two storeys high. It was just visible between the trees as the bus swung round a tight bend. I only caught a glimpse of it, but I still noticed the fence, which made it look more like a prison. The bus stop was a couple of hundred metres further on, and rather than going back down the road towards the institution, we walked down a narrow gravel track towards the summer camp. Julia seemed distracted, walking with her hands in the pockets of her thin cardigan, her gaze fixed on the treetops or the sky.

The youth summer camp at Jumkil comprised five red wooden buildings with white window frames, arranged in the shape of a horseshoe. It didn't look like the sort of place where someone could get stabbed and sustain life-threatening injuries, but then most things are not what they seem. It was run by three youth workers. They were all men, ten years older than me, broad shouldered, with tattooed arms and warm smiles. 'Role model' wasn't quite the right phrase, but that was the first thing I thought. One of them introduced himself without smiling, and showed us to one of the five houses.

The surroundings were warm and inviting; but as Julia and I approached the threshold, I had the sensation you'd get from a formal visiting room. There was something about the compulsory nature of the place — the fact that Grim had been ordered to participate in the camp — that made it feel uncomfortable.

'We don't actually have a visiting room,' the youth worker said, 'but we've made a common room into a temporary one. You're from Salem, aren't you?'

I nodded.

'Then you know how it is. The only positive thing about coming from a place like that is that everyone's got their eye on you. If you do put a foot wrong, we can help you back on track. That's what we're trying to do here.'

'By giving them knives?'

'It was a table knife. He'd stolen it, and sharpened it himself.' The youth worker shrugged. 'I'll be outside. Let me know when you're done.'

The common room was a mess of tables and chairs, not in any particular order; there was a pool table and a dartboard, but no darts. A big TV on one wall was silently showing music videos. On a noticeboard there were flyers and leaflets from various organisations. I recognised several from Rönninge High because they'd visited and told us about their work against crime and drugs.

Grim sat reading at one of the tables. He had changed during the three weeks he'd been away. He was tanned, but he'd shaved his head. Instead of his mop of blond hair, he only had short, straw-coloured stubble left. As we walked in, he smiled weakly and put the book down.

'Hello.'

'Hello.'

Julia and I sat down at the table, which was covered in carved doodles, spiky and uneven, as though they'd been made with keys or something. Some had been coloured in with pencil. I felt the carvings with my fingertips. Grim looked like a boy who'd suddenly got very old.

'How are things?' I asked.

'All right.'

'Only a week left now.'

'I know.'

'Pretty good deal,' I attempted. 'Nicking the travel kitty gets you a month out in the country.'

Grim chuckled, but the laugh never reached his eyes.

'Yes, I suppose so.' He sniffed the air. 'You smell good.'

'Do I?'

'It reminds me of the smell of our place,' he said.

'Sometimes your sense of smell isn't as good as you think,' Julia mumbled, and I was sure she was blushing, but I couldn't see because she was sitting next to me.

'That's not what people say around here,' Grim said.

'Do you get cred for your sense of smell?' I asked.

'Something like that.'

'What does that mean?' Julia asked.

'Nothing,' Grim said with a smile, rubbing his hand across his stubbly head. 'Just that ... it's okay here.'

'Your mate got stabbed the other day,' I said.

'He wasn't my fucking mate,' Grim hissed, and a dark shadow shrouded his eyes. 'Jimmy's my mate.'

'Jimmy?' I said.

'The one who did the stabbing.'

JIMMY WAS A PALE, wiry guy with long brown hair, Grim explained. His dad drank too much, and his mum was even worse. She didn't live with them anymore; she'd moved in with a Finland-Swede from Botkyrka who supplied her with drugs. Jimmy was also the victim of bullying at school. So one day he'd had enough and was halfway through smashing this kid's face in with a staple gun before anyone could stop him. That was how he'd ended up at the camp. An alliance had formed between five of the campers, led by a guy called Dragomir, an ice-hockey player from Vällingby. To begin with, Jimmy had kept out of the way, as had Grim. That's how they'd found each other. 'Found each other' — those were the words Grim used.

'We didn't do that much,' Grim said. 'We just talked mostly, about lots of different stuff.'

After a week, it had emerged that Grim had a unique sense of smell. He had, for example, found the cupboard containing the petty cash — money that he and Jimmy had split. The others soon found out. They took Jimmy's share of the money, but let Grim keep his. Grim then split his share with Jimmy, without telling anyone.

'But I didn't stand up for him,' he said, and seemed ashamed. 'Not in front of the others. I was with them more than with him, even if we did meet up and talk about stuff in secret.'

About two weeks into the camp, Grim was walking across the yard one evening after playing basketball in one of the buildings, which was kitted out as a fully functioning sports hall. Behind one of the houses he could hear a group trying to keep their excited voices down. He saw Dragomir's silhouette and several others standing around him.

'It's time, you little slag.'

Grim went over to the huddle and looked down at what was waiting in the centre of it: straight brown hair and Jimmy's terrified face.

'Not my hair,' he whispered. 'Please, not the hair.'

Dragomir was holding clippers, which started buzzing intensively.

'Shall we play hairdressers?' Dragomir asked, and held them up towards Grim.

'I looked Jimmy in the eye,' Grim went on. 'Shook my head, and took a couple of steps back. Once my back was turned, I heard the rasping noise of the clippers as they worked their way through his hair.'

Grim had tears in his eyes. That surprised me. Julia stretched her hand out towards her brother's, but he moved it away. I looked at his shaved head.

'Is that why you …?'

'After that,' he said, rubbing his eyes quickly, blinking a couple of times, 'a day or so later, he was sitting in the dining room, and I asked if I could sit next to him. He just shrugged, but I was happy that at least he hadn't said no. There were still little tufts of hair here and there; it looked awful, and I asked him if he wanted me to sort it out. He just looked at me and smiled, shook his head like it really didn't matter anymore. I'm sure he had a table knife, but at the end of lunch I noticed that he was eating with just a fork. He must've hidden it away at some point during lunch, right in front of me. A few days later, he put that knife in Dragomir's stomach, in the same place where they'd shaved Jimmy's hair off. That's what happened,' Grim concluded. Silence fell, and it was heavy.

WE LEFT JUMKIL that evening.

'See you in a week,' I said.

'Yes, that'll be the end of the quiet life.'

He knew. I was sure of it. He had smelt her on me. I think he'd smelt me on her, too, but he didn't say so, at least not so I heard it.

'It will be good to get you home,' Julia said, and stroked his back. At first, her touch made him tense up, but then he let her carry on.

'WHAT HAPPENS IF you put twenty kids together, all with similar problems to John, if not worse?' Julia muttered, on the bus journey home. 'This is what happens. People get hurt, and the people they're supposed to be helping come away from there much worse than when they arrived. It's insane. I don't understand what Social Services are thinking.'

'I think he knows,' I said quietly. 'About us.'

'He doesn't know it. He just suspects it.'

'Are you sure about that?'

'He's my brother. I know how he works.'

'What happens if he finds out? Shouldn't we tell him instead?'

Julia didn't answer. I asked her if everything was all right, and she met my gaze and smiled, said that, yes, everything was all right. Even though I suspected that it might not be true, I chose to believe it.

Me and Grim could talk about everything. Everything except Julia. He'd often asked if I was interested in someone, or insinuated things about some girl we knew. I always answered him vaguely. When it came to Julia, I couldn't predict how he might react if I told him.

It's not that it was in itself a serious betrayal of our friendship. I'd seen similar scenarios in films, and it usually worked out okay.

138

Sometimes it didn't, in which case it would usually end in disaster.

Grim might be okay with it, and then it would be fine. It might be weird and uncomfortable at first, but that might pass. He might, on the other hand, think that it was unacceptable, and he wasn't going to blame Julia. They were brother and sister. It was as though I would be forced to choose between them. If I even got the chance to choose. It was possible that Grim might disown me, and make it impossible for me to see her. Then I would have lost them both.

It hadn't actually been going on for that long — not more than a month — but it felt as though time were being stretched, slowed down, making every day special.

I'd never been with anyone before, but a classmate had a long-distance relationship with a girl he'd met on holiday in Skåne. He went down there every other weekend, and I thought to myself that this was what it must be like for him, those days when he was with her. Simply because they were so few, because they would soon be gone, they were more precious, and to carry on as normal would seem like a waste.

If something had been wrong when we visited Grim at Jumkil, there was no sign of it now. Julia was back to normal. We went swimming. I held Julia's hand on the way there, and in the water her skin became strangely smooth and light. When we got back to Salem, Julia asked if I wanted to come in. She was home alone, she said. When we got to their floor and Julia opened the door, it was obvious that we weren't alone at all. There was a strong cooking smell in the flat. In one of the armchairs in the living room was a woman with curly hair and a beautiful face. She didn't look up when we came in. I could hear the clattering of dishes being washed by hand coming from the kitchen. Julia froze next to me, letting go of my hand.

Her dad's face peered round the doorframe. It was tough and severe, the skin slightly red, and he was swollen around the eyes, as though he had just woken up. He looked surprised. He was holding a plate and a tea towel.

'I didn't think you were home,' said Julia.

'But we are.' He tried to smile, and looked at me. 'Have we met?'

'No, I don't think so.'

'No point,' said the woman's voice. It was monotonous, but had a slightly husky quality that was attractive. If she'd varied her inflection she could've worked in customer service for a company with angry customers. 'She never sticks to anything anyway.'

'Mum,' Julia said, carefully, but I saw that her teeth were clenched.

'It's true.'

'Leo,' I said. 'I'm Leo. I live in the next block.'

'Leo,' Julia's dad said, as though he was trying to place the name.

'I'm friends with Gr—, with John. We go to the same school. Not in the same class, but the same school. We've been friends for a while.'

I couldn't stop talking, and I could feel my cheeks going red. Julia might have noticed, because as she was taking her shoes off, she carefully put her hand on my shoulder for support, giving it a gentle squeeze.

'I understand.'

That's all he said. The plate he was holding was dry, and he disappeared back into the kitchen.

'Would you like some food?' he called. 'It'll be ready in a few minutes.'

'Maybe, Dad,' Julia said, grabbed my arm, and quickly dragged me into her room.

'What are their names?'

'Klas and Diana. Why do you ask?'

'Just wondered. Neither you nor Grim have ever said.'

'Sorry.' She shook her head. 'I really didn't think they'd be home. They'll tell John.'

'Not if we just say I was here to pick something up, or that you were showing me something, or … Yes.'

'Would you be okay with that?'

'Yes.'

'I'm no good at lying,' she said.

'Me neither.'

Klas and Diana Grimberg. I'd heard so much about them.

'They aren't like I imagined,' I said.

'Mum and Dad?'

'Yes.'

'What were you expecting?'

That's just what I was trying to work out. That they were always shouting, never spoke to each other? A visual recollection popped up: seeing Grim's CD player being thrown out the window and falling to the ground.

'I don't know,' I said.

A gentle knock on the door.

'We're eating now,' Klas said. 'Want some?'

Julia looked at me, and I shrugged.

The table was laid simply. It was just another weekday evening, and my being there was of no significance whatsoever. They weren't trying to make an impression, at least not in that sense. There was something appealing about doing it this way, especially in comparison to my parents, who always tried to impress people on those occasions when we did have guests, which I found hugely embarrassing.

'Spaghetti bolognese,' her dad said. 'You do eat meat, don't you?'

'Of course,' I said.

'Well, it's not that simple anymore,' he muttered. 'People's eating habits are getting stranger and stranger.'

The sound of footsteps came from the living room, and Diana Grimberg came to sit at the table, opposite her daughter. As she passed Julia, she stopped, looked at her, and stroked her cheek tenderly.

'You look so pure, do you know that?' she mumbled.

'Thanks.'

'And you.' She looked at me. 'Don't forget she is a catch.'

The corners of Diana's mouth twitched, and her expression was one of surprise, as though it was something that didn't happen very often. Eventually, her lips separated, and a laugh squeezed through — a laugh that I didn't know how to take.

'Leo just came to borrow a CD,' Julia said, as she spooned big dollops of sauce onto her plate.

'I understand,' Klas said.

'But I couldn't find it,' she went on, without looking up at them. 'Maybe it's in John's room.'

'Yes. Maybe.'

I poured myself some water from a jug, and Julia and her dad pushed their glasses over towards me. I filled their glasses, and looked at Diana, who hadn't touched hers. She was sitting looking at something out the window. I took the glass and poured her some water, then put it back.

She was startled by the noise, and looked at me.

'Thank you,' she said. 'Sorry, I was just thinking about something.'

'What were you thinking about?' Julia asked.

'Nothing.'

'How long have you and Julia,' Klas began, and interrupted himself to finish chewing and swallow, 'how long have you known each other?'

'A couple of months,' I said. 'About as long as I've known John.'

'He calls himself Grim,' Diana said, and drank some water. 'Strange. Or is it just me who thinks so?'

'No, it's not just you,' Klas said. 'But he's seventeen. You never have such funny ideas as you do when you're seventeen. Isn't that right, Leo?'

Klas smiled, and something was behind his words — something

that didn't come out.

'I suppose so.'

'He's going places,' he said. 'Anyone can see that.'

'Yes, but which places?' Diana said, and looked at me. 'Don't you hurt her.'

'Mum!' Julia said sharply, and I felt her hand on mine, under the table.

'Diana, keep cal— '

'Is it surprising that I get worried?'

Julia put her fork down next to her plate and looked up.

'I'm sitting here. You don't need to talk about me in the third person.'

Diana looked at Klas's tumbler.

'Are you drinking water?'

'Yes?'

'But you're on holiday now. You don't have to put on a front because they're here. I'm sure Leo already knows, don't you, Leo?'

'I, no, I ...'

'Stop it now, Diana.'

'Shall I get the bottle then?'

She looked at Klas's hands. It was only then that I noticed them trembling slightly.

'I can see you want it.'

'I'm drinking water.'

'But ...'

'That's enough.'

'He blames it on you,' Diana went on, in a monotone as before, and she glanced at Julia before turning her gaze back to the window, fixing it on something outside. 'You know that, he needs it to cope with living with you after t— '

'Diana.' Klas's voice was so sharp that I tightened my grip on the fork, and Julia's hand disappeared as she straightened up with a jolt. 'That's enough.'

I left the Grimbergs' flat confused and CD-less, which was hardly surprising.

LATE THAT NIGHT, I met Julia at the water tower, which stretched up towards the sky, and in the gloom seemed darker than usual — rougher than it normally did. I'd always thought of it as mushroom-shaped, but now it looked more like a courtroom gavel. Julia threw her arms around me in a way she'd never done before. It felt more urgent, almost desperate, and I let her do it. I asked her something she didn't hear.

'Eh?' she mumbled, with her warm breath against my upper lip.

'Is it always like that at home?'

'More or less.' She looked up at the tower. 'Come.'

Julia made her way up the tower, climbing in the darkness above me. I followed her until we got to the highest ledge.

'This is where I first met Grim,' I said.

'Oh, right.'

She lifted her hands up inside her dress, and something small and black fell to her ankles.

'Unbutton your jeans,' she whispered. 'And sit down.'

Julia's breath was burning hot on my neck. Over her shoulder, I could see Salem stretched out beneath us, and the sky, which was getting darker and darker. I strained to keep my eyes open.

I'm sitting in the car outside your place. I can see you at the window, but you can't see me. That makes me sad. I want you to know. The incident tapes are flapping, lonely in the wind. The first time you see them, they make you feel bad. Do you remember that? But back then we were pretty much still just kids, and we saw a lot of them. We got used to them.

Just before Dad dies we spend a lot of time talking about Mum.

'I only really remember her from photographs,' I say, which makes him angry, even though he's very weak. I try and tell him that it's good that I remember her that way, and that the other memories are things you want to forget, even though there must have been good times. But he doesn't listen, he doesn't have the strength.

Did I say how they met? I should have, because I remember you told me about yours. It was at a bar in Södertälje. She worked in a music shop and apparently all the guys there wanted to sleep with her but she only went with two before she met Dad. She was in the bar with a few friends from the local music scene, and he was there with a couple of welder mates after work. At the bar she asked him what sort of music he liked and Dad said:

'I don't listen to music.'

Mum smiled and said: 'Perfect.'

That's how Dad tells it anyway. When I arrived it was without complications, and Dad says they were extremely happy, that their only worries were financial. They'd always lived on the edge of their means and they carried on doing so, even though Dad was already drinking quite heavily. Then Mum got pregnant again. I don't remember any of this, I was too young of course, but I understood some of it later. How Mum had fallen into a coma after the birth, for some reason, and how she had changed by the time she woke up a couple of days later: passive and apathetic with sudden unpredictable outbursts. Dad tells me that, after a while, when they started to worry that she might never get better, he cried every night over losing the one he loved.

'That's what it felt like at least,' he says. 'But then maybe we'd lost each other long before.'

I tell him he's wrong, that they hadn't at all, although I realise deep down that I really don't know what I'm talking about. Dad probably feels the same way, but he doesn't say so, he just puts his hand on top of mine and says it's hard to know with families, and he gives me a confused smile.

They were so alike, her and Mum. He screamed at her and hardly ever gave her praise when she did something good. It tormented him, because he knew why he did it, yet couldn't stop himself. He tried to avoid drinking around her because he didn't trust himself.

He didn't just start to turn on Julia, everyone got it. He could never leave Mum, she was too dependent on him for that, she needed him too much. He was unhappy, chronically unhappy, and found it harder and harder to get up in the morning and go to work at the welding company.

Dad exhales, weakly. He asks for water. I give it to him. He asks how I am. I say he's all I've got left. He smiles and says that's not true, but he knows nothing.

XV

POLICE OFFICER SUSPECTED OF MURDER.

Sam has her phone out, and is showing me *Expressen*'s latest headline. I look from her phone to mine.

I think you should watch the news

Annika Ljungmark's article is short but succinct. As of ten o'clock this evening, several sources within the city police have confirmed the latest developments in the investigation into Rebecca Salomonsson's murder. Police are now pursuing a specific line of enquiry, one in which a police officer is implicated. 'He can be placed at the crime scene around the time of the victim's death,' claims a source.

It will only be a matter of hours until the police officer's identity is revealed. That's always the way. I lean against the bar, and look up from my phone. My head starts spinning. Sam looks at me, worried.

'Leo, it ...'

'It's not me,' I manage to say.

'I know that.'

I look at her, unsure whether she has understood what I mean.

'Good.'

Sam looks down at my phone.

'What's that?'

'Someone's been sending me messages.'

'Who?'

'I'm not entirely sure.'

What happens next is strange and yet it feels so familiar, so obvious: Sam grabs hold of my arm. From the corner of my eye, I see how Anna is watching us.

'Be careful,' Sam says.

'I'm doing my best.'

'No you're not.' She doesn't let go of my arm. 'You have always been so careless.'

As though she realises what she's about to do, Sam lets go of my arm. And there it is; I can see it in her eyes because I know just how it feels: for a second, she sees a flash of Viktor in my face.

'Unless there's something else, I have to go,' she says.

I follow her to the door. It's still raining outside. The black streets shine and sparkle, and above us the clouds race across the sky. She leaves without saying anything, but she looks back over her shoulder. I light a cigarette and stare after her until she disappears round the corner.

'Absinthe, please,' I say when I get back in and stand by the counter.

'What was that all about?'

'What?'

Anna puts down a glass and pours my drink.

'That. Her, you?'

'We were together once.'

'You said.'

'We were expecting a son. We even had a name.'

'What happened?'

I drink from the glass. The knots under the skin by my temples start to loosen.

'A car accident.'

'He died?'

'Yes.'

Anna is standing with her elbows on the bar, holding her face in her hands. The edge of the bar pushes her breasts up, making her cleavage deeper than it is normally.

'You're a psychologist,' I say.

'Psychology student.'

'What do your books say about me?'

'No idea.' She looks at the clock. 'I can close up if you like.'

'Why?'

'You look like you need … distracting.'

She smiles. I've drunk the absinthe too quickly. It has already reached my head, and is starting to make things murky.

'I think you're absolutely right,' I mumble and glance at the door. 'But it's not … sorry, but it's not you I w— '

'I know,' she says. 'I don't care.'

So I allow myself to go along with it, just this once.

Anna walks over to the door and locks it. On her way back, she calmly unbuttons her shirt and takes it off, lets her hair down. She sits down on the barstool next to me, and I take a step forward, between her legs, and she puts her hand on my chest, strokes carefully down my stomach, and starts unbuttoning my jeans. I need this, and when I close my eyes I notice to my surprise that the inside of my eyelids are in fact not black, but dark, dark red.

AT SOME POINT — maybe during, maybe after — the memories seep in, unexpectedly, like when someone you haven't seen for ages comes up to you in the underground and you chat for a bit, and after the brief meeting the past sweeps by.

I am thirteen years old. I've had enough of getting hit by Vlad and Fred, and I start to pay it back, but to someone smaller than me. His name is Tim. Above us, the sky is heavy, like wet snow. I punch him in the guts.

I am five; I've just learnt to ride a bike. My dad's trying to film it, but every time he gets the camera going I fall off, and the only thing that ends up on film is my brother, cycling around in the background, carefree and self-assured, on a bicycle that is much bigger, with bigger wheels and more gears.

I am twenty-eight or twenty-nine; I've just met Sam. Something I say makes her laugh. We're on a boat. I recognise a face among the passengers — someone who looks like Grim, but it's not him. Sam asks if everything is all right. I say yes.

I am sixteen; Grim and I are standing at the foot of the water tower. He's been arguing with his parents. It's late spring, and Klas Grimberg has received a letter from his son's form tutor. She writes that she has tried to contact him and Diana by telephone, without success. Grim has hit a classmate, and if it happens again the tutor will have to involve the police. Klas gets angry and drinks while he's waiting for his son to get home. When he does, they row, and it ends with Klas shouting at Grim to behave himself at school and not end up like him; if he doesn't sort himself out, he'll knock some sense into him. At least that's what Grim claims he shouted at him. We go up the tower and shoot birds. Grim laughs when I say that one of the clouds is like someone we know, a fat boy who everyone calls 'Ram'. Another cloud looks like Julia. I don't say this to Grim.

The same year: it is early spring, and Grim and I are out in Handen, waiting for someone to sell us some hash. Neither of us has tried it before. Grim's wearing a T-shirt with MAYHEM printed on it, and we prowl the streets. Four men with boots, studs, and long hair appear from out of the darkness. They come over and ask what we're doing, wearing T-shirts like that. They point to Grim's T-shirt, visible under his open coat. Then they kick the shit out of us, and my ribs hurt for weeks afterwards. We find out later that people connected to the band Mayhem have been burning down churches in Norway and Gothenburg, and we get scared. Grim gets rid of the T-shirt. We never mention it to anyone, not even Julia. It's something that just I and Grim share. On the local train home that night, someone plays The Prodigy on their ghetto-blaster, way too loud.

A day or so after the fiasco in Handen, we buy some hash

from a guy who comes up from Södertälje. We do the handover in Rönninge and smoke it sitting on the water tower. I don't feel anything, and I suspect Grim doesn't either, but we giggle till our bellies hurt, because we've heard that's what people do when they're stoned. The second time I smoke, I get really sweaty and feel sick. Grim looks dozy. That time we're on the football pitch on the outskirts of Salem, lying on the grass. It's evening, and the air is cool.

Grim is interested in technology but he's no good at maths. When he gets maths homework, I have to help him, till one of us has had enough. He's always on time, never late. He has trouble respecting people who aren't punctual, just as he can't accept the police lurking around Salem at night. Every time Grim sees a police car, he gets down. It's the start of the summer, 1997, and Grim hardly ever talks about his dad, I realise. On the few occasions he does, he says nothing flattering, yet I sense something behind the words, something that doesn't come out. As though he identifies with him. Maybe that's why they clash the way they do. I plan to ask Julia about it, present my theory to her, but it never happens.

Two months later, I meet Klas Grimberg when we have to eat dinner with them. I'm struck by how like his father Grim is. I think about mentioning it to both Grim and Julia, but I don't, because I'm not sure what it implies.

'What happens if the most important thing you have,' Grim says one afternoon, on a northbound local train, 'was never even supposed to exist at all?'

'What do you mean?'

'Imagine that there's some kind of fate, or whatever the hell you want to call it, and we were never meant to be a family? If somehow it wasn't supposed to happen? If it just ended up this way, by accident? I mean, look at us. Considering what life is like at our place, everything could be an accident.'

'All families are fucked up.'

'No. No, they're not.'

I AM SEVENTEEN. It's been several months since Julia died. I smile for the camera. It's for the class photograph, and I don't recognise any of the people around me.

XVI

When Grim returned from Jumkil, he arrived in one of Social Services' anonymous white vans. The air was close, and a short while earlier I'd seen Vlad and Fred walk past, a street away. I wondered what they were doing in Salem, and struggled to breathe. I sat down on a bench between the blocks of the Triad and tried to make myself inconspicuous until they'd disappeared from view.

The van parked in front of the Triad, and one of the back doors opened. Grim climbed out with his bag, the same black hold-all that he'd had the air rifle in the day we met. It felt like a long time ago, but in fact we'd only known each other for less than six months. A man with an off-licence carrier bag, dirty cap, and wild white beard was sitting on a bench close by. He stared, alarmed, at the white van before gathering up his possessions, rising shakily to his feet, and walking off with forced dignity. Grim closed the door, and the driver — a man, I couldn't discern any more than that — turned his head, did a U-turn, and drove off, as though he had urgent duties to attend to somewhere else. I stood up, which gave Grim a fright. When he saw it was me, the confusion was replaced by a smile, and he raised his hand. I was smiling, but him coming back felt weird for me, as though the freedom I'd had access to had been temporary, and had once again been replaced by a sort of straightjacket.

LATER ON, we went up to the water tower. The air was still, and the sun shone down on us. Most of the cars that passed us on the road below were full of camping gear and families. It was the end of July, and there was ages left of the summer holidays. Grim was wearing a short-sleeved shirt and shorts, yet still wiped the sweat from his forehead several times.

'I'm going to Uppsala tomorrow,' he said.

'What are you doing there?'

'Seeing Jimmy. He's still on remand.'

'Do you know how he's doing?'

'No. But I think he's okay. He's doing better than the guy he stabbed, anyway.'

Grim was the one who wanted to go to the water tower. I would have preferred to do something else, ideally somewhere without any connection to Julia whatsoever. Instead, we went up the tower, and Grim sat down on the ledge, exactly where I'd been sitting a few days earlier as Julia climbed out of her knickers and straddled me. It felt absurd, unreal.

'What are you laughing at?' he asked.

'Eh?'

'You laughed.'

'Oh. No, nothing. Just had a funny thought.'

'When we met at the camp,' Grim said as he pulled out a bottle of spirits and two glasses from the little rucksack he was carrying, 'we never had time to talk about you.'

'It felt like there was more important stuff going on,' I mumbled.

'How's your summer been?'

'Good, I suppose. Micke moved out. Me and Dad helped him move, and neither of us have seen him since.' I hesitated. It would have seemed strange for me not to mention it. 'I had dinner at your place.'

Grim filled the glasses and pushed one towards me. I drank some, and after that so did he.

'It's fucking strong,' said Grim. 'I think it's absinthe or something.'

He drank from his glass. 'You were at our place?'

'I was going to borrow a CD from you.'

'Which one?'

I shrugged.

'I can't remember now.'

'Oh. Other things got in the way?'

'Yes.'

'Dad made you stay for dinner.'

'Exactly.'

In the distance there was a bang — a crashing noise — and a car alarm started wailing.

'It is,' Grim started, 'not Julia's fault, but Mum … have I told you she has problems?'

I already knew this, but I wasn't sure whether Grim knew that I knew. At that moment, I couldn't remember who had told me — whether it was he or Julia. Everything had gotten so complicated.

'I can't remember. Maybe.'

'Well, she does anyway. She has had as long as I can remember. It goes in waves, up and down. When I got sent to camp, it got a bit worse, if I understood right. And Dad has subconsciously — at least, I think it's subconscious — put the blame on Julia. Which makes everything about … I don't know, but I end up on the outside. And that doesn't bother me; it suits me fine. It's better to be outside when you see what it's like for Julia. But it makes it really hard to be at home.' He laughed. 'Despite all the shit at the camp, it was nice to be away from home. Can you imagine? I guess I hadn't grasped how bad it was, until I realised that's how I felt.'

'You can ask for help.'

'From who?'

'I don't know. Social Services?'

'Social Services can fuck off. They've already been around and stuck their noses in.'

'Well, someone else then.'

'Who?' He looked genuinely tormented. 'Who do you ask

for help? Who are you supposed to turn to? And is it really my responsibility?'

'I don't know,' I said.

'Stop saying "I don't know."' He tilted his head back, leant against the water tower, and closed his eyes. 'When I went up to dump my stuff just now, it was chaos. I think Mum had forgotten her medication, and Dad had been drinking. He's just started back at work, and he always drinks more than usual then, presumably because his job is so fucking brain-dead.'

We said nothing for a while. I wanted to leave, go and see how Julia was. The frustration was getting to me, making my palms cold and clammy.

'I saw Vlad and Fred.'

'Uh-huh?' said Grim.

'Vlad and Fred.'

'The idiots that used to give you grief?'

'Yes. I saw them earlier on. Do you think ...?' I took another sip. It scraped my throat horribly, burned my stomach. I did my best not to sound scared. 'Do you think they've moved back?'

'Why would anyone move back here? I bet they were just visiting or something.'

He took his Discman out of his bag, gave me one of the earphones, and we sat listening to music and drinking until the batteries ran out, which didn't happen until very, very late. After that, I hobbled home, terrified I might bump into them — but I never did.

'YOU SEEM A BIT DOWN, Leo.' My dad looked up from the paper, and put his coffee cup down on the table.

'I'm just tired.' My head was pounding, and every time I blinked my eyelids hurt. 'I was up late last night.'

'Late.' He nodded thoughtfully. 'I didn't hear you come in.'

'I don't know what time it was.'

'Considering how you smell, at least it's not hard to work out what you were up to,' he said.

'I don't smell.'

'You stink.'

I chewed my toast slowly.

'Don't tell Mum.'

'Where do you get the booze from? Is it smuggled?'

'No, Dad,' I sighed.

'I can't stop you from drinking. We never stopped Micke. But ...'

'Oh yes we did,' Mum's voice came from the bathroom, followed by her footsteps as she came into the kitchen. She looked at me with a stern expression. 'If you drink again, you won't be allowed out.'

'Annie,' Dad began, 'he's not — '

'No,' she said sharply and stared at him. 'I've had enough. He's never home anymore.'

'Annie, let me talk to him.'

She looked at me, then Dad, then back at me.

'You pull yourself together, starting right now,' she said before she left the room.

Dad looked tired. He drank some coffee and stared at the half-eaten toast on my plate.

'Aren't you going to finish it?'

'I'm not hungry.'

'You need to eat.' He hesitated. 'Your mum and I would both be a lot happier if you just got a job.'

'Dad, for fuck—'

'Yeah, yeah,' he cut me off and held his hands up, apologetically. 'I know.' He put his forearms against the edge of the table and leant over. 'She's right, Leo. But there's something else, isn't there?'

'What do you mean?'

'As I said, you look a bit down.' He waited, but when I didn't say anything he added, 'You can talk to me if you need to.'

I looked up, unsure.

'How well do you know the people who live in the Triad?'

He raised an eyebrow.

'No one knows anyone here really, not even those living within the same four walls. So I can't claim to know them at all.'

'Okay.'

'Is it someone in this block?'

'No.' I nodded towards the window. 'Someone in that block.'

He followed my gaze towards the block where the Grimbergs lived.

'I see.'

'You don't know anyone who lives there?'

He shook his head and drank some coffee.

'It's a girl,' he said, matter-of-factly.

'What makes you think that?'

'Dads see that sort of thing.'

I took a deep breath, and Dad looked hopeful. *He tried*, I thought to myself. I stood up and left without saying anything, and went to my room. I closed the door and sat down by the window, looked over at the block they lived in, and studied the windows of their flat, hoping for a glimpse of Julia.

NOTHING HAPPENED. I started feeling pathetic, and Dad didn't come in, so I lay down on the bed instead and listened to music for the rest of the day. I thought about ringing them, but I was worried that Grim would answer; he would notice that something was wrong, I was sure of that. And if Julia answered, Grim might ask her who she'd been talking to, and then she'd have to lie. She wasn't good at lying, which was one of the things I liked about her, but this time her inability to lie was not helpful.

Eventually I rang anyway.

'Diana Grimberg.'

'I ...' I began. 'It's Leo. Could I ...?'

'Wait,' she said. 'Julia. Phone.'

Diana's voice was so quiet that it really shouldn't have been possible to hear it unless you were standing right next to her. Maybe you develop hypersensitive hearing or heightened awareness if you live with someone like that, because I soon heard footsteps coming towards the phone.

'Who is it?' Julia asked Diana, but got no reply.

'Hello?' she said instead.

'Hi,' I said.

'Oh, hi. Hang on.'

Footsteps. A door opening and then closing. Music in the background that slipped away and disappeared.

We talked as long as we could. In a few days' time I was going to Öland for a week. My uncle lived there with his family, and we spent a week there every summer, at the end of the holidays. That was the only time I used to leave Stockholm. My brother had always come, too, but this time he couldn't because he had to work.

'Why didn't you say anything?' she asked, sounding hurt.

'I haven't ... I was thinking about not going at first.'

'Why not?'

'Because of you.'

'Okay,' she said hesitantly. 'But now you are?'

'I think so.'

'What's changed?'

'I don't know ... nothing.'

'Must be something.'

I lay there for ages, listening to her breathing. I wondered if Grim was lying on the other side of the wall, listening to us talking.

ON ÖLAND, the time dragged. We came back after a week, and in that short time something had happened in Salem: I met Grim outside the youth centre, and his eye was purple-blue and swollen. He was trying to hide it behind a pair of Wayfarer shades, but it wasn't working — the bruising was too big. We sat on a bench in the sunshine. He told me how he'd made an ID card for a guy who'd tried to use it to get into a club.

'There was nothing wrong with the card,' Grim said. 'The problem was with this idiot. He wanted to get in to places where you need to be eighteen, and I sorted that out for him. Would you believe that the idiot goes to a twenty-plus club? He was denied entry, of course. What does he do next? Drives out to Salem with two mates, looking for me, because he thinks I've ripped him off. They even came to our place. When Dad found out, he was drunk, and he chased me out of the flat. The guy and his two mates were waiting outside, and I got a smack in the face before I could get away.' He shrugged. 'Fuck it.'

'But why did your dad chase you out?'

'He wasn't chasing me out — he was just chasing me. But it was better to try and get out than to get caught.'

I tried to imagine Klas Grimberg chasing his son. During that dinner at their place, there had been something in his look that suggested he was probably capable of it, despite his measured calmness. But he had been sober then.

Grim pulled out a folded envelope from the inside pocket of his jacket, just as someone came round the corner of the youth centre. He was our age, with baggy jeans and big clonking Adidas, a hoodie, and a cap. He didn't go to our school, I was pretty sure of that.

'Everything all right?' Grim said when he came up to us.

'Yeah, man,' he mumbled, and glanced at me.

'He's safe.'

The guy looked around and gave a little nod. His hoodie had a pocket on the front, from which he pulled out neatly folded five-hundred-krona notes and then handed them to Grim, in exchange for the envelope. It all happened so quickly that if I'd blinked I would have missed it.

'Have you copped a beating?' he asked, looking at Grim.

'Some guy misunderstood something, that's all.'

'Shall I do him?'

'No.' Grim looked around. 'See you round.'

'Okay.'

He turned and trudged off, and we headed back towards the Triad. Grim counted the money.

'Fifteen hundred,' I said.

'I'm getting more and more expensive,' Grim said.

IN A LOT OF WAYS, we were very different. But more than anything else, this meant that we complemented each other. We would now sometimes think the same thing, say the same word. We'd started using each other's phrases. Without realising, I'd started buying clothes that were more like his, and he had several pieces of clothing that could have come straight out of my wardrobe.

I assumed that these sorts of changes were almost inevitable when two people spend a lot of time together, understand each other, and share so much, but perhaps there was also a deeper bond between us. I was the only one who knew about Grim's fake-ID business. Apart from his customers, of course — but he told most of them that he was just the middleman. He claimed that no one would have believed that a seventeen-year-old possessed the skills he did. He was probably right. That would lead to suspicion, and suspicion was bad for business.

IN SALEM, high summer had made way for a cooler end to the season. It was the end of the holidays, and when they were over Julia was going to join me and Grim at Rönninge High School. We would be walking the same corridors, maybe meeting up at break-times.

The day after I came home from Öland, the phone rang. Dad answered, and knocked on my door, smiling.

'For you. Julia.'

I pushed him out of the room and closed the door.

'Hello?' I said.

'Hi.'

'Hi.'

I had missed her voice.

'How are things?' I asked.

'Good.' She cleared her throat. 'I'm home alone today.'

'Are you?'

'John's gone out. Mum and Dad are at Granddad's.'

Diana Grimberg's father lived in a nursing home outside Skarpnäck. It was death's waiting room, but while they waited for the next life, each month there was a big dinner for the old folk and their relatives. Julia had gone along once and said it was a real drag, a view shared by both Grim and Klas. The only one who had enjoyed the dinner was Diana, who was apparently determined to make dinnertime as uncomfortable as possible.

'Do you want to come round?' Julia asked.

'Yes.'

When I went out that day I had a feeling that something significant was going to happen. It couldn't go on like this. The door to the Grimbergs' flat wasn't locked, and I walked into their hall.

'Julia?'

'Come in.'

She was sitting on the edge of her bed, and she looked up at me.

'You've done something with your hair,' I said.

'I've put curls in.' She hesitated. 'Don't you like it?'

'I ...'

'Actually, you know what, don't say anything. It shouldn't matter. You know? It shouldn't matter what my stupid brother's stupid fucking mate thinks of my hair. It doesn't matter. So don't say anything.'

I sat down on the edge of the bed and said: 'Lovely.'

'Eh?'

'I think it looks lovely.'

Julia sighed heavily. Her room was a mess. It didn't look like it had been tidied since the last time I'd been there.

'This was just a laugh,' she said. 'For me, anyway.' She avoided looking at me. 'Something I was drawn to, maybe because it's taboo. I mean, my brother's best mate. It's the sort of thing you only see in bad comedies.' She laughed, but there was no joy in the laughter. 'Maybe I've always been drawn to this sort of thing. I mean, to things that are just a bit wrong. Like the coat with the weed, that I told you about. The one I stole at school?'

I nodded. I remembered.

'I hadn't really thought about it before now, this week you've been away, but maybe it's my fault. I never meant it to get serious.'

'But it got serious?' I asked, unsure how I was supposed to be feeling.

'I think so.'

Then she snogged me, violently, before she reached for the stereo remote and turned it on.

'Julia, we should talk. We should talk some more.'

Julia turned up the volume. It took a couple of seconds before I realised it was 'Dancing Barefoot', and I only knew it because Julia once told me — I can't remember when — that it was one of her favourite songs.

The volume made it difficult to distinguish words from sound, and the music just turned into a pulsating wall of sound that, I thought at the time, was beating in time with my heart. Her necklace dangled above my face, and in an odd moment I lifted my head, kissed her neck, and took the necklace in my mouth, and felt how cold it was. I closed my eyes.

Something made Julia stop. I opened my eyes, she reached for the remote again, and everything went very quiet. The barrel of the lock clicked around, and someone opened the front door.

'It's John,' Julia whispered in my ear, and quickly climbed off me, making the bed underneath creak. 'Lie still.'

She looked annoyed as she stood up. She pulled on a pair of denim shorts, and opened the window.

I lay there on the bed, not knowing what to do. A split second before the knock on the door, she pulled the duvet over my head and whispered: 'Don't move.'

'Are you home?' I heard Grim's surprise as he opened the door.

'You're on summer holidays, too, aren't you?' Julia asked.

'Yeah, but …'

I wondered what he might be looking at.

'Is everything okay?' he said.

'Yes?'

I was pretty sure that I heard him sniffing the air for something.

'You need to tidy up. And make your bed.'

'Yes, Dad.'

He disappeared from the doorway and Julia closed the door, then sat down on the bed with a heavy sigh.

'Shit,' she whispered, and I carefully pulled the duvet away from my head. 'That was close.'

'Yes.'

'Shh.'

'I'm whispering.'

'You're whispering loudly.'

'How can you — '

'Shh.'

Two, three, four bangs came from outside the window. The sound of gunshots. A light wind found its way into the room, making the curtains flutter. It was afternoon, and the summer had stretched itself unnaturally. Julia turned around and looked at me. She had her hand on her necklace, pulled it from side to side on its little chain.

'This can't go on,' she whispered, and I knew she was right.

'I'm going to have a shower,' Grim's voice said outside her door, a few moments later. 'What are you up to?'

'Leave me alone,' Julia attempted.

'Are you alone in there?'

'Of course I am.'

He stayed there, outside the door, I could hear that much, but he didn't say anything else.

Julia was staring at her hands, and I realised that I was holding my breath. Soon a door opened and then closed, and Julia nodded to me.

'He's in the bathroom now — get out of here.'

I opened my mouth to say something, I didn't know what; Julia looked away, and I knew that there was no point in trying to think of something to say, so I carefully stood up and left her room. Through the bathroom door, I could hear Grim as he turned the shower on.

XVII

Dawn is breaking, and the city is waking up. I'm standing on the balcony watching a young constable remove the incident tape. He seems to be taking his assigned task very seriously, and he is carefully wrapping the tape around his hand. A stinging sensation behind my eyes, a sudden hunger, takes hold of me, and I go back in and eat an improvised sandwich made from leftovers while I stare at an invisible dot somewhere in front of me.

'Counterfeiter'. It's not really the right word, but that's what the police call it anyway, since most of them started just like Grim did, forging ID cards for sixteen-year-olds who want to get into bars. Counterfeiters exist; everyone knows that. Their task is a difficult one, and if they're not up to the job they soon disappear, one way or another. But they are out there, and those few have major resources because their services are so expensive. In this town, money buys anything, and in a time when disappearing is impossible, there are few things more valuable than a new identity.

Since John Grimberg hasn't been on any up-to-date registers for ten years, and yet earns a living supplying people with new identities, it might be safe to assume that he, too, has another name. Maybe more than one. Probably, I decide. He obviously no longer uses the original one, and it would be unlike him to restrict himself to just one alternative identity.

My phone rings. It's Levin's number.

'Hello?'

'Leo. Good morning.'

'Good morning.'

'I understand you're looking for a John Grimberg.'

'How do you know that?'

'My secretary said so.'

'Oh.' I'd forgotten that. 'Yes, that's right.'

'I don't know much,' Levin says, 'but I can tell you what I know.'

'Can we meet?'

'That's why I called. If you hurry — I'm about to leave.'

OUTSIDE THE ENTRANCE to my building, on Chapmansgatan, something bright flashes in my face, and I am temporarily blinded. The noise — humming voices — is coming from journalists. A black TV4 mic is pushed under my chin, and I blink again and again to try to get rid of the white dots floating across my field of vision.

'According to police, you are a potential suspect in the murder of Rebecca Salomonsson; would you like to say anything?'

'You were at home when she died, weren't you?'

'Is this revenge for your suspension?'

The questions patter down. I look for the young officer, hoping for help, but he seems, appropriately enough, to be looking the other way, strangely absorbed by the incident tape. The last question grabs my attention, and I look for the face it came from.

'I recognise you,' I say.

'Annika Ljungmark, *Expressen*. What have you got to say about the allegations?'

'I haven't done anything.'

The questions start up again, but it becomes a wordless hum and my pulse is rising, and I do the one thing you should never do: I push between two of the reporters and start running.

They follow me for a while, but with their cameras, bags, and dictaphones in their hands, they soon give up. I make it to Hantverkargatan, out of breath, and head down into the darkness of the underground.

I'm outside Köpmansgatan 8 in Gamla Stan. No reporters. It's still early.

A buzz comes from the heavy door and I push it open, step into the cool stairwell, and realise for the first time how warm I am. I might have a temperature; I think I do. In the lift, everything starts spinning, and I feel nauseous and double over, convinced I'm about to bring up my breakfast. Nothing happens; I just stand there, panting, and the lift door opens and waits for me to step out. Something is wrong with me.

'Leo,' Levin says, and behind his little glasses his eyes widen as he sees me standing outside the door. 'How are you feeling?'

He takes me by the arm; presumably it looks like I need it, and apparently I do because I stumble just inside the door, and have to hold on to the hat-stand while I take my shoes off.

'Okay. The lift made me dizzy.'

I manage to get my shoes off and I wave Levin's hand away. He asks me to sit in the kitchen, and I walk in and slump onto one of the chairs next to the little round table. The chair creaks but is noticeably comfortable, and I feel like I could fall asleep. Levin takes a glass from the cupboard, pulls out a tube I don't recognise, drops an effervescent tablet into the glass, and fills it up with water. It starts fizzing and bubbling pleasantly.

'I haven't slept much,' I mumble and stare at the glass. 'What is that?'

'For tiredness.'

'But what is it?' I insist.

'Like twenty cups of coffee. The military use them. I got them from a good friend, a major. I've never taken one myself.'

I pull the glass towards me. Levin straightens his glasses and stares at it.

'Drink it.'

I take a swig, and it's harsher than I was expecting, like a fizzy drink with way too much carbon dioxide. It burns my palate, my tongue, my teeth, everything.

'Is it nice?' Levin asks, and the corner of his mouth twitches slightly.

'Not exactly.'

'John Grimberg,' Levin says. 'How come, may I ask, you are looking for him?'

I take a deep breath, just as the discomfort in my mouth starts to subside and a smooth sensation spreads inside me. It's subtle, but unmistakeable. Warmth gathers in my stomach, moving up to my chest, out to my fingertips. My eyes seem sharper, my movements more precise. Whatever it is Levin's just given me, I'm going to make sure I get myself a tube.

'Well?' Levin says.

I tell him about Julia, and her death, but not everything. I can't face that. I tell him about Rebecca Salomonsson again, about the necklace in her hand. How Grim once paid Sam a visit. With each word that leaves my mouth, I become more and more vulnerable. Levin's gaze slips from me, to the glass in my hand, to something outside the window, to the pattern in the wooden tabletop, to the time on his wristwatch. For some reason, he decides to wind his watch back a minute or so, and stares at his hands. He might seem bored, but in fact he is listening attentively. I drink from my glass again, and the anxiety is muffled, but still there.

'So,' I say eventually. 'That's why I need to know whatever you know.'

'I see,' Levin says. 'I'm afraid you're going to have to come with me to Kungsholmsgatan.'

For a second, I am convinced that I have made a serious mistake.

'No, no,' he adds quickly. 'Not like that. Not for that reason. But I'm late. My taxi is waiting down by Slottsbacken. I'll explain on the way.'

I stare at the glass.

'What is this, seriously?'

'If I remember rightly, it's amphetamine.'

I stare at him.

'You've got me high.'

'Just a little bit.' He stands up. 'Come on.'

XVIII

Levin walks alongside me, down towards Slottsbacken, tall and gangly in his gloomy grey jacket and black jeans, his bare head pale and round. A wind blows from somewhere, and on a corner, half-hidden by a skip, someone is sitting — maybe homeless, but maybe not — and shaking a collecting tin with one hand and holding a mobile phone in the other.

'Señor, please.'

Levin shakes his head, and I raise my hand dismissively without stopping.

'What a fucking city,' Levin mutters.

'You get that in small cities, too.'

'Not like here.'

The taxi is waiting there with the engine running. Behind it, the Royal Palace towers over us. A boy is standing there with his tourist parents, staring blankly at it. The palace stares back, just as blankly. We say nothing for a while, and Levin suddenly looks troubled, his gaze fixed on something beyond the windscreen.

'I did a bit of extra work at one time,' he says, as the taxi slowly turns down Myntgatan, towards the Vasa Bridge.

In the distance, the Parliament building and the City Hall stand proud, with the three crowns like pale-yellow sequins against the white sky somewhere above.

'They wanted me on the recruitment unit — go out to schools and explain what applying to join up involves, what demands are made, and so on. Quite a pleasant job, a bit of a change. So I took it, did it when we didn't have too much on. Later, I was asked about going to see kids and young people in care homes, not so much to recruit but to show them a different side of the force from the one they would normally experience. It was a pretty thankless task, but who could blame them for having problems with the police? Most of the force have got a problem with young people; a surprisingly large part spend most of their time chasing kids for minor theft and vandalism, as though they were witches. Why shouldn't young people have something against the police?'

'I'm from Salem,' I say. 'I know what it's like.'

'Of course,' says Levin. 'Naturally. Anyway, one autumn, I think about twelve or thirteen years ago, I visited the young offenders' institution in Jumkil — the place where one lad tried to kill another by tipping a big drying cabinet on top of him. The staff knew enough from previous experience to make sure it was properly secured to the wall, so the attempt didn't get very far. But still, this had happened during a near-riot only a week before my visit; as you can imagine, even I felt pretty uncomfortable about the whole thing. It wasn't that I was afraid — more that I thought they would see my visit as a threat or a mockery. I would have, had I been in their position. I tried to get the visit postponed, but Benny — you know, old police chief Skacke — refused. He said it was now more than ever we needed to show ourselves there. Maybe he was right, I don't know. So I didn't really have much choice. I went.'

The taxi swings onto Vasa Bridge, where the traffic is heavier than before. It's still so early that I can see the mist rising around the heavy white bulk of Central Station. The warmth from the weird drink is still present, and I feel awake and alert. I think about the timescale of what Levin is telling me. Grim would have been about twenty then.

'I started with a sort of introduction, a presentation in one of the big halls, and after that I followed their daily routine for a couple of hours. That part, the tagging along, wasn't planned, and I don't think Skacke would have approved, but the head there at Jumkil invited me to do it, and I felt it was the least I could do to minimise the distance between me and the youths there. So I did it, and made sure I was available to anyone who might have wanted to talk to me. There was certainly hostility there, but not as bad as I'd feared. Several seemed to be interested in police work. One of the ones who didn't say a word to me, neither during the presentation nor afterwards, was John Grimberg. He sat right at the back during the introduction, and kept himself to himself for the rest of the day. I did notice him, but didn't give it much thought.

'Before lunch, I had a quick meeting with the director of the institution in his office in the main building. We were supposed to have had it earlier, but hadn't had time. They were still busy with the aftermath of the unrest. We sat there talking for a while, and Westin told me about the problems at Jumkil, about the clients — that's what he called them — and the offences they committed there. He was, of course, worried about the number of assaults, the number of threats and thefts. No one really knew how bad it was there, but the things that the staff got to hear about were undoubtedly, as they say, the tip of the iceberg.'

The taxi stops at the end of Vasa Bridge, and I look at Rosenbad and at Fredsgatan, which runs down to the right, the windows of its mute buildings lit from within. I remember chasing a suspect through there once, a man who was accused of robbing a bureau de change. He hadn't. The robber was the man's fifteen-year-old son. The man I'd been chasing had merely supplied him with the weapon.

'On Westin's desk was a little box,' Levin continues. 'I looked inside, and saw that it contained a collection of ID cards. "What is this?" I asked. "Items we've confiscated," he said. "I see," I said, "From whom?" and then I picked up the box and flipped through its contents. "John Grimberg," Westin said. According to Westin,

Grimberg claimed that he wasn't going to do anything with them, that he'd just made them to kill time and to hone his skills. They were …' Levin goes quiet. 'They were outstanding. Really outstanding. They weren't just cards, but various invoices, certificates, benefit-office claims and correspondence, flow diagrams about the tax authority's procedures for registering and de-registering citizens, lists of registers that one is automatically entered on at birth, lists of other registers and how you might end up on them. He even had copies of real police reports, with his illegible notes in the margins, maybe to denote what information had been garnered from surveillance and what must have come from an insider. The internet featured heavily in his notes — it was all quite new then, don't forget. He could see the threat it posed, that was for sure. He seemed to have tried to work out what information was available, and from how many different sources. And I promise you, Leo, judging by what I saw, he was practically qualified for employment with the fraud squad even then.

'I asked Westin whether Grimberg had committed other offences during his time at Jumkil. "None whatsoever," he replied. That was it. I couldn't help smiling, which I'm a bit ashamed of now. But I told him not to worry about the naughty kids who go round punching each other or stealing CD players. The vast majority will have respectable jobs and probably kids of their own by the time they're thirty. It's the likes of John Grimberg you need to be careful with. Westin, of course, looked completely bemused, and had no idea what I was going on about. Which, I suppose, was understandable, even if that's the sort of approach which had led to incident after incident that could have been avoided.'

The taxi turns up Hantverkargatan, past the streets where barely an hour ago I had managed to escape the reporters waiting on my doorstep. I look for them, expecting them to still be standing there, on corners, but the only people visible are still-sleepy Stockholmers, standing at traffic lights, staring intently at the red lights, the ground, invisible dots somewhere just in front of them. The first cafés are opening. The noise of the city is slowly building.

'I asked if it might be possible to meet John, to talk to him one on one. Westin looked a bit bewildered, but he nodded and asked me back to his room. The long corridor of closed doors was alarmingly prison-like, and when Westin unlocked the door, John wasn't there. He asked me to go in and wait, and I asked if it was really okay for just anyone to go into someone's room without the client's — I used that word — *consent*. "Of course," Westin said.' Levin shakes his head. 'There's no respect for privacy in those places. I think it's even worse now; I've heard that certain rooms even have CCTV cameras. Anyway, I went in and sat on a chair by the desk, with my back to it, while Westin went to get John.'

'What was his room like?' I ask.

'Bare. Compared to most young men's rooms, these quarters are always bare, but even compared to the others, John's felt unusually simple. He had few clothes. The bed wasn't made — a breach of the rules. His desk was what I was most interested in, but it seemed too private for me to investigate without John being there. I could see from the corner of my eye that there were a few things on it, but I assumed that they were of no value to John or the likes of me. He was too clever for that. If he was still at it, he would have hidden it away. The box of stuff that Westin had shown me earlier had been found in a cavity behind the wardrobe — by chance, he claimed, and I'm pretty sure that was true.

'John had been sent to Jumkil for GBH, but that was just the main offence. The full charge-sheet included threatening behaviour, possession of an offensive weapon, forgery, and attempted serious fraud. If I understood correctly, he had been trying to sell ID cards to someone. A physical altercation occurred, and John had threatened the buyer with a knife. It had been an open-and-shut case — loads of forensic evidence and several witnesses. I believe he was no longer living in Salem at that time. His sister Julia, who you mentioned, had died a few years earlier, and even if the family had always had problems, apparently it was her death that ripped the family apart. He was on the electoral roll as a lodger at an address in Hagsätra. It was there, on the street outside the house, that the crime had taken place.'

For a moment, he's quiet, as the taxi stops at the junction between Bergsgatan and Polhemsgatan. Kronoberg Park is very, very green, but I think the drink Levin gave me has made all the colours appear unnaturally vivid. Everything has a shimmer to it, which makes the world seem like a more hopeful place.

'John came into the room, led by one of the staff. He was surprised to see me — that much was obvious — but he soon regained his composure and just nodded slightly in my direction. "Is it okay if I sit here?" I asked. "Sure," he said, and sat down on the edge of the bed, as though prepared to quickly stand up again. He was tense and nervous. "How long have you been here?" I asked, and John answered that he didn't know. "You lose track of time in here," he said. But he thought it was just over eighteen months. He had in fact been there for exactly eighteen months when I was there, almost to the day. He had way more of an idea than he wanted to let on. That in itself is remarkable; most criminals of that age are the opposite. They want us to believe that they are cleverer than they really are. I asked him what he was in for, and he asked me whether I didn't already know. "Yes," I said. "Sorry, it was a stupid question." I got my police badge out instead, and held it up in front of him. "Have you ever seen one of these, up close?" I asked. "Only constables'," he replied. "Never a superintendent's." He took it off me and inspected it carefully — the back, the edges, the pattern in the plastic, the little chip. Held it up to the light. He knew exactly where to look to find the important details. "You could make one of those, couldn't you?" I asked. "Police badges are difficult," he answered. "They have a different pattern. And the chip just becomes a useless bit of plastic. You can't store the necessary information on it." "How did

176

you find that out?" "Practice," he replied. "And what do you plan to do with your talents?" "Who knows?" he said.'

The taxi has stopped outside the entrance on Kungsholmsgatan.

'Excuse me,' the driver says, looking for eye contact in the rear-view mirror. 'We're here.'

'Yes?' Levin says and looks up.

'We're here,' I say.

'Yep.'

I pay, and Levin opens the door and climbs out while the driver prints the receipt and hands it to me. I give it to Levin, who looks blankly at it.

'Ah, yes. Thank you.'

He walks up a couple of steps and sits down, scratches his shiny head, and straightens his glasses, which have slipped down his nose.

'John knew full well what he was planning to do with his talents. It was plain to see. I asked him where he'd got the police reports from. It could've been a leak, I thought to myself — and blow me down, it was. But I never found out who the mole was. He said nothing, of course. "Are you interested in police work?" I asked instead. "Yes," he said. "You've never thought about joining the police?" This was the first time he displayed any kind of emotion. My question made him laugh. I ignored that, and explained that, with his background, and above all his criminal record, proper tests would be necessary, and I would need to pull all manner of strings in Solna, but that it was far from impossible. "Would you be willing to do that?" he asked. I said that what I'd seen in Westin's box was evidence of his skill.

'As I said, he was pretty much ready for the fraud squad. Unfortunately, you do have to take the traditional route, but people have been known to climb very fast. Within six, seven years he could, with some further training, be working on the stuff he was already doing. I even offered him the chance to keep himself up to date with his field of interest alongside the training. There was so much upheaval in the world of Swedish registers and ID documents around the millennium, and it was important that he kept up with the changes.'

One of the officers from the NOVA group, the organised-crime unit within Stockholm Police, climbs out of a black car with tinted windows and goes up the steps, past us. He nods to Levin and looks puzzled at my presence, but doesn't say anything.

'You're thinking: did Levin think he had a chance? Well, yes, I did, because I did have a chance, I could tell. John considered my proposition. He was going to get out just before the application deadline. He had time to prepare and send in the application. "But," I added, "make sure all the information on the form is genuine." That made him laugh, too. People like John Grimberg ... I'd met a few before him, one or two since. Five, six people during my forty years in the force. And the reason I tried to get him to join was actually two-fold. It's always a shame when a talent is misused. As a criminal, there was a risk that he wouldn't last long; it's that sort of world. I wanted to give him another chance. That's always been my weakness, and my strength, I think, as a cop. But my reason was also simple crime prevention. A crook like John could cause a lot of damage, and use up a lot of police resources.'

'Did you say that to him?'

'The first part — not the second.'

'How did he react?'

'Not at all. He said nothing. It was time for me to leave, and I gave him my card, asked him to call when he'd made up his mind. He never called.'

An elderly couple pass on the other side of the road, and Levin's eyes follow them. They look tired but unbowed, happy almost.

'About a year later,' he went on, 'his name cropped up in an investigation. A failed armed robbery. The problem was that the culprits were all wearing masks, so we didn't know who they were. But we had our usual suspects, of course, and we put them under surveillance. One of them was spotted with someone who the snoop didn't recognise. I got to see the picture and, right enough, it was John Grimberg. Shortly afterwards, our suspect disappeared — vanished into thin air. John was interviewed, but it led nowhere. He was released, and after that I never heard his name again until Alice said that you had asked about him.'

'He's changed his identity,' I say. 'For the last ten years he's only been in the Whereabouts Unknown register.'

'Uh-huh,' Levin says.

'You don't seem surprised.'

'No,' he says. 'There's something about certain people, as though they start to disappear right in front of you. As though they're always in character, wearing a mask — not just in front of others, but even for themselves. To be devoid of identity like that has an effect on human beings. It's dangerous, of course, but people who change themselves so drastically often do so to protect themselves from something even more dangerous. What it was in the case of John Grimberg, I couldn't tell you; in fact, you probably know more about that than I do. There's nothing weird about role-play in itself; it's a matter of practice and competence, an ability that most of us can acquire. It's a part of this job, even for you and for me. But, unlike us, unlike those officers who sometimes claim to be someone else, or the opportunistic fraudster flashing a false ID card, who can go back to their real selves afterwards, the likes of John Grimberg don't have that option, and they don't want it either. There is something about that emptiness a person can create in themselves which makes me very uneasy.

'Now, in retrospect, I wish I could say that I knew all along, but I didn't. It was no more than a hunch, a flash of insight into how things might turn out for him. And that flash came just at the point in our conversation when he almost started to become transparent in front of me. There was nothing behind his facial expressions or the look in his eyes, just more facial expressions, other looks, none

179

of them any more false or more genuine than the other.'

Levin goes quiet and sits there a while, before shaking his head, standing up, and brushing off his trousers with the palm of his hand. 'Sorry about this rambling, Leo,' he says, visibly embarrassed. 'I'm getting old.'

'Did you see anything else in that box in Westin's room that could give any clues as to where ... or who he is today?'

Levin shakes his head.

'I'm not sure; my memory lets me down these days, Leo. But I don't think so.'

'No signature, no initials, nothing?'

'Nothing. As far as I remember.' He clears his throat. 'I remember his language.'

'His language?'

'I remember that he was very eloquent. That's unusual among kids on the estates.' He blinks rapidly. 'Yes, that's right. I remember one other thing, but it might not have anything to do with John Grimberg. That robbery I was telling you about, the unsuccessful one, when he popped up during the investigation ...'

'Yes.'

'The detectives thought that the robbery was linked to drugs, like most things in this town are. The robbery was apparently instigated because a kilo or two of heroin had disappeared, and the victims of this theft had to pay their debts to their suppliers. They were desperate, I suppose, which isn't really that surprising. When desperate people need to get their hands on a lot of money, fast, it often ends in a robbery. The heroin was found later at the home of a woman called Anja, I think her name was. She wasn't much to look at, as they say, but she was light-fingered, and she knew one of the people convicted of the robbery. That's how they found her, via her contact network. Somehow Anja had managed to lift the consignment, with the intention of using some of it herself and selling the rest, climbing a rung or two in the hierarchy. She was arrested for possession with intent to supply, and she was sentenced to jail; I can't remember if was two or three years in Hinseberg Prison.'

'When was this? You said "about a year later" before.'

'Oh,' Levin says. 'It must have been ... maybe 2002 or 2003, I can't quite remember. Anyway, the detectives thought that she must have had someone else, not necessarily an accomplice in that case, but someone who was close to her and who moved in the same circles. Because Anja had no one — her parents were dead, and she had no family of her own. And when they checked through her phone, which was of course stolen, they found a number they couldn't trace.'

'You suspect it was him.'

'That's right. Someone had made a list of Anja's known contacts; it was in her file, and someone had written "JG?" on it. There were a lot of relevant people with those initials around at the time, men and women — Johan Granberg, Juno Gomez, Jannicke Gretchen. But I had a feeling that it might have been him.'

'What gave you that feeling?'

'Hard to know. Intuition, maybe.'

'Where is she now?'

'In the Forest Cemetery.' Levin looks downwards. 'She hung herself in her cell at Hinseberg. It was in the papers.'

'I didn't start reading the papers until I was thirty.'

This makes Levin laugh. Then he looks at me.

'You should tell all this to Gabriel.'

'Birck?'

'Yes.'

'Maybe.'

'Leo.' Levin 's expression is grave. 'You may be in danger. In more than one sense.'

'Yes, maybe.'

Levin looks up and examines an advertising hoarding on one of

181

the external walls: DO YOU WORRY ABOUT WHAT YOUR DOG GETS UP TO? KEEP TRACK OF YOUR DOG ON YOUR SMARTPHONE!

'Keep track,' Levin says thoughtfully. 'Not surprising that people want to disappear. Not surprising that in a society like ours, people hate the police, they don't trust us. Ten thousand or twenty thousand police won't make a difference. It's the wrong job, at the wrong time. In the wrong system, in the wrong part of the world.' He breathes out, heavily. 'So his sister died young,' he says, more quietly. 'You knew each other, you and her?'

'Yes. He thought her death was down to me.'

'Was it?' Levin asks, with no visible emotion, as though his interest in the answer were purely professional.

XIX

Towards the end of the summer holidays, someone sprayed one of the doorways in the centre of Salem with black spraypaint. FUCKING NIGGERS GO HOME, read the text, written in spiky, uneven letters, and framed with swastikas. The next day, a well-known skinhead was seriously beaten, close to Rönninge High School. Neither of the two perpetrators were Swedes. I knew it, since that's how it always worked. The events made the press, but the story was soon dropped. There was nothing to suggest that the skinhead who'd been beaten had written the graffiti on the doorway, but that was neither here nor there. Three days later, a black kid got kicked in the face. His name was Mikael Persson, born in Sweden but with an Egyptian father. Another few days passed and another skinhead was assaulted near the water tower in Salem. The victim had a shaved head, denim jacket, and combat trousers, and was a member of the Swedish Left Party and several anti-racist organisations. His assailants didn't know that. They thought he was a neo-Nazi, because he looked like one.

These events coloured the end of the summer, although their effect on me was only fleeting. Julia and I split up after that time when Grim came home while we were in her bed. It wasn't something we talked about and then decided upon. The ending just crystallised of its own accord, unsaid yet unmistakeable.

At first I kept away from Grim, too; just the thought of him made me think of Julia, which made me heartbroken. I'd never known pain like it, and for four days I didn't talk to a soul, not even my parents. They got worried, and went and got my brother, which just made things worse. On the fifth day, I realised that I couldn't deal with this on my own. I needed someone, and the only person I could contemplate was Grim. I couldn't tell him, but he could distract me. When I called him, he sounded worried.

'I've been trying to get hold of you,' he said. 'Why don't you answer? Has something happened?'

'Sorry. Nothing. I've been ill.'

'Ill?'

'Just the flu. But today's the first day with no fever.' I hesitated. 'Shall we meet up?'

GRIM NOTICED THAT something was wrong, I could tell. We didn't need to do anything; the only thing I felt was the need to have him close by. To not be alone. He understood that. We spent time in hidden-away parks, or on forgotten benches — me with a book or music, and Grim with his ID cards. He practised non-stop, but since his time at the summer camp, Klas was much stricter about what he got up to in his room, so he had to practise in other places. We sat at my place several times, and for a while my desk was more Grim's than mine, until my dad noticed and asked in a nervous voice what we were doing. We used our fake IDs and went to Wednesday Club on Södermalm, got drunk on cocktails, and giggled at the forbidden nature of it all when the barman wasn't looking.

I wondered how Julia was getting on. If this was even affecting her. After a while, probably so that I could deal with everything, I convinced myself that this was easy for her. But my friendship with Grim had been saved. Perhaps it would all work out in the end. I thought about what Julia had said that time, that if she could travel in time she would go forwards, to see how everything turned out. I was starting to understand what she meant. The uncertainty, this feeling of having lost something, perhaps for nothing, was almost the hardest part.

One day, I had my bedroom window open. So did someone else, nearby, because I could hear N.W.A.'s 'I Just Want to Celebrate' through distorted speakers. I went over to the window and felt the warmth of the sun. Julia was down there, out walking with a friend, a blonde girl called Bella. I'd met her a couple of times that summer, with Julia. They were laughing about something, and Julia seemed to be happy.

I tried to focus on the fact that I'd got Grim back, but all I could think of was how I'd lost Julia.

Something was boiling, deep, deep inside me.

It was then, in those last few days of the summer holidays, that I saw that Tim was back in Salem.

TIM NORDIN was a year younger than me, and the first time I saw him he was sitting on his own by a playground on the outskirts of Salem. I was thirteen at the time, and I was so angry I was close to tears. Soon the rage turned to shame, and I didn't want to go home. Vlad and Fred had been more aggressive, more threatening, than usual. It was one of the few occasions when I'd tried to fight back, and it had resulted in one of them putting a knee in my guts. That humiliation of attempting yet failing to resist was worse than not doing anything; it made everything feel even more hopeless. It was like a confirmation that I was weak. Whenever I hadn't tried to fight back, I could always tell myself that I could have, if I'd wanted to — however childish that may seem.

I'd managed to get away, and after struggling to get some air in my lungs, I started wandering around aimlessly. When I saw Tim at the playground, something burned inside me. Something forced its way out of me — the need to fight back against powerlessness, humiliation.

I went over to Tim, who didn't seem to have heard me. He was a wiry little kid; he wore a cap with the peak facing backwards, and baggy clothes that were too big, to make him seem bigger than he was.

'Hello,' I said when I got within a couple of steps of him.

He didn't respond.

'Hello.'

Tim still didn't look up. The rage burned inside me and I looked around. We were alone. I took the last paces over to him and smacked his cap off. That made him jump and pull his earphones out.

'Why don't you answer when I'm talking to you?'

'Sorry,' he said and waved the earphones demonstratively. 'I didn't hear.'

He was scared. I could see that in his eyes, alert and dark, dark brown. His thin face, with its sharp little chin and thin lips, made his eyes look round and unnaturally large. *He's actually scared of me*, I thought to myself again.

'What are you doing here?' I said.

'Nothing,' he said and bent over.

'What are you doing?'

Tim stopped.

'My cap.'

I smiled.

'It's not your cap.'

'I got it from ...' he began, but didn't complete the sentence.

'From your mum?' I mocked. 'Did you get it from your little old mum?'

He looked at me, without reacting.

'Answer me!' I screamed.

Tim nodded silently and looked away. I picked up the cap, scrunched it up, and stuffed it into the back pocket of my jeans. On the bench beside him was an orange-yellow peel, and I was standing so close to him that I could smell clementine or orange on his fingers.

'A purple cap,' I said. 'Purple. Are you bent?'

'Eh?'

'"Are you bent?" I asked. Are you deaf, too?'

He shook his head.

'What are you shaking your head at?'

'I'm not deaf,' Tim said quietly.

'Well, answer me then. Are you bent?'

He shook his head again.

'Eh?' I said and leant in to him. 'Louder.'

'I'm twelve,' he whispered. 'I don't know what I am.'

I laughed at him.

I DIDN'T HIT HIM THEN. That would come later. As I left, I passed a building site. I chucked the purple cap in a skip, making sure that it fell so far that Tim wouldn't be able to reach it even if he did notice it, which was unlikely.

I felt relieved, as though I had deserved restitution and had got it, which may be why my conscience never reacted.

For two years I used Tim Nordin as a tool to purge myself with, to feel superior, just as Vlad and Fred had used me, I suppose. Maybe that's how it was — everything just a reaction to something that had happened earlier. Someone always ended up in the firing line, everyone turned on someone else, and I was neither better nor worse than any of them. I just was.

Then something happened that caused Tim Nordin to move away from Salem. Maybe it was to do with his family; I don't know. He disappeared, and I didn't give it a lot of thought. I never told anyone what I'd done, and I don't think Tim did either. After that, nothing, until Julia mentioned him when we were sitting up on the water tower.

NOW HE WAS BACK, taller but just as wiry. He walked past the Triad one morning when I was sitting having breakfast. I didn't recognise him at first, from so far away, but as my eyes followed him, it was obvious that I was watching someone who didn't want to be seen.

Tim always walked like that. The trouble with trying not to be visible is that the effort it takes is so obvious, and itself becomes visible.

'Leo,' Dad said, on his way out to work. 'Is everything okay? You've seemed ... different this past week.'

'Yes,' I said. 'Everything's okay.'

'Sure?'

'Sure.'

He nodded, disappointed, and took his keys, walked out, and locked the door behind him. An hour later the scene was repeated, with my mum this time. I stayed by the kitchen window, waiting for Grim to call. This time I was going to ask him how Julia was. I needed to know how she was feeling. People laugh for lots of reasons, and the fact that I'd seen Julia doing it didn't mean she was fine.

An hour later he rang, and we brought a football along and kicked it ahead of us on the way down to the rec. Grim didn't like sport — the only thing he'd ever shown an interest in was shooting on television — but he said that kicking a ball as hard as he could was a good feeling. I agreed with him there.

The recreation ground lay deserted, waiting for us. I picked the ball out of the net that Grim had just kicked it into.

'You know who Tim Nordin is, don't you?' I asked.

'Tim ...' Grim said and frowned. 'Yes. He was Julia's friend when she was little, but I think he moved away. No one, not even Julia, knows why.' He dropped the ball to the ground. 'Why do you ask?'

'I thought I saw him earlier.'

'What, you know him?'

'No, no. But a friend of mine went to nursery with him, so I know who he is.'

I never asked about Julia; I couldn't. From tomorrow on, she would be going to the same school as me.

THAT FIRST DAY BACK, I didn't see Julia at all. Didn't see Grim either. I hung out with my classmates instead, and that felt weird. It wasn't that I didn't like them; it was more that I'd hardly seen any of them over the summer, which had been so long and in which so much had happened. I had lived in another dimension for those long months.

The second day, I had maths in one of the classrooms at the furthest end of the factory-like building. When I came round the corner, the big corridor was empty. I was a few minutes late, and the lesson had already started. Rows of lockers lined the walls; several of them had already been defaced with graffiti tags. A big, black swastika had been painted on one of the locker doors.

The door to one of the toilets opened and closed, and Julia came walking towards me. She had a ring-binder and a stack of books under one arm, her eyes fixed on a piece of paper that flapped in time with her strides. When she looked up, she froze, and it was this — the look in her eyes — that made the world rock underneath my feet.

'Hi,' she said, without stopping.

'Hi,' I said, and stopped. 'How are things?'

'Confused,' she said. She looked down at her timetable and carried on past me.

I watched her, hoping that she would turn her head, but she didn't. That was the thing that made me feel silly, duped. Crushed. I wanted to cry because this was how it was going to be from now on, and I couldn't see an end to it.

Later that day, I found out that Tim Nordin had come back to Salem because his parents had divorced, and Tim's dad wasn't exactly the kind of person who could raise a child. Tim had to live with his mum instead, and they'd moved back because she missed Salem. I mean, that on its own was enough. He should clearly have refused to move back.

THAT WEEKEND, there was a big outdoor party at the recreation ground where Grim and I had been a week earlier. Word got around, thanks to scraps of paper pushed into lockers and passed around during lessons. Me and Grim went with a Coke bottle each, half-filled with booze that we had decanted from our parents' drinks cabinets. I'd only managed a few measures of vodka, so I had to dilute it with pop. The bubbles made it taste worse than normal.

'Do you know if Julia's coming?' I asked.

'I don't know,' Grim said. 'I didn't mention it to her, so I hope she doesn't. I can't be arsed keeping an eye on her.'

'Why do you need to?'

'It's my sister, for fuck's sake. And she's been a bit weird recently.'

'I don't get it,' I said, and could feel my pulse rising. I unscrewed the bottle top and took a deep, burning gulp. 'You can't be so overprotective all the time. She's nearly sixteen, man. She can look after herself,' I went on and then, unable to stop myself, added: 'Stop treating her like a child.'

Grim avoided eye contact.

'You don't get it, do you?'

'What's to get?'

'She's the only reason we stick together, that our family works. And Mum and Dad can't protect her.'

'But why does she need protecting? And why does it have to be you that protects her? Social Ser —'

'It was their fucking fault I ended up in Jumkil. If they take me or Julia, we've had it.'

I took another swig from my bottle. I remember thinking that perhaps one of them had the problem, as opposed to the problem being between them, in the make-up of the family. That the problem wasn't that they risked being pulled apart, but rather that they tried so hard to be a family. I couldn't really articulate the thought.

'But is it that important? That you stick together? I mean, maybe there's something negative about that, too.'

I just didn't know how to express it.

'You only have one family,' was all Grim said. 'Only in good

190

families do people think, "I'd be better off without them."' He looked me in the eye. 'So shut your mouth. You haven't got a clue.'

For the first time, I was scared of Grim, without knowing why. Maybe it was because I was starting to feel drunk, but there was something about his stare. It was a foreboding fear like when you imagine what severe pain might feel like, the kind of fear that instantly makes you feel shaky and insecure for no reason.

THE RECREATION GROUND was full of people sitting around in groups, laughing, drinking. Music was being played from heavy ghetto-blasters, and some people entertained themselves by climbing up the goalposts and sitting on the crossbar. Grim and I sat with a few people he knew. They asked him about the camp and the guy who'd been stabbed. Grim shrugged, not wanting to talk about it. They asked what he'd done to his hair, and Grim told them that he'd thought it was getting too long, so he'd cut it off. That's when I saw Julia walking towards us, wearing dark jeans and a white T-shirt with the word JUMPER written across the chest. She had a Coke bottle in her hand, and seemed to be looking for someone.

I looked at the bottle in my hand. It was dark now, and to see how much I'd drunk I had to hold it up above my head, against the sky. This movement made Julia turn her head. She carefully raised her own bottle to me, and I felt embarrassed. She thought I was waving. Julia smiled like she did when she was a little bit drunk.

Grim spotted her and sighed.

'I knew it.'

He waved to her to come over and sit with us.

'What are you doing?' I said.

'Well, if she's got to be here, it's better if she at least sits with us,' Grim slurred.

She came over and knelt down.

'What are you talking about?'

191

A girl behind us squealed as one of the guys who'd been sitting on the crossbar fell down. Everything except the music went quiet, until we heard the guy laugh, still lying there, beer can still in his hand. We laughed, too, all of us.

Julia's knee touched mine, and I found it hard to control my hands. Scenes from the summer, good scenes, whizzed past me and I longed to go back. She took a swig of whatever it was in her bottle, and winced. Nearby, from one of the ghetto-blasters, Radiohead was singing 'Karma Police', and more people arrived at the recreation ground. Most of the pitch was covered with people from school. Older guys turned up, but soon left again. They just wanted to be paid back for the alcohol they'd bought for people. Some started arguing, but it was soon settled. I wondered what Julia was thinking, wondered if she knew that Tim Nordin had moved back, whether that news would make her happy, whether she'd regretted us splitting up. My head started spinning, and the thoughts led nowhere, just round and round.

'I need a piss,' Grim said, and looked at me. 'Are you coming?'

'No,' I said.

His eyes flitted between me and Julia.

'Okay,' he said, and headed down to the bushes.

Only then did I notice that Julia was nervous. She was drinking quickly and laughing a bit too much at stuff the people we were sitting with were saying.

'Good party,' I said.

'Yep.'

'Did you come with anyone?'

'Yes.' She looked around. 'But I don't know where they are.'

'I like your top,' I said.

'Do you?'

'Doesn't everyone like Jumper?'

Julia didn't answer; she drank. I carried on instead: 'At school, when we walked past each other ... you said you were confused.

192

You meant that you were confused about school ...' I looked at her. 'Right?'

'Sure,' she said, with a faint smile. 'If you say so.'

'I don't say so, I'm asking.'

'And I'm answering.'

I leant towards her, about to say something, but I was interrupted by Grim, who was back, and who sank down beside us.

A while later, everything started spinning around me, and when I got up to go over to the bushes for a piss, it was like the whole recreation ground was sloping. All the shadows, sitting there with their bottles and cans, went blurry round the edges, and I stumbled on something, but I got up again.

When I woke up, I was lying sideways across a bed. I still had my clothes on. I moved my head to see what time it was and it really hurt, made me close my eyes. I was at home, at least.

My hand reached for something — water — but the bottle on my bedside table was too far away. I rolled over and grabbed it. It was empty. It was then, as I looked at the empty bottle, that I noticed my hand. It was covered in red spots.

I REMEMBERED GETTING UP to go for a piss in the bushes. I remembered the fear I felt that I couldn't explain. After that, everything was shrouded in mist until I woke up. I looked at my hand and tried to recall whether I'd eaten anything before I went home. The red might be ketchup or tomato sauce. I lifted my hand to my nose to smell it, but couldn't detect anything other than the faint whiff of cigarette smoke that clung to my skin. I got out of bed, and tried to work out whether I had pains anywhere other than in my head. I didn't.

WHEN I CAME BACK from the bushes, Grim and Julia had gone. I asked someone we'd been sitting with where they'd gone, and he mumbled something about them having fallen out.

'Why did they fall out?'

'Fucked if I know.'

I'd gone to look for them, nervous. I remember the track that played again and again that night, 'I Just Want to Celebrate', and how the nausea twisted up inside me, and how I hobbled away from the recreation ground, with bright spots sweeping across my field of vision, and wondering if someone had put something in my bottle.

I WENT for a shower. I'd left the window open in my room to let a bit of air in. I wondered where my parents could be, but then I remembered the flyer I'd seen on the kitchen table — something about an August flea market in Rönninge. I was home alone and scrubbing my hands to get rid of the red. Slowly, it dawned on me: it must be blood. Under the water it dissolved quickly, and streaks of red ran down and turned pink against the white bathtub. As I washed my face, my top lip throbbed. It was tender and a bit swollen, and that's how it came back to me.

I'D GIVEN UP looking for Grim and Julia, and tried to find someone else instead — anyone. A girl was standing leaning against a lamppost not far from the rec, and I walked over to her. I couldn't remember what I asked her, but I could still feel her body against mine. She was small and skinny, like Julia. I must have pushed myself against her. She pushed me away, and I tried again, but this time I got a smack in the face. Maybe from her, maybe from someone else; that sequence was unclear. I fell to the ground, I think, not from the smack, but because of my bad balance. Then: someone laughing, mockingly. Humiliation, how it twisted inside me.

I lay there, ashamed, until they'd gone, and after that I headed home. Somewhere along the way, I met Tim. It seemed like he was on the way home, too. Had he been on the rec? I hadn't seen him.

I stopped him.

'So you're back,' I slurred.

We stood on the pavement, in the gloom between two streetlamps. Tim seemed sober. He smelt healthy, like fabric softener.

'Yes.'

'Where are you going?'

'Home.' He squinted. 'What's happened to your lip?'

'Nothing.'

'It looks like you've been hit.'

'Nothing,' I screamed, and he stared at me. 'You knew Julia, didn't you? Julia Grimberg.'

Hearing the name surprised him. Something flickered in his eyes.

'Yes. Why?'

I didn't know what to say to that. Instead I put my hand on his shoulder and pushed him backwards, forcing him to take a step back.

'Let me go,' he said. And then, quieter: 'You will regret it if you don't.'

'Don't what?'

'If you don't let me go.'

I remembered that I laughed. Not at him, but everything else. How absurd everything was, how complicated it had got. I laughed at the fear I felt, laughed at Grim. At Julia. And then I hit Tim, again and again. Once in the face, in the stomach, between his legs. He offered no resistance, just lay there looking at me with an empty stare, which is what provoked me even more. That look reminded me of Grim's and there was something unsettling about the whole thing.

It might have been the hangover, or Julia, or Grim; maybe it was Tim's blank stare and his equally empty, meaningless threats. Probably all of those things. I bent double in the shower, gasping for air.

It is the year 2000. Mum has been dead for a year. I'm twenty-one and I've left Jumkil Young Offenders, I'm living in the tunnels under the city, along with the others. They don't trust me and I don't trust them. I daren't sleep, worried they'll take my stuff. To stay awake I take speed, just like everyone else. I'm rarely out in daylight and that affects my eyes, my vision is cloudy. I steal phones for a living, run around with a rucksack full. When I do eventually fall asleep I wake up with no possessions, no phones. I have to start from scratch on a comedown from the speed. Doesn't go too well. One guy refuses to let go of his bag and I nearly kill him. Afterwards I don't remember anything, those images don't come back until much later.

I leave the tunnels and move in with a friend in Alby. His name is Frank, he's a smackhead and he gives me my first bowl. I love it and I leave the speed behind, sleep on a mattress. He's got this girl there and she's fit and she's nice to me. When he's not home we have sex. For some reason she has to leave the country a few months later and I help her, make her an ID card she can use.

She gets on a train and I never see her again.

The day before she leaves I'm lying on the floor, high, half-leaning against one of the cupboards. I'm out of it and I can't focus, just see Frank has something in his hand and he crouches down in front of me. He asks me if I've done this before.

'Done what?'

'These.' He waves one of the cards in front of me.

'A few times.'

Frank says I'm good. He asks if I can do it again, for some more gear. I say yes, but that I need the materials and the tools and that I'm wanted for a robbery and I don't dare leave the house. Frank sorts what I need, steals it from warehouses. He comes back with the wrong stuff several times and has to take it back. He says that seems weird.

Later he introduces me to the guy known as the Man With No Voice, Josef Abel. Through him I get to know someone who you must know. Silver. He's the same age as me but far more powerful. Silver asks me to help him with a guy who needs to lie low for a while. I do it in exchange for heroin. Soon Silver tells me about a friend who runs a company, but the company's about to go under. He asks me if I would take on the company in exchange for a payment. It's a lot of money, which I can buy a shitload of junk with. So I say yes to the money and the company, and in exchange, he says, a few people might come and ask questions.

I end up as a front for the company without realising what that entails. The law on limited companies means that it's the shareholders who are ultimately responsible for the company. I've got fuck all to do with it but it turns out I'm the one liable when the company ends up going bust a few months later. The debt is half a million and all my gear is gone. It's the first time I ever think about topping myself. It's around then that I realise it would be a good time to pull off the ultimate trick, the greatest illusion of all: to disappear.

XX

Time, I'm running out of time. The feeling is unmistakeable, but I don't know what to do about it. Levin has disappeared into the building, and I walk around Kungsholmen with my hands in my pockets. I'm trying to think.

Recollections of this morning — the reporters on the doorstep — come back to me, and for some reason I can't shake them. That feeling of being watched and hunted grows inside me, and I turn around, time and again, convinced that someone is following me. I slip into a café, a hole-in-the-wall place on a side street near Kungsholmen Square, and I choose a seat where I can see the window and the door. Out on the street, an old woman is dragging an equally old man along the road, as though they are in a hurry to get somewhere. The man seems to be resisting, until I realise that he just can't walk any faster.

My phone rings. I recognise the number. It's a Salem number. I put the phone to my ear.

'Hello?'

'Leo, it's Mum. I ... How are things?'

'Good. Has something happened to Dad?'

'No, no.' She clears her throat. 'No, all's well here. We were just wondering, we read about what has happened and ... I just wondered if everything's okay.'

I close my eyes.

'Everything is fine.'

'Is it? Because ...'

'It's no big deal. Just a misunderstanding.'

'Because I was thinking, what with everything that happened in the spring, you know.'

I haven't told them any details, those few times I've been to Salem. In fact, I've stayed away as much as possible just to avoid that.

'Micke's worried, too.'

'Tell him it's all okay.'

She sighs.

'Mum, it's okay. Honestly.'

'Oh well, if you say so. It was nice to see you the other day,' she says instead.

I do my best to keep talking to her a bit longer, but before long the stress falls down onto my shoulders again and I finish the call. I drink some water and it goes down wrong, making me cough.

Rebecca Salomonsson was robbed. She went to Chapmansgården to sleep, and someone ended her life by going in there and shooting her. She had Julia's necklace in her hand. I try to work out whether there's a connection between the robbery and her death, but I don't get anywhere. I try to imagine Grim as the perpetrator, but it doesn't fit. He would never be that careless.

My phone vibrates.

have you worked it out yet?

I hesitate.

grim?

yes

My pulse is racing.

we need to meet, I write.

yes

where are you?

soon

what does that mean?

I stare at my phone. It is mute and black, until it lights up and the ringtone vibrates through. It's Birck. I don't answer, and carry on waiting instead. When nothing happens, I send another text.

hello

Still nothing, until Birck rings again. I ignore it and drink some more water. A bus slows down and pulls up at the bus stop. A big advert covers one side of the bus: a middle-aged woman and an equally middle-aged man, both flawlessly beautiful, and the words YESTERDAY'S SKILLS, TOMORROW'S LIABILITY — KEEP YOUR CV UP TO DATE. In one corner of the café, a dad is sitting with his child, a boy. The boy says something that makes him laugh. I look away. He's the age Viktor would have been.

The phone rings for a third time and I give up. I answer.

'What?'

'Why the hell didn't you answer?' Birck says. 'I was about to file a missing person's report.'

'What do you want?'

In total, five hundred and thirty-six tips about the murder of Rebecca Salomonsson have been received and registered. It often takes far too long for the police to wade through that number of tips, for obvious reasons. People are unreliable. The details they give must be verified, either by comparing them to one another, or to cold, objective facts, like forensic evidence. I've done it myself, for a short time towards the end of my training. In cases of homicide, the tips are prioritised but it is still very time-consuming. The aim is to get through the witness reports within the critical first seventy-two hours.

It is only now, a little more than sixty hours since the crime, that they've finished doing it on the Rebecca Salomonsson case, and a few have proved to be of some interest.

'More specific witness testimonies described a man who was like … well, like you.'

Birck clears his throat.

'Someone is trying to stitch me up,' I say. 'I think I'm starting to grasp who it —'

'Calm down.'

'What?'

'We got lucky this time. It turned out that one of the witnesses recognised him. She's a former whizz-whore who now earns a living as a bartender, and by coincidence she often works at the bar where a certain Peter Koll likes to drink expensive Spanish liqueur.'

'Koll? Spelt like Koll as in —'

'As in Kollberg, yes. The similarities end there.' Birck clears his throat, again. 'We're pretty sure that it is him. There's just one problem.'

'Which is?'

'He doesn't want to talk to us.'

'Well, I never.'

'You don't understand what I mean. I ... shit, hold on.' I hear Birck struggling with something and clicking on his computer. 'Right. Should work now. Listen.'

First a rasping noise, then the background noise caught by a microphone. I push the phone harder to my ear.

A voice with a slight and hard-to-place foreign accent:

'I don't want to talk to you.'

Then Birck's voice:

'Who do you want to speak to then?'

'...'

'Who do you want to speak to then?'

'I have been instructed to only speak to one person.'

'And that is?'

'...'

'Must I ask every question twice?'

'Junker.'

'Leo Junker?'

'Yes.'

201

'And who gave you these instructions?'

'...'

'Who gave you these instructions?'

'...'

Birck clicks the mouse button again, and the sound stops.

'We've got a lot to talk about, you and I,' he says.

IT'S ONLY A SHORT WALK to police HQ, but as I step out into the street a taxi stops at the junction and drops off a passenger. I raise my hand, climb into the car, and try to collect my thoughts during the two-minute journey.

I'm now more used to answering questions than asking them, but there is a subtle elegance to a well-executed interrogation. It is pretty much always about providing the officer in charge with a bureaucratically correct piece of the puzzle ahead of the trial. The protocol must be followed; everything needs to be recorded, transcribed, and approved by the interviewee. It then needs to be labelled, added to the documents, and archived. In the digital archive, there are years and years' worth of sound recordings, of people just talking. To listen to all of them would take lifetimes.

'PETER ZORAN KOLL,' Birck says, as he moves through HQ half a step ahead of me. 'Thirty-six years old, born in what was then Yugoslavia, but raised in Germany. His parents fled the war. He came to Sweden in 2003; his first conviction was in May 2004, for illegally possessing a firearm. Since then, suspected of more than twenty crimes, basically everything apart from rape and treason, but never convicted of anything other than petty offences that carry suspended sentences or a tag. He ...'

Birck stops, and looks me up and down. His face is close to mine, and I can smell his breath, a sour mixture of mint and coffee.

'Are you high, Leo?'

'Me? Er, not anymore.' I blink. 'I think. No.'

Birck breathes out, his cheeks clenched.

'I can't have someone high in an interview.'

'I'm not high, I told you.'

Birck looks at me, sceptical.

'You can't have a suspended officer in the interview either,' I remind him. 'Strictly speaking, I mean.'

'You're coming in,' he says frostily. 'You're coming in, but you keep your mouth shut.'

I shrug. He keeps walking and I follow him. 'Do you know anything about this guy?', he asks.

'Not exactly, no.'

'Koll is the type of criminal who does as he's told. Provided you can afford to pay his prices.'

'So he's a consultant?'

'Something like that.'

Birck calls the lift and waits. He looks worn out; his clear eyes are bloodshot, and his skin is paler than yesterday.

'So,' he says, 'if you don't know who he is, how come he wants to talk to you?'

'He's been instructed to.'

'Yes,' Birck says impatiently, 'but by whom?'

The lift arrives. One of the chief constable's secretaries steps out, professionally uninterested and with a serious demeanour.

'I think I know why she died,' I say.

Birck looks at me as the lift doors close and the metallic-grey cube starts moving upwards.

'I'm listening. Why?'

'Because of me.'

Birck keeps staring. I think he's trying to work out if I'm joking or not.

'A further analysis of the prints on the necklace,' Birck says slowly, 'revealed that your print was very old.'

I REMEMBER a forensic-science teacher we had during police training. He started his lecture with a story about Babylon and China several hundred years BC, where fingerprints were used as signatures. The use of fingerprints is ancient and widespread, but their use by the police is much more recent. A Scottish teacher — I think his name was Faulds, or something like that — published an article about them at the end of the nineteenth century, and he turned to the police in London since he felt that they could use his method. The London police thought it was stupid, and dismissed him. I think that little detail is what makes me remember all this, because even then the forces of law and order were extremely conservative and sceptical players.

In any case, this caused Faulds to contact Charles Darwin, who was too old and famous to start working on Faulds' observations himself. But he must have guessed that Faulds was on to something, because he gave the information to his cousin, Galton. He was an anthropologist, and he probably wasn't terribly busy, considering that he went on to study fingerprints for ten years before publishing his masterpiece. Fingerprints stick on almost any surface, and Galton had shown that they were statistically unique. No two people had the same prints, so the whole world of forensic science was turned on its head. I remember we were still reading short extracts from Galton's *Finger Prints* when I did my training.

I remember that, and this: fingerprints are deceptive things. How long a print stays on a surface depends on a host of factors: what kind of surface it is; how much exposure to the elements it gets; how salty, oily, or fatty the print is; and so on. But there is no set point at which a fingerprint will be destroyed. A fingerprint can, in unusual circumstances, outlive us.

I look at Birck.

'So?' he says.

The print must be fifteen years old. If that's right, if it's still there, the necklace must have been stored very carefully. I don't know what to say.

'I don't know if I'm right,' I say. 'Maybe Koll can help ...'

The lift door opens. I get out before Birck. He sighs.

PETER ZORAN KOLL is sitting in Interview Room 3 — the same room, the same chair as I was sitting in about twenty-four hours earlier. He's shorter than I expected, has a square face and the sort of haircut you only see in American war films. His shoulders and his chest are broad. He's wearing light jeans, a T-shirt, and an unbuttoned short-sleeved shirt. A constable in a light-blue shirt and tie is standing watching him just inside the door. Koll has a smug glint in his eye. His hands are cuffed, and the cuffs scratch against the tabletop when he moves.

Birck has collected a folder and a dictaphone from his office, and nods silently to the constable, who leaves the room without looking at me. Koll's eyes follow her.

'Something interest you, Koll?' Birck asks, pulls out a chair, and sits down.

'I'm used to keeping an eye on people.' He looks at me. 'Leo Junker.'

'That's right,' Birck says, and opens the folder, while I hesitantly pull out the chair next to him. 'Leo is here now. Let's talk.'

Koll laughs — a short, mocking laugh.

'You have misunderstood.'

'What have I misunderstood?'

'I'm not talking to you. Only to him.'

'You're not the one who gets to decide around here,' Birck says calmly.

'Oh yes I am.'

'And what makes you think that?'

'I know something you don't know.'

'And what might that be?'

Koll smiles. He has clean, white teeth.

'I have strict instructions to only speak to him. Alone.' He attempts to fold his arms, but doesn't manage it. The handcuffs stop him. He looks surprised, as though he'd forgotten they were there. 'No sound recording.'

'Who has given you these instructions?' attempts Birck.

'I only talk to him.'

Birck stares at him for a long time before looking at me.

'One moment, Peter. We'll be back soon.'

We come out, and the police constable sweeps past us as she goes back into the room to keep him under supervision. Birck leans against the wall, pinches the bridge of his nose between his thumb and forefinger, and closes his eyes tightly. He opens his eyes, blinks a few times, and runs his hand through his hair.

'Right,' he says. 'Do it. In exchange, we demand that he does the interview again later, with just me.'

'But I'm not up to speed on the investigation.'

'That's why this is strictly between us. You don't say a word to anyone about this. Got it?'

'Yes.'

He looks very focused.

'Well, then.'

'RIGHT,' I SAY to Koll. 'Tell me.'

'What do you want me to tell you?'

'You've been instructed to only talk to me. Who instructed you?'

'You're stressing,' Koll says, irritated. 'Calm down.'

'Okay,' I say. 'We'll start somewhere else. I'm not really sure what you do. How do you make a living.'

'I do what people ask, you know.'

'Which is what?'

'You name it.'

'Like killing people for money?'

'Not really,' Koll says. 'I don't like that.'

206

'But you did it this time?'

'Yes.'

'Why?'

'My family's in Turkey. I'm in touch with a police chief there. He can get them to Sweden, for a price.'

'You've bribed a Turkish police chief? Is that what you're saying? Have I understood correctly?'

The look in Koll's eyes darkens.

'Not exactly. I contacted him a few years ago and asked him what it would take to get them to Sweden.' He clears his throat. 'Four million. Per person.'

'Aren't you from Yugoslavia?'

'What's that got to do with it?'

'I just wonder why your family is in Turkey.'

'That's where they went. They've got friends there. But my brother committed a crime and ended up in prison.'

'And the others? Are they inside, too?'

'No.'

'Can't they help your brother?'

'They can't do what's required, you know. They don't have, what do you call it, resources.'

'So you're saving up.'

'Yes.'

'Through crime.'

'Yes.'

'In Sweden, there are easier ways to get hold of money than going round committing crimes.'

'Are there?' Koll asks, with raised eyebrows. 'Like what?'

I realise that I don't have a good answer for that one.

'How much have you got?' I ask instead.

'I've got enough now. That's why I said yes.'

'So, did your employer know about your situation?'

'I think so, can't be sure.'

'What makes you think so?' I ask.

'Seems weird that someone comes and offers me exactly what I need. Don't you think?'

It does, undeniably.

'So,' I say. 'Let's go through this one more time. You take a job from someone, who gives you exactly the sum of money you need to get your family to Sweden. Is that correct?'

'That's correct.'

'And you've been instructed to only speak to me.'

'Correct.'

'Have you been instructed to get caught, too?'

Koll laughs — a mocking laugh, again.

'No. But if it was to happen, I was going to get more money, and I should demand that I only speak to you.'

'That was part of the deal?'

'Yes.'

'You don't seem too upset about having been arrested.'

'I am, but I know that I'm going to be, what's it called, compensated.' He hesitates, before he lifts his head, with an honest expression on his square face. 'I don't actually like killing people.'

He is more malleable now, I can tell, but it's still too early to ask about his paymaster. That hasn't been said, but it rests between us, like a silent understanding.

'The one you were given the task of killing was Rebecca Salomonsson at Chapmansgården.'

Koll stares blankly at me.

'I didn't hear a question.'

'Is that correct?' I say.

'Did anyone else die there that night?' he asks.

'No one else died at Chapmansgården that night.'

'Well, then, it was her.'

There it is: the confession. It's been a long time since I sat in an interview with a suspect — too long — but the feeling of getting that out of him is surprisingly familiar, satisfying.

'Tell me about it,' I say.

'What do you want to know?'

'Rebecca Salomonsson died shortly after midnight, didn't she?'

'I didn't check if she was dead, if that's what you're wondering. I don't like killing people, but I know how to.'

He smiles. I want to punch him in the face.

'Tell me what you did that night,' I say.

'I went to a place on the other side of the road, a flat, from about eleven at night. I knew that she was usually among the first, so I made sure I was there in time. The flat was on the second floor, two windows facing the street, no curtains. I sat there and waited, looked through the windows at Chapmansgården. I could see the dorm, and bits of the other rooms. I waited for her to arrive and lie down in one of the beds.'

'Whose was the flat?'

'I don't know. No furniture, so I suppose someone had just moved out. But there was still a name on the door.'

'What name?'

Koll squints, studying the tabletop that separates us.

'Wigren. C. Wigren.'

'With a V or a W?'

'W.'

'How did you get hold of the flat?'

'It came with the job. I got the keys, and the money.'

'How did you get them?'

'A P.O. box. I always use P.O. boxes.'

'How long did you sit there?'

'Till I saw her arrive, till she went in and lay down.'

'Did she have anything with her? A bag or anything?'

He shakes his head.

'I checked the people coming and going through the doorway. It wasn't hard to work out when someone who was on their way

there turned up. You can tell who belongs there, they often have
… they're junkies and whores. I'd done some reconnaissance in the
days leading up to it, so I knew she usually slept there and that
the door was unlocked, that you could open the windows from the
inside — just open that little catch. And that the woman who runs it
always starts with the washing up. That was good, because it would
mask the sound. She walked down the road much earlier than I
was expecting, you know; it can't have been later than midnight.
She was high as a kite, could hardly stand up. I think she felt sick,
because she kept, what do you call it … heaving, and had her hand
in front of her mouth. She went in and lay down on one of the beds.
I waited a while, but I didn't want to wait too long; I was worried
that others might turn up, you know?'

'I understand.'

'I just had to go out, cross the road, and go inside. That woman
was there in the kitchen, doing the washing up. I snuck past, into
the bedroom, put a bullet in her temple and put the jewellery in her
hand, then left via the window, back down onto the street again.'

'The jewellery,' I say. 'Tell me about it.'

'It annoyed me. I wasn't told about it beforehand. It was in my
P.O. box that same day, in an envelope with one of those yellow
sticky notes on it. It said I should put it in the girl's hand.'

'Have you still got the envelope?'

'Of course I haven't.'

'What kind of jewellery was it?'

'Like a necklace. I didn't pay much attention.'

'When you left Chapmansgården,' I say, 'did you see anyone on
the way?'

'This is Stockholm. Of course I did.'

'Who?'

'No idea. I didn't exactly inspect them.'

'What were you wearing?'

'Eh?'

'What clothes did you have on?'

'Why do you ask?'

'Answer the question.'

'Black jeans. A black jacket. A dark-grey shirt.'

That matches the witness statements. I realise that I'm nodding, and that Koll notices. I stop nodding.

'What did you do after that, once you'd left Chapmansgatan?'

'Went home.'

'And where is that?'

'I've got a studio in Västra Skogen.'

'So you were on Kungsholmen, and you live in Västra Skogen. You took public transport home? The underground?'

'Yes.'

'And which route did you take from Chapmansgatan?'

'Does it matter?'

'Yes.'

'I went down to Norr Mälarstrand, took the first left. I think it's Polhemsgatan?'.

'That's right.'

'Then down a street that I don't know the name of, and up another road, Pilgatan, which I followed up to Bergsgatan. Then I took a right, down to Rådhuset underground station.'

According to Birck, the crucial witness had seen Koll at the junction of Pilgatan and Bergsgatan. It fitted.

'Bar Marcus on Pilgatan. Is that a place you visit often?'

'They have good Spanish liqueurs. My dad and I always drank Spanish liqueurs. There was a bar in my home town, and they had loads; Dad used to bring some home. I still like it.'

'Is that a yes?'

'That's a yes.'

'And the barmaid, do you know her?'

'No.'

'She recognised you anyway. Why might that be?'

211

'What do you think? Probably because I go there.'

'She knew your name.'

He shrugs.

'I always pay cash. But I must have told her once.'

This is what Birck needs. Strictly speaking, the question of who killed Rebecca Salomonsson has been answered. But the question of the conspiracy to murder her remains. I usually feel a rush of adrenalin and relief at times like this. This time, I just feel confused.

'The person who gave you the instructions concerning the necklace was the same person that asked you to kill Rebecca Salomonsson?'

'That's right.'

'Why?'

'What do you mean?'

'Why were you asked to do it?'

Koll furrows his brow, and his eyes dart around, as though he's hesitating.

'I don't usually ask questions like that, you know, that's why people come to me. But this time ... there was something weird about the whole business. I think she'd seen something she wasn't supposed to see, or heard something she wasn't supposed to hear.'

'What makes you think that?'

'I asked around a bit. This thing seemed extremely low-key, if you get my meaning. Lots of people had no idea.'

'Your impression was that she knew something. About what?'

'I don't know.'

'I don't believe you. I think you know. Why are you keeping it to yourself?'

'It's not something you talk about, okay? Do you know what I mean?'

'No.'

Koll sighs and shakes his head.

'I think that somehow she found out about his true ... who he is.'

'Your employer?'

'Yes. The rumour, and I'm pretty sure it was true, was that someone she knew went to him for help, not long ago. And that she found out then, don't ask me how. And you know what the whores at Chapmansgården are like — they've got nothing. So I think she was trying to blackmail him, threatening to reveal his identity.'

'She threatened to go to the police?'

'Where else would you go?' Koll waves his hand dismissively. 'I'm talking too much, man, I'm talking too much; I don't want to say any more now.'

'Just one more thing,' I say. 'Before we finish. Why were you instructed to only talk to me?'

'He said you'd understand why,' Koll says.

'I don't,' I say, but at the same time I'm aware of a slight sense of relief: if Koll's right, she didn't die because of me.

'Well, then, that's your problem.'

'What did he say his name was?'

'Daniel Berggren.'

'And that was what Salomonsson found out?'

'No, no. Berggren was just a ... you know ... an alias. If I got it right, she found out his real identity.'

Daniel Berggren. Just ordinary enough — there will be too many out there to find the right one — but not so common that it looks like a made-up name to hide behind. It's well thought out, elegant almost. It's got Grim written all over it.

'His real identity?' I say.

'Yes.'

'And you don't know what that is?'

'No idea.'

It can't be John Grimberg. That's been untouched for ages. He must be using a third, one that I haven't come across yet.

'What do you know about him?'

'Not much. He stays under the radar. Does jobs for people, gives them new identities.'

'Was he going to do one for you?'

'No. He offered me one, but I wanted the money, that's why I did it.' Koll leans forward. 'I mean, I didn't like him. And now there's something in your eyes — fear. I'm good at spotting stuff like that, you know. I don't like it when things don't go according to plan, when things aren't prepared in advance. It's unprofessional. I'd worked it out to the minute, and then all of a sudden that fucking necklace is in the picture … it slowed me down. If it hadn't been for that, I probably wouldn't have got nicked. So I'll give you a tip.'

Koll pauses for effect.

'Yes?' I say.

'You're never going to find him. There are too many Daniel Berggrens. So,' he says, lowering his voice to a whisper, 'you need to find Josef Abel. An old man. He can help you.' Koll scans the closed door behind me. 'But don't say this to your colleague. It mustn't be recorded.'

'Josef Abel,' I say. 'How do I find him?'

'Go to Åby. Ask around. There's only one Josef Abel. The Man With No Voice.' Koll hesitates. 'I'm only saying this because I don't like him. You understand?'

I study him carefully.

'So you haven't been instructed by him, by Berggren, to tell me exactly this?' I ask. 'It's not the case that this is all part of it?'

Koll smiles weakly.

'You're not stupid, are you?'

'So I'm right?'

'You can be clever and still be wrong, you know.'

'Am I wrong about this?'

'Does it matter?'

Yes, I think to myself. There's something about this contrived situation, a suggestion that he's watching me the whole time, shadowing me. As though I'm following an invisible, predetermined path right into a trap. Koll's right. I am scared.

'Am I wrong?' I attempt, again, and strain to hide the fact that my hands have started shaking again. 'Are you dropping him in it, or is this part of the job?'

'Who knows?' is the only answer I get out of him, and he refuses to say any more, even though I'm putting the pressure on. I end up grabbing Koll's shirt and raising my clenched fist towards his face to get him to talk, but that's as far as I get. The door opens behind me, and Birck comes rushing in and grabs me, and he's much stronger than me.

XXI

I stood outside the gates of Rönninge High School that Monday at the end of August. It was a beautiful day, I remember. I was waiting for Grim, who'd said that he would come to the early lesson.

'Leo,' said a voice behind me, and as I turned my head I saw Julia walking towards me.

'Hi,' I said.

'I tried to call you yesterday.'

'Did you?' I said, surprised.

'There was no answer.'

I couldn't remember the phone ringing, but then again the whole weekend was like a thick white fog.

'Weird,' was all I said.

We started walking in silence. As long as we did that, it felt like we had everything under control, as though everything was okay.

'Do you remember Tim?' she said. 'I've mentioned him before. I thought I saw him on Friday.'

'Where?'

'In Salem, on our way home. But it was from a distance, and I was quite pissed.'

'I ... how was that? Seeing him? After all this time, I mean.'

'Good,' she said. 'I think. I'm glad he's back, even if we didn't know each other that well at the end. It still feels good having him here, somehow.'

'Well, that's good then,' I forced out.

'We need to talk,' she said, stopped, took a step towards me. 'I ...

first of all, I think John already knows about us. Not suspects, knows. And then, I ...' She looked at her watch. 'I've got English now.'

'I've got R.E.' I hesitated. 'We can walk in together anyway?'

We carried on, and from the corner of my eye I saw Tim walking ahead of us and through the entrance. It must have been his first day at school, his first day back here. He seemed nervous or stressed, but he was probably just late. Seeing him gave me this stabbing sensation. I could just about see a black eye, like a print. But I knew there was more: aches in his stomach from those blows; the spinning, streaking pains in his ribs; and the dull ache between his legs. And the other pain, the pain that doesn't show. The one in his heart.

Julia didn't see him. Halfway across the schoolyard, she put her hand in mine and held it there until we went separate ways down the corridors. We'd been seen by many; Grim wasn't one of them, but by that point I'm not sure I would've cared if he had been.

THE LUNCH BREAK. Sometimes it was only forty-five minutes, but it was usually ninety. One-and-a-half hours. We used to spend that time eating, not in the school but at the burger stand round the corner, and smoking cigarettes or listening to music.

That lunchtime, Julia and I ate at the burger stand. We talked about the party on the rec, and she told me how she'd started feeling ill while I was away. She had wanted to stay and wait for me, but Grim had taken her home to the Triad. She'd thrown up pretty much all the way home.

'You were drinking fast,' I say.

'I was nervous,' she muttered. 'What happened later, after we'd left?'

'Nothing,' I said, and drank some pop. 'I went home, too.'

Our lockers were at opposite ends of the school, and Julia didn't know which one was mine. I didn't know which was hers. We went to mine first.

I remember this: there weren't many people in the corridor. Outside, the sun was shining brightly, and there were twenty minutes left of the lunch break. Some people were standing by their lockers; others were sitting on the worn-out benches. The common-room telly was broken. The screen had been smashed in a fight late that spring. I showed Julia my locker, and she noted the number, asked me to open it.

'Why?' I said.

'I want to see what you've got in there.'

'It's not tidied.'

'Surely that doesn't matter.'

I started opening the locker, took the padlock off. Just as I opened it and peered in to see just how bad it was, someone screamed, and in that same instant I heard Julia's voice.

'Leo, watch out.'

She grabbed my shoulder so hard that it turned me around. Julia was standing in front of me and my eyes met hers, clear and warm, and then, bang, her grip tightened on my shoulder, before her hand went limp and fell away.

'Ow,' she whispered.

More screams. Something metallic fell to the floor; I looked up. Tim Nordin was standing five or six lockers away with his arms hanging by his sides, and a toy gun on the floor in front of him. He stared at me, his black eye almost shining. Then he turned around and ran, through the corridor and down the steps. I looked around, trying to work out what had happened, where the bang had come from. I couldn't make the connection between the toy gun and the scene playing before my eyes: Julia collapsing; more screams. Everything stopped. I could smell burning.

I couldn't say anything. I didn't even know what to do. I picked her up and put my arms around her, pressing as hard as I could on her back. I tried to stop the flow of blood, but I could feel it running between my fingers, forcing its way out in waves. I could feel her heart against my chest, at first very, very hard and fast, but soon slower and slower, weaker and weaker. I don't think I cried.

I DON'T REMEMBER what happened after that. I can't even remember how I got to the hospital in Södertälje. I didn't go in the ambulance. Julia had been hit in the back, on the left side, somewhere around the heart. That's how it looked, anyway, but all the blood made it hard to say where the wound was. The ambulance was there, I've since found out, after just a few minutes. That's what gave me hope — that it came so quickly. At least school nurse Ulrika said it should. She got to us before the ambulance arrived.

When Ulrika came, she took Julia from me, and shortly afterwards we heard the ambulance sirens. Julia's forehead was shiny and her skin was pale, but she was breathing. It was strained, as though an invisible weight were lying on her chest. My jeans were flecked with red.

I BLINKED, and found myself at the hospital. Grim was there, somewhere. Klas and Diana, too. Julia was in theatre. The bullet had missed her heart, but had ripped apart several major arteries. They struggled to repair them, but she had lost so much blood that they couldn't say whether she would survive the strain of the operation.

A police officer, a woman who said her name was Jennifer Davidsson and that she was a detective inspector, wanted to talk to me. She wondered if it would be okay to ask a few questions. I only remember small details from that conversation, me saying that the police had arrived quickly. The inspector told me that Tim Nordin had made his way from the school to the police station in Rönninge and handed himself in. He admitted that he'd shot someone. But he had hit the wrong person.

'He said that he was aiming for …' she began and then hesitated. 'Well, you. Do you know why that might be?'

'I used to … He was … I bullied him.'

I knew deep down that I had done something much worse, but at that moment I wasn't capable of explaining it.

'That doesn't make what he's done okay.' She put her hand on my shoulder, where Julia had grabbed me, and I pushed it away. 'I'm going to see if I can find you some new clothes,' she said quietly.

I was still wearing my flecked jeans, my red-splattered top. I nodded. The inspector looked at me for a long time.

'She might have saved your life. And maybe you have saved hers.'

After that, she didn't say any more.

I'VE NEVER BEEN ABLE to get used to the noise, the lights, the commotion that is a hospital, since that day. Sitting there in one of the many waiting rooms, waiting for my parents, it seemed bizarre that this was just another workplace. People came, got changed, did their jobs, got changed again and went home, cooked meals for their kids, and watched telly with their families. Like factory work. Absurd, that they had people's lives in their hands.

I'd got some new clothes — Adidas tracksuit bottoms and a too-big T-shirt that the inspector had gotten hold of. The school had been closed. People were worried that Tim Nordin might not have acted alone, that maybe he'd made a pact with someone else, that others might be at risk. The police assured everyone that nothing pointed to that, but the school was closed anyway.

A nurse took me into a treatment room, measured my blood pressure and took my pulse, and checked that I was okay physically. Then she said that someone would soon be along to talk to me.

'About what?'

'He'll give you information about things that can make it easier after this kind of … after what you've been through.'

'Oh, right. Okay.'

I sat there on the trolley. She left me alone. Julia had been in theatre for over two hours. The door opened after a while, and my parents and my brother rushed in. I didn't say very much. They asked what had happened, but at that moment the door opened again and a white-haired man came in. He asked them to go and talk to the police for a little while. Once they were satisfied that I wasn't hurt, they nodded and left.

The man was a psychologist, and he asked matter-of-fact questions. I answered as best I could, because I liked him. He gave me a load of leaflets and brochures, and said he'd be back.

'Do you know how she is?' I asked.

'No.'

I wondered if I'd already asked him that. I asked everyone I saw.

BACK IN THE WAITING ROOM. Three hours since the operation started, and still nothing from anyone. The scene in the corridor was playing on repeat in my head. The shot that echoed between my temples. The warmth of her blood on my hands.

Someone sank, silently, into the chair next to mine. I turned my head.

'Hi,' Grim said.

His voice sounded absent, had an almost mechanical ring.

'Have you heard anything?' I asked.

'Not about Julia.' He looked up at the clock. 'She's having an operation. But I've heard something else.' He avoided looking at me. 'Like it was you he was after.'

I glanced over at his fingers, which were solidly knotted together, as though he was bracing himself.

'Tim. Is that right?'

'I think so.'

'Why was he after you?'

I didn't answer.

'If it turns out that he did it because of you, and if she dies … I will never forgive you.'

'I understand that,' I said, looking at my hands.

'You had a ... you were together, weren't you?'

'Yes.'

He nodded slowly.

An hour-and-a-half later, Julia Grimberg was pronounced dead on the operating table. The time of death was 5.27 p.m.

XXII

Because Tim Nordin had intended to shoot me, and had missed, he was convicted of attempted murder, aggravated manslaughter, and weapons offences. The prosecutor had wanted a custodial sentence because of the premeditated nature of the crime, but the court sentenced him to secure care under the supervision of Social Services.

I remember the trial like a sort of grey mist. As the intended victim, I was in the defence team's line of fire, and in the end I was sure I was going to faint. Since we were both minors and the crime was so serious, it was all conducted in closed sessions. Behind those doors, the past was unravelled.

It came out that I had tormented Tim Nordin for two years.

It came out in front of everyone, except Julia Grimberg. She was dead.

And I had lost my best friend.

He banned me from going to the funeral. There were no photographs, so I couldn't even see what it had been like. It was only then — several weeks later — that the shock started to recede and I realised I would never see her again.

I couldn't stay in school. It was impossible. I switched to a school in Huddinge. Grim changed schools, too, but he went to Fittja. Shortly after that, the Grimbergs left the Triad and Salem. I don't know where they went — possibly Hagsätra. Just before they moved, I'd tried to get back in touch with Grim, without success. The only one who would talk to me when I called was Diana.

'You know,' she said. 'His hatred towards you is ... so strong right now.'

She sounded surprisingly composed and normal, I remember thinking. Perhaps this was just what was needed to shake Diana out of her depression, to let her move on. That was a horrible thought.

And wrong. I later heard from someone in the triad that Diana Grimberg was being cared for at a psychiatric unit in Södertälje after a failed suicide attempt. She was probably going to be staying there for a long time. Grim's dad drank more than ever, got sacked, and ended up unemployed.

NOT LONG AFTER THAT came the anger. I wanted to hurt Tim Nordin. I wanted to hurt Vlad and Fred, who'd hit me, left me wanting to do the same — and then I found Tim. I wanted to hurt whoever had hurt them. After a while I could see that there was no point; the chain was infinite. I would never be able to find where it all started, never find the source. The original force that had set everything off might never have existed. I didn't want to hurt someone, I realised; I wanted to hurt everyone.

I tried to find out where Vlad and Fred lived. I spent several nights wandering around with a knife inside my coat, looking for them. I went from one estate to another without finding them. I alternated between a feeling of unbearable shame and guilt, and a feeling of being the victim of injustice. Was it my fault? Was it my responsibility? Tim was the one who'd held the gun. Julia had stepped in between us. I hadn't done anything, but was I innocent? I was the one who'd started on Tim; if I hadn't done that, he would never have gone so far. And I was the one who Julia was in love with, the one she wanted to protect. I was the common denominator. But if it hadn't been for Vlad and Fred ... I was tying myself in knots, confusing myself. There was no end to it.

That's when I realised I needed help. I looked up the white-haired man who'd talked to me at the Södertälje Hospital. His name was

Mark Levin — apparently, he'd said so the first time we met — and he could see that I needed to start treatment and therapy straight away. He took it upon himself. I only started feeling better when Julia had been dead for six months, but I hadn't been to her grave yet. Mark Levin reckoned I wouldn't be able to move on until I'd done that.

I DREAMT ABOUT HER, almost every night. It went on for years. It surprised me, just how much I could bear and yet still be able to stand on my own two feet. The thought of what we are actually capable of living with scared me, but maybe when it gets unbearable the brain switches off, and the grief comes up in your sleep. When your defences are down. Losing Julia felt like losing something fundamental, one of the elements. As though the air had disappeared, and all that was left was a gasping for something that wasn't there.

When I set out to visit Julia's grave for the first time, it was the end of February and it was cold — so cold that new record lows were being reported every day. All over Stockholm, homeless people and animals died because they couldn't cope with the strain and they couldn't make it inside in time. Despite that, there was only a dusting of snow on the ground as I passed through the gates and made my way over to the new part of the cemetery where Julia lay. I saw fresh footprints in the snow, and I felt strangely reassured by the knowledge that I wasn't alone there. It was the middle of the day, and the sky above me was white and matte like paper. From a distance, I noticed a shadow standing by one of the graves. It was a woman wearing a long brown coat, whose hair was the colour of wire wool. I walked past, and further along there was another person. As I looked down at the ground, I saw that the footprints in the snow led to him — another shadow, with a shaved head and a thick black jacket with a fur-trimmed hood.

He was standing with his hands in his pockets, staring at the grave. I heard him sniffing. That was the first and only time I saw Grim cry.

I moved off the gravel path, in behind a tree, while I tried to decide what to do. My back was warm and I undid my coat, and felt the cold rush in. My hands were shaking. I never thought I'd react like this. While I stood there I saw him walk past, on his way out. His eyes were swollen, but he seemed composed.

I took a deep breath, waited until he was out of sight, and stepped back out onto the path, following Grim's tracks in the snow.

It was smaller than I had expected. But until I got there, I hadn't realised I was expecting anything at all.

JULIA MARIKA GRIMBERG
1981–1997

The grave was framed by frost-ravaged flowers and a burnt-out candle. A thin layer of snow had settled on the rounded headstone, and I carefully leant down, struggling against the resistance that seemed to exist between my hand and the stone, before brushing away the snow with my palm.

I think I whispered something. I felt my lips moving, but I couldn't tell what I'd said. That she was gone, that she no longer existed, was incomprehensible. It was a hoax, a bad joke; someone had tricked us all. She must still be there somewhere, just out of reach. That's how it felt.

I stood there for a while. I think I said sorry. That it was my fault. After that, I turned around, did up my coat, and started walking away. Beyond the trees loomed the water tower — dark grey, mute.

HE WAS STANDING THERE with his hands in his pockets, and his stare was fixed on the tower, perhaps on the ledge where we'd met less than a year earlier.

'Are you spying on people now?' he said, without looking at me.

'What do you mean?'

'In the cemetery.'

'Right. Sorry.'

'It's okay.'

His voice was calm and quiet.

'Do you visit it often?' I asked.

'The grave?'

'Yes.'

'As often as I can. It's a bit of a way from Hagsätra. You?'

'That was the first time.'

'It'll be my last visit for a while.'

'How come?'

'I've been done for assault. And possession. My sentence starts tomorrow, in Hammargården on Ekerö.'

Hammargården was, like Jumkil, one of the young offenders' institutions that closely resembled prisons. Hammargården wasn't quite as infamous as Jumkil, but not far off. According to the rumours, active criminals worked as guards there, and were therefore able to get drugs and weapons to the residents in exchange for cash.

Assault and possession. That wasn't like Grim.

'What did you have on you?'

'Acid tabs. I needed to shift them to pay for more tools.'

'What sort of tools?'

'For making ID cards and stuff.'

'But they don't know about that.'

'No.' He looked down. 'They've got no idea about that.'

'How's Hagsätra?'

'I'm moving after the stint in Hammargården.'

'Where to?'

'Alby. I've got a mate there; he lets me stay over sometimes. I might as well move in. I can't stand living at home any longer. Dad drinks most of the day and night. I try and keep on top of the bills, but the money's not there anymore. And Mum … doesn't live at home.' His eyes moved up to look at the tower again. 'You have ruined everything. Not Tim. It wasn't him; you were the one who drove him to it. You're a fucking bully. After everything we talked about, just that kind of shit, it turns out you're just like them. And you were the one who got Julia to … she was clever, Leo, she would never have gone that far.'

'Got her to do what? Get together with me?'

'And you never said a word,' Grim went on, as though he hadn't listened to me. 'Not about Tim, nor Julia. You said nothing at all.' He laughed. 'Jesus, you must have told so many lies. I can't even remember all the times you must have lied, there's that many.'

'She didn't say anything either.'

I felt a blow to my chest; he grabbed my jacket, and my legs disappeared from underneath me. My neck cracked onto the frozen soil, and the pain streaked through my head. Grim pushed his forearm hard against my throat, his face a hair's breadth from mine and his eyes black. I couldn't move.

'You don't blame this on her,' he said. 'You got that?' A second time, screaming: 'You got that?'

'Sorry,' I managed, my voice cracked.

Grim's arm made it hard to breathe. He stared at me. Then he blinked once, let go of me, and stood up. I struggled to my feet. My neck was aching. Grim already had his back to me and was on his way. He stopped and turned around, opened his mouth to say something, but nothing came out; he let the air go. I stood there, breathless, looking at him.

'Might see you round, Leo,' he eventually said.

THAT WAS THE LAST TIME I met Grim. I didn't hear from him again, and I didn't see him either. The summer arrived, and this time I managed to get a job as a cleaner at a local company in Salem. My parents were pleased, but said nothing. I carried on with my therapy,

228

carried on my treatment with Mark Levin. I let people get close to me again. It took time but it worked, and when I realised that it was actually possible to move on, I was astounded. I still dreamt about Julia, and visited her grave. Every time I walked into the graveyard I expected Grim to be there, but he never was. I heard on the grapevine that he'd been kicked out of Hammargården and sent to Jumkil — not the summer camp this time, but the institution itself. It was apparently down to him having stabbed someone, which in turn was the result of an argument that had ended with the other guy telling Grim to fuck his sister.

WHEN I WAS TWENTY, I left Salem. The next winter, Daniel Wretström, a young skinhead visiting the capital, had his throat slit. I remember wondering whether it was just chance that it had happened in Salem. It didn't feel like it. I recognised several names among the accused. They were my old friends' younger brothers.

I never met Tim again, although I planned to visit him several times. I heard that he was trying to kill himself. The first attempt was the night after the verdict. He'd tried to take an overdose. The second was a few weeks later, this time with a razor blade he'd managed to smuggle in. The third attempt was a month or so later, but again he didn't succeed. He died about a year later, I think, from an overdose.

I think about everyone that's disappeared, like Vlad and Fred. I don't know where they are now, or even whether they're still alive. The same goes for several of the others, the people I knew in Salem: they seem to keep disappearing, as though the ground has opened up and swallowed them.

Sometimes I see people, couples, walking hand in hand. They look happy, laughing as though there are no troubles in their lives, as though they've never lost anything and they're not going to lose each other. If they only knew how fast it can happen. I know. And you know, don't you? You remember. But it wasn't about you that time, not really.

When I see them I sometimes want to do something drastic, pull them away from each other. Maybe because it fills me with envy, but maybe also because I want them to understand that nothing lasts forever. Am I entitled to do that? When I know that sooner or later something's going to happen to people, have I got the right to tell them?

I loved somebody, once. Anja. We got to know each other at a friend's place. It started with an argument: we both wanted our mutual friend's last gram of horse. She ended up hitting me in the face and taking the bag, but she felt so bad about it that she wanted us to share the last bit together. That was nice, I thought, and I could soon see that there was something about Anja that I'd never experienced before, something about the way she seemed to see inside me. I fell violently in love, so much so that we kept it a secret so that others wouldn't come between us and ruin it. Does that sound familiar? I think it does.

One day I went to her place and she wasn't there. All that was left was furniture and the aftermath of a house raid. She was on remand in Kronoberg and was sentenced to two years in Hinseberg for serious drug offences. I didn't dare visit her. I was scared they might pick up my trail. We tried to talk on the phone, but it was hard, partly because I needed to be so careful, but above all because Anja got more and more out of reach. I don't know why, she'd always been a bit unstable, even on the outside, but nothing like this. Losing her freedom was eating away at her.

I heard that she'd hung herself in her cell. She'd tried to send me a letter, but it had been stopped by Hinseberg, for some reason. It had been intercepted and incinerated. That was 2002 and I never found out what it was she wanted to say to me. That's what made me finally do it, got me to take the risk that disappearing entails.

The happy ones walking hand in hand, sometimes I want to hurt them because they have each other, because the world isn't fair. I wonder how far I might go. Do you wonder that too?

XXIII

Above the towering hulks of Alby's high-rise blocks, the sky hangs low, as though straining not to lose its grip and fall to the ground. It's late in the evening, and the small rectangular windows are illuminated here and there. I pass the underground's turnstiles and look around as though Josef Abel might appear on my command.

AFTER BIRCK DRAGGED ME out of the interview with Koll, he confronted me. He asked me to explain what the hell had happened in there. I said I didn't have time to explain, that I had to go.

'You're staying here,' Birck said, holding my shoulder in a tight grip.

'How much did you hear?'

'Of what?'

'Of what he said.'

'Not that much, but enough to know that you threatened him.' He looked at me. 'Why were you trying to hit him?'

'I don't know,' I mumbled. 'I lost concentration.'

'You look like a fucking mess, Leo. That, and everything else ...' He shook his head. 'I don't know what we're going to do.'

'Can't we deal with this later?'

Birck's stare was icy.

'The prints on the necklace, Leo. I need to know how they got there.'

'I can tell you tomorrow. You need to find someone called Daniel Berggren. You should probably call NOVA.'

'Don't tell me what to do.' He took a deep breath. 'We'll wait till tomorrow.'

'Why?'

'If NOVA get involved it's not going to end well. Besides, they have no resources. They're busy with the security-van robbery in Länna.'

'Tomorrow might be too late,' I said and turned to leave.

'Leo,' Birck said sharply. 'You go home and wait while I have another go at Koll. I need to get that prick to start talking. I would rather have you here, but it's going to get too late and I have to do this by the book. You come back here tomorrow and tell me what you know.' He looked at his watch. 'I'm putting a car outside your place. I want to keep an eye on you.'

'Don't. People on Chapmansgatan have seen enough police cars.'

'And enough corpses,' Birck said flatly. 'I'd be happy if they didn't have to see any more. Above all, yours.'

I went home, and my head was spinning. I now realised that it had to be him; there was no doubt. I tried to work out what I was feeling. Grief? Something like that. I felt sad, that he'd gone this far to protect his own identity. But it still didn't explain why he'd got Koll to put the necklace in her hand. I thought about sending him a text, but suddenly I felt unsure. He seemed more unpredictable than ever.

I saw the squad car roll in and park up on the road. One half of the occupants got out and crossed the road, entered my building. I went to the draining board and drank a glass of water, took a Serax, and waited for the knock on the door.

'Is everything all right here?' he asked — a man with a serious expression and pale-blue, friendly eyes.

I looked at his insignia, embroidered on his shoulder.

'Are you an inspector?'

'Have been for two years now. Why do you ask?'

'Makes me feel important.' I managed a smile. 'Everything's all right.'

He nodded and left. I waited a little while, ate some food, and left the lights on before leaving through the side door, the same way I'd left after Rebecca Salomonsson had been found dead. Nobody seemed to be following me. I went to Södermalm and passed Sam's studio. She was there, and the lights were on. I looked around, but didn't notice anything unusual. The street was sleepy, and Sam was unhurt. I turned around and walked past the studio again. Sam didn't look up. Instead she sat, needle in hand, bent over a young woman's back. I used to do that a lot, go past her place, especially after the split and Viktor. I've never told my psychologist, never told anyone. I wonder if Sam knows anyway. Probably.

IN THE DISTANCE, a flashing neon sign: ALBY CONVENIENCE STORE 24/7. It doesn't look open, but maybe it's not supposed to.

It's a small shop, packed to bursting point with goods. It stinks, a mix of spices and cleaning products. Somewhere in there I can hear laughter, and someone speaking a language I don't understand. Some of it's Spanish, but mixed with something else. The little shop seems bigger than it is, because the shelves are arranged in a labyrinth-like structure and you have to go right through it to get to the till. There's no belt, just a counter like you'd get in a kiosk. Two young men and two equally young women are standing in a semicircle, as though under the spell of the man I glimpse behind the counter. They seem to spot me.

He's old enough to be their granddad, with big brown eyes, prominent, bushy eyebrows, and tufty, frizzy hair that was once black but is now flecked with grey. The beard is thick and well groomed.

'Can't find anything you want?' he asks when he sees my empty hands.

'Not yet,' I say.

'Are you a cop?'

'Depends.'

'Depends on what?' asks one of the young men.

He and his friend are both tall, lanky. One is wearing a leather jacket; the other, a dark-blue hoodie with RATW printed across the chest. I wonder what the letters stand for.

'Does it count if you're suspended?'

The older man squints at me, before he rattles off something quick to the others. One of the women is wearing a bright-green short skirt, tights with holes in, heavy boots, and a short denim jacket covered in safety pins, chains, and badges. She crosses her arms, and when her jacket pulls tight over her breasts, one of the men glances at them.

'Oi! Stop staring,' she says.

Her mouth clicks as she speaks, like a piercing hitting her teeth. The man laughs at her.

'I'm looking for Josef Abel,' I say.

It goes quieter than I'd expected.

'Why, my friend,' says the man behind the till, apparently unmoved, 'are you looking for him? And why do you think we know who he is?'

'I've been told that there's only one Josef Abel, and that people out here tend to know who he is.'

'Tend to?' The man behind the counter looks quizzically at the girl in the denim jacket, who says something — *tender* — in Spanish. 'Ah-ha, almost the same,' he says. 'Yes, people do … tend to.' He smiles, perhaps pleased with the new addition to his vocabulary. 'You only go to Josef when you need help.'

'I need help.'

The man squints at me, as though trying to decide whether or not I'm lying.

'Are you armed?'

I shake my head.

The man in the leather jacket comes over and starts frisking me — my shoulders, down my back, hips, stomach, legs. He does it very thoroughly, and as he moves I can smell cheap aftershave. When he's done, he turns to the man behind the counter.

'He's clean, Papi.'

'A bit rude, disturbing old men at this hour,' Papi says, and runs his hand through his beard. 'Whatever it is must be important.'

'Yes. But I just need some information. A name. Nothing more.'

'You police negotiator, eh?'

'No, no, I'm not.'

'How do you know that Josef can give you information?'

'Peter Koll said so.'

He drops his head, examining the countertop — covered in stickers and adverts for cigarettes and tobacco — and seems to be contemplating something for a second, before nodding at the woman in denim.

'Karin. Take him with you.'

She stares at me and then at her friend, who still hasn't said anything. Her eyes are brown and blank, as though she's seen too much of what the world is capable of.

'Okay,' she says and looks at me, takes something from her coat pocket.

'You don't need to get that out,' I attempt, looking at the knife.

'Yes,' she says. 'I do.'

OUTSIDE THE SHOP, on the way to the high-rise blocks, Karin walks alongside me with the knife in one hand, the other hand stuffed in her pocket. It's a good knife, the sort you buy in a hunting shop; it gently follows the contours of the hand, with a little round trigger that releases the blade. I wonder if she's ever used it. Something tells me she has. I wonder how old she is — definitely no older than twenty, maybe not even eighteen, but she's tall, and I've always found it hard to guess how old tall women are. Karin's boots boom heavily on the tarmac. As she walks, her clothes rustle slightly.

'How do you know Josef?' I ask.

'He's the one who's really called "Papi". It's just Dino and Lehel who call Goran "Papi", because they're actually related.'

'And what does Papi mean, then? Dad?'

'More or less. Josef is like a dad. Well, he's more like a granddad these days. He's old, but he's still Papi. Our dads, I mean our own dads, they've got some stories about him.'

'Is it right that he gets called "the man with no voice"?'

'Yes.'

'Why?'

'He can't talk.'

'And why not?'

'Whoa. Too many questions.'

'SHALL WE RING the bell?'

Karin shakes her head. We're on the top floor of one of the blocks.

'He already knows,' she says, and opens the door. It's a simple wooden one with a letterbox and ABEL written on a label that was once white.

The hall is large and neat, and a red-and-brown rug with a crocheted pattern muffles our steps. Straight down the corridor, the flat divides, with a room on each side. To the right is what looks like a big kitchen with a dining table and chairs; to the left, something resembling a living room. Karin takes her boots off, and gestures to me to do the same. She goes into the room on the left, and says something in Spanish to the two young men sitting in armchairs, each holding a video-game controller. In front of them, a TV is showing a meeting between two football teams. On a little table in between them lie two black pistols. One of the men pauses the game and looks up, says Karin's name and then Papi, and something else.

'What's he saying?' I ask.

'That you can go in,' she says. 'But only if I go in, too.'

Beyond the men are two doors, both closed. The man gesticulates wearily towards one of them and watches us pass.

The door is opened by yet another man, about Karin's age. He has thick black hair and pale skin, piercing blue eyes, and a pronounced, sharp nose that projects over his lip. He looks at Karin.

'It's late,' he says.

'I know. Thank you,' says Karin.

The room consists of a single bed, an armchair, a television, and a bookshelf. The floor is covered with a carpet. Someone is sitting in the armchair — a man with yellowish skin and a white halo of hair around his head, his eyes fixed on a book. He's wearing a white shirt, and grey suit trousers held up by simple black braces. The shirt is unbuttoned, revealing a vest and a chestful of bushy white hair. His nose is bony and low; his eyebrows, thick and straight. His shoulders are relaxed, hunched over the book. They are shoulders that once belonged to a wrestler or someone whose job involved moving pianos.

'Josef Abel?' I ask, standing a metre or so away from him.

Abel looks up, pulls a black leather-bound pad from his shirt pocket, and finds a pen. His breathing comes in noisy puffs. As he writes, I notice the scar circling his neck like a necklace: light pink, uneven, and thick from one side to the other, just above the collar bone. He shows me the notepad.

do I know you

Then his eyes come alive, and he tilts his head slightly to one side, scanning across my legs, my hands, my shoulders. He adds two words:

do I know you mr officer

'Leo Junker,' I say, and slight surprise is just visible in the old man's face.

you were involved in that mess on Gotland

238

'Yes, unfortunately. I need your help. Daniel Berggren — does that name mean anything to you?'

The man holds up a finger and turns around. He looks over his shoulder, picks up a book that is lying on the floor next to him, and pulls an envelope out of it, which he shows to me. It's white, postcard-sized, and soft, as though it contains several sheets of paper. *leo*, is all that's written on it, written in handwriting I don't recognise.

'It's from him, is it? From Daniel?'

Abel nods, and that makes the envelope seem warm against my fingers.

'When did he leave this?'

came by courier don't know any more

'I don't really believe that.'

suspicious, eh?

The old man laughs — a mocking, panting laugh.

'You've been in contact with Daniel Berggren, then?'

has something happened?

'How well do you know him?'

His face goes tense, sombre.

quite well please don't tell me you're bringing bad news

'I'm afraid I am,' I say.

The old man is blinking. If he's shocked or surprised, you can't tell; maybe there's a hint of a shake in the next word he writes on the pad:

suicide?

'Almost,' I say. 'Murder.'

victim or murderer

'Murderer,' I say as I look around, pull a chair over, and sit down on it.

you're lying that can't be true

'I'm afraid it is.'

Abel shrinks into a heap, as though he'd got a puncture. As he turns the page in his pad, he discovers that he's just filled the last page. The old man opens his mouth and speaks, breathing in the words, his voice like a cracked ghost. It's a terrible noise, the sound of someone speaking with glass shards in their voice box. A little while after he's gone quiet, the words sink in:

'New pad.'

The man who's been standing next to Karin leaves the room and comes back with a new pad. In the meantime, Karin goes over, squats down on her heels, and chats to Abel. He's pleased to see her. His eyes light up and he smiles, stroking her cheek when she tells him something. Karin is holding his hand between her palms. I'm holding the envelope. The sweat is making the envelope damp.

D isn't a murderer

'Maybe not directly,' I say. 'But indirectly. I need to know what you know. He was my friend, once. Now I'm afraid that he's going to hurt people.'

what do you want to know?

'How did you come to know him?'

he came to me

Abel strains to remember, before he continues:

after Jumkil

He looks at me, curious.

'I know about Jumkil,' I say.

his friend introduced us

'The friend he was living with at the time, here in Alby?'

'Yeah,' Abel hisses, nodding. The sound is hollow and wheezy, makes me think of reptiles.

D had certain skills

'I know.'

I made sure he used them he helped a lot of people

'He helped a lot of people to disappear?'

and he helped a lot of people get here from their home countries

Abel hesitates before adding: *for money*

'And you had money,' I say.

That makes the old man crack a smile, showing his sorry excuse for a mouth with its many missing teeth; those that are still there are crooked, deformed, and unhealthily yellow.

understatement, he writes.

'I see. Drugs?'

Abel tenses up in his chair, stares at me for a long while, as though this is a crucial moment.

among other things but that was then I'm old now

'You were hardly young twelve years ago.'

I was younger mr officer

'Did you know that Daniel was really called something else? That his name was John?'

don't remember

'John Grimberg.'

Abel taps the words he's just written, as if to emphasise them, and adds: *we called him the invisible man*

'Why?'

The old man writes a longer reply.

he got in trouble after a thing with S, he disappeared then, didn't see him for some time, then he came back, like an apparition

'When did you last see Daniel?'

a couple of months ago

'Under what circumstances?'

'Whoa.' I hear Karin's voice behind me, and feel a hand gripping my shoulder, tightly. 'Is this an interrogation, or what?'

'No.'

'Take it easy, right?' she says. 'Lean back.' She lets go of my shoulder. 'He doesn't like being pushed.'

'I'm not pushing.'

'I'll be the judge of that.'

Abel smiles apologetically and blinks at Karin. On the TV, in the background, a music video is flickering. A big whale is floating through space, and looks as if it's about to swallow the earth. Looks welcoming.

'A couple of months ago, you met Daniel,' I say. 'What was the deal?'

he was here on business

'Someone was going to disappear?'

Abel nods.

'Does he still use the name Daniel Berggren?'

that's the name he's always used with me

'How do you get in touch with Daniel if you need to get hold of him?'

send a letter

'To what address?'

He writes something down and rips it from the pad, gives it to me. It's a P.O. box.

'This isn't a real address.'

it's the one I've got

'So what happens when you contact him by letter?'

he comes here

'After how long?'

2–4 days

I look at the address in my hand and stand up from the chair. I wonder where the box is. Wherever it is, it's likely to be close to Grim's home. That box must be important for him.

'Thank you,' I say.

you don't want to thank me you want to lock me up for drugs and violence, he writes, *because you think I've hurt the children of Alby*

'Yes,' I say.

I nearly say something, but I don't really know what. I stare at Abel, try to decide if there's anything I could threaten him with. There isn't. I take a couple of steps back, on my way out. He writes something else on the pad and waves me over again.

242

do you think you make the world a better place?

'I think I did think that, once,' I say. 'But that was then. I have changed.'

people don't change mr officer, he writes, *they adapt*

XXIV

Sitting in an underground train, I open the envelope. The carriage is almost empty — just a few passengers dotted about, sitting with their heads leaning against the windowpanes. The lighting is pale yellow, making my skin look sickly.

It looks like some kind of diary, several pages long, written in the kind of handwriting Grim probably doesn't use anymore. In some parts he writes differently, modified and distorted as if to conceal his identity. You can tell, though. It's like he was trying on some old clothes for the first time in ages, and wasn't sure what persona, what character, they conveyed.

In the period leading up to my disappearance I go to a psychologist. She becomes increasingly flippant and I can't understand why. I remember one afternoon in her office, she asks me what's wrong. I say that I don't know, that it may or may not have something to do with my family, or my friends, I don't know. Anja's dead, maybe it's that. Maybe it's the junk. She asks how my family are these days. I say fine, everything's fine. There's only Dad left and he's fine.

'What about me?' I ask.

'What do you mean?'

I don't know what to say, I feel so disorientated.

'Yes, what about me?' I repeat, feeling helpless.

'It will be okay,' she says, 'when you get a bit older everything will be fine. You grow out of things.'

'I don't know,' I say, 'I don't think so.'

She tilts her head slightly. She looks down on me, she doesn't say so but I know it's true. I've met so many people like her now, and they are all the same.

I manage to disappear. It takes time. Giving someone an ID card and a pat on the back is one thing, but really disappearing is another. Especially if, as I have, you've ended up in all sorts of unusual registers. I don't manage to fix all of them. Certain entries are too old to be altered, buried deep in the machinery of Swedish bureaucracy. I bribe whoever I can, threaten civil servants via decoys, and report false changes of address and bank details. I try and get myself certified dead but for that you need a corpse and I'm not prepared to go that far. 2003 and everything else is in place. I choose the name with great care and at twenty-four John Grimberg is a man who vanishes into thin air.

I switch to a lighter drug because I need a clear head right now. It doesn't work out and in the end I'm back on the horse. To keep functioning I start taking black market medication. No clinic would prescribe Subutex for the likes of me. I'm still taking them, but no one knows about that — well, apart from you. Twice a day I take methadone, sometimes more often than that. Recently it's been more.

After a while, once I've managed to become someone else, things start ticking over on their own. Through Abel I start helping people get new identity documents, start investigating whether it's possible to completely erase any trace of someone. It's one thing getting rid of yourself. Someone else is a much bigger ask.

Before long I'm all over the place, helping people left and right and earning insane amounts of money. If I told you how much you would laugh, it's ridiculous. But during all that time, all those years, even when things were at their worst, not even then did I think of you. I hadn't forgiven you, but I'd moved on. Besides, I had no idea who you were, where you were, or even if you were alive. That uncertainty felt good.

And then, just three weeks ago, everything fell apart. Imagine it taking that long! Since then I've been writing this to you, Leo.

Are you listening? Can you hear me? I'm going to make sure that you listen.

Dad got sick and after a while he died. I'd tried to see him as much as possible before he had to go into hospital.

I think we both knew we'd had it, but neither of us said anything. I think he knew what I was up to, but he didn't mention that either.

We played cards, watched films, went and played darts every now and then in some bar, that sort of thing.

I don't know if he felt the same, but it seemed to me that we had an unspoken agreement. We just made sure we had each other, that's all. We both needed that.

Then he had to be admitted and I visited him in hospital. I used a false name and Dad heard it, I think, because he called me it once, and smiled. The last time we saw each other he was very weak and it took a while before he recognised me. That's when something grabbed me, when I saw his face.

I'd put so much distance between myself and everything else that had anything to do with Salem. I had to, to survive. So when I saw him there it was a shock, as though everything came back to me. Suddenly, no time had passed, despite the fact it's been nearly sixteen years. He was all I had left. And then he died. I didn't know what to do with myself. I started dreaming and the dream was just one thing: the colour red, how I was ensnared by it, and couldn't get free. I floated through the funeral in a daze.

I was the only one left, and had to take care of the estate. Dad had taken care of Julia's and Mum's deaths. He claimed to have thrown everything away and I hadn't been down in the basement, so when I did go down there I got a shock. Everything was there. He hadn't even thrown my old clothes away. As I'm writing this I just don't understand why he didn't say anything, why he claimed to have thrown it all away. But as I stood there all I could think about was how he'd fitted it all in. Even the furniture from Julia's room was down there. Her bed, desk, shelves, everything. The bed was still made. Can you imagine? The bed was still made! The bedclothes were full of mould but you could still see the pattern, the little colourful dots. For some reason I took the boxes off the bed and pulled the cover back. There were some of her clothes lying in there. They were half-rotten, just like the bedclothes, but I still recognised them.

You've no idea how the little everyday things can bring the past crashing back, like a black hole inside of you that sucks you in. That was the first time I had a relapse with the heroin, in there. I went out and scored and sat down among the stuff and just shot up.

When I started going through the boxes I found clothes I hadn't seen for ages. They belonged to you. That blue hoodie with the Champion logo on, do you remember that? I don't suppose you do. I even found Julia's notepad, where you had written each other's names. I found Mum's old photo album, which she'd put together during those moments when she felt a bit happier. I remember she was very particular about the order, which photo should come after what. It started when it was just her and Dad, then I popped up here and there and then Julia. She was wearing her necklace in several of the photos.

That storage room was like stepping into another time. Everything swirled around me. Memories of Mum, Dad, and everyone else. It was just like I told you, do you remember I said several times that if anything happened to Julia we wouldn't be able to stick together? And that's what happened, slowly but surely. I don't think I cried. I lived down there for several days (don't bother looking, I'm not there anymore), going through all that stuff, not doing anything else. I watched those old films we made, the ones we recorded ourselves. First up was one called 'LOVE KILLER'. Do you remember that one?

I burnt the lot in a steel drum in the yard. Everything, apart from the stuff that was too big to fit. I took that to the dump. But everything else, every last fucking memory, I torched the lot. I am no one. Have nothing. On the outside, everything's fine after Dad's death, but inside it's like I'm disintegrating. I feel so incredibly lonely. Invisible. For the first time.

Maybe it's because I'm getting older. When I was twenty I could live like this, didn't think about missing anything. That I was just gliding through life. These thoughts keep me awake at night. The isolation is complete. I feel anonymous, it's like everything's suddenly caught up with me. I've started hallucinating. Sometimes I manage to sleep but sometimes I can go days without.

The methadone doesn't help anymore, I feel constantly drawn back to the smack. What is this life of mine anyway? I'm not in touch with anyone, I've got no ties to anyone.

How did I find you after all this time? That's the fantastic part, how the pieces all fall into place even though everything is in bits after Dad's death. It starts a couple of weeks before his death, when I finish a job for someone I don't trust, but I need the money. He's got an acquaintance, a girl, who I trust even less. Rebecca. Somehow she finds out my identity, the one that I normally live under. You have to have them on you — ID documents — and one evening, when I'm meeting someone, I haven't had time to switch to the identity I use the rest of the time. She must have snooped in my jacket or something, although I'm almost certain that I never let it out of my sight. I don't know because I'm so shaky and I've taken a big dose of methadone. The world is a little bit murky and I don't feel safe. Maybe one of them, Rebecca or her friend, gets to see my name.

She starts blackmailing me, saying she'll go to the police if I don't pay her to keep quiet. To begin with I do as she says but it escalates, just gets worse and worse. She demands more and more money, she even follows me to Dad's funeral, and causes a scene at the reception. I'm scared all the time, always looking over my shoulder. Everything that I've built up is at risk of falling down around me. I start planning for a new identity but I can't cope with it, the state I'm in. I need to get rid of her somehow. I start following her. One night she ducks through that entrance on Chapmansgatan. I wait outside, in the car. A man comes out a few minutes later, and that man is you.

My world stands still. And it's that, my reaction when I see you, which makes me understand what I have to do.

I know what you're thinking: I've lost my mind. Maybe I have. But everyone has something that will push them to the edge, and maybe over it. Most people don't know what that is, but I do. I know where it started to go wrong.

I kept you under surveillance after I'd found you. Now it's your turn to spiral down, down, down.

XXV

As I emerge from the tube and up from the underground, I take a few deep breaths, trying to compose myself after reading the whole diary.

Daniel Berggren's P.O. box is in an office on Rådmansgatan. It takes a while to work that out, but not as long as I'd thought. In central Stockholm the P.O. boxes are located at a number of addresses, and sitting at a computer at an all-night 7-Eleven I manage to find the right address by using search engines and a process of elimination.

When I leave the 7-Eleven, it's gone midnight. Stockholm doesn't feel like a capital city anymore. The streets are almost empty, the pulse lower. My hands are shaking.

I head to Rådmansgatan, and stop outside the door of the office, which turns out to be closed between midnight and five in the morning. I push my face against the glass — it's secured on the inside with heavy bars — and I see row after row of P.O. boxes, the size of ordinary letterboxes, stacked on top of each other endlessly. The insignia of the Post and Telecoms Agency hangs on one wall.

In the corner of the ceiling, what must be a CCTV camera blinks away. A car pulls up behind me, and the reflection is visible in the window, the word SECURITAS on the bonnet. A bulldog of a man climbs out and starts walking towards me.

'Everything all right?' says the bulldog.

'Everything's all right,' I say. 'Just curious.'

Outside Chapmansgatan 6, the patrol car is still there. Inside, one half of the patrol is awake, his face weakly illuminated by the screen of a mobile phone; the other seems to be in a very deep sleep.

QUARTER PAST FIVE. That's what time it is when I open the door to the P.O. boxes on Rådmansgatan. My eyes are stinging from the tiredness, and I'm pretty sure the insomnia's made me ill. I swing between sweating and freezing, until I realise that it's been far too long since my last Serax. It could be withdrawal symptoms. Standing inside the door, I rifle through the inside pocket of my coat until I find a pill and swallow it, feel it gliding down inside me while I get the note with the address. P.O. Box 4746.

The boxes are arranged in columns of ten. Row after row fill the whole of the vast space. Bigger boxes are along the wall, some about the size of a couple of shoeboxes; others, so enormous that you could easily hide pieces of furniture in them.

I locate box 4746 somewhere in the middle of the labyrinthine warren, and I examine it, being careful not to touch it. It looks just like any other. Using a pen, I open the flap slightly, and carefully push my finger down inside the box. There's post in there. That means he needs to pick it up; he needs to come here. I look around for a suitable place to keep watch from. I might need to be here for some time. I pick a spot a long way from the entrance but from where I can still see the door and the box. Time passes; Rådmansgatan is just visible through the window, and out there the city is coming to life. People pass by, carrying bags and children; buses roll past. The sun rises and lights up the street.

Women and men — early birds — come in, walk briskly to their boxes, collect the post, stuff it in their bags, and disappear again. I watch them carefully. They're most probably self-employed people of some kind; most of the post looks like business letters. It's an effective camouflage by Grim. He's just one of many well-dressed and independent people collecting their post in the morning. I start feeling thirsty, and my legs hurt. Once the place is empty I do a couple of laps around the boxes, pretending that the camera in the corner isn't even there.

Quarter past eight. After three hours' wait, someone walks past the window. I notice out of the corner of my eye: a tall man, black clothes, straw-coloured hair. I can't see his face. He crosses the road and walks towards the entrance, and in the blink of an eye he disappears from my field of vision, and I hold my breath until the door opens and he steps inside. He's wearing black jeans and an equally black jacket. Underneath that, he's wearing a simple blue T-shirt. The straw-coloured hair is neatly styled; the angular face, relaxed yet pale and sunken, hollowed out. At first I wonder if it is him, but then he does this movement — casts his eyes left, and his head follows suit — that convinces me. It is Grim, but so much older, and the feeling is overwhelming and unreal, as though for a minute I'd taken that step over to the other side and seen the dead.

His face still makes me think of Julia. I wonder what she would have looked like now.

Grim walks with his hands in his jacket pockets. He might already have seen or heard me, although I don't think so. I'm standing behind a row of boxes, and I'm watching him through a little gap in between them.

He opens the box, takes something out — I can't see what it is — and heads for the exit. But he doesn't go out. Instead he goes and stands between two rows of boxes, forcing me to move so I can see what he's doing. My strides are hasty, and in my ears my pulse is beating hard and fast, and I tilt my head, look out, and hold my breath. Grim has stopped by another box; he opens it and takes out what looks like a metal cigarette case. He takes something small and black from his inside jacket pocket and puts it in the box. Then he locks it and heads for the door. I ought to step out, confront him, maybe beat him unconscious, I don't know, but I should do something, and in spite of that I can't move. All I do is keep my eyes on the box to memorise which one it is, while I get my phone out.

He goes out the door and disappears round the corner.

My legs feel weak as I go over to the post box Grim just left, and I make a note of the number. Then I call the phone number Levin gave me, the one that goes to someone calling herself Alice. She answers, perfectly uninterested, as though she sits answering calls all day long. Maybe she does. I ask for her help, tell her I need the name of someone who has a P.O. box on Rådmansgatan.

'Listen, are you okay?' she asks.

'What do you mean?'

'You sound like you've just been crying.'

'Can you just give me the name?'

'Number?' she says; I can hear her tapping away.

'Fifty-six forty-six.' I hesitate. 'Are you looking at the Tax Agency's register right now?'

'Uh-huh.'

'Can you check another post box, too?'

'One thing at a time, Junker.' She clears her throat. 'Fifty-six forty-six, I'm guessing you're standing in front of it right now?'

'Yes. Yes I am.'

'There's no single name associated with it. There are two. Looks like they run a company of some description. Tobias Fredriksson and Jonathan Granlund.' She clicks away. 'Born seventy-nine and eighty. Neither have previous. Both single. One lives in Hammarbyhöjden; one near Telefonplan. It looks like their business premises are near Telefonplan, but it isn't the same address as Granlund's.'

She coughs. I wonder if she's a smoker.

'And the other box?' she asks.

'Forty-seven forty-six.'

'Same address otherwise?'

'Yes.'

A short silence.

'Daniel Berggren. The only match I can find is on the electoral roll. Daniel Berggren, born seventy-nine, fifteenth of December, listed as living in Bandhagen.' She carries on clicking. 'Hmm, he's got a P.O. box for his residential address. I've seen that before. Usually just a front.'

'Have you any details, other than addresses, for Fredriksson and Granlund?'

'No, not even a phone number. Do you want the addresses?'

She reads them out, and I jot them down, amazed.

Grim's identity is cloaked in a fog of deceptions.

'Thanks, Alice,' I say.

'Uh-huh,' she mumbles, and hangs up.

BIRCK CALLS just as I'm on my way down to the underground at Rådmansgatan station. He's snorting down the phone, asking where I am.

'You were supposed to be here. We agreed. I need you, your information.'

'How did you get on with Koll yesterday?'

'Get down here. Now.'

'If you tell me how it went with Koll.'

A heavy sigh.

'He's not really saying anything, keeps saying that he's under orders to only speak to you. All I got were little snippets that don't tell us anything on their own, but which might support the forensic evidence we've got. And then he's saying that he did it for money, a contract. I pushed him on that name you said, Daniel Berggren, but he just looked fucking delighted and refused to tell me anything. So get down here now.'

'Can't we do this on the phone?'

'Definitely not.'

I pass through the tunnel under Sveagatan, past the threatening red painting of Strindberg that covers the wall.

'He did it on the instructions of Daniel Berggren, but that's just a front for two other names,' I say. 'One Tobias Fredriksson of

255

Hammarbyhöjden, and one Jonathan Granlund near Telefonplan. Both are the right sort of age. On paper they own some kind of business, but I'm certain that it's just a front. His real name is John Grimberg, but Grimberg is only recorded in the Whereabouts Unknown register. I don't believe that Granlund, Fredriksson, or Berggren is the alias he's using at the moment. He calls himself something else. And I think that's why she died, because she found out about that.'

'She got wind of his identity?'

'Exactly. I got lucky and found the right Daniel Berggren, so I am —'

'How did you manage that,' Birck says coldly, 'from your flat, where I ordered you to remain?'

'I was lucky. And you can't give orders to people who are suspended.'

'I don't understand where you fit in to all this. It's time to talk now, Leo,' he attempts, almost pleading.

'Daniel Berggren, or John Grimberg, as he was known then, used to be my friend.' Down on the platform, the train thunders out of the tunnel with the brakes squealing. 'Before he started hating me.'

'Because?'

'That doesn't matter.'

'So the necklace was put there as a warning to you? Or a threat?'

'I don't know,' I say, thinking about the diary pages that are still in my inside pocket. It's true. I really do not know. I board the train, look around the carriage, convinced that someone is watching me. 'His dad died three weeks ago. Since then, everything's gone downhill fast, and he's now behaving extremely irrationally. And I think he's dangerous.'

'How long have you suspected this?' he asks.

'Only a day or so.'

'Only a day or so,' he repeats, and sighs. 'I'll let Pettersén know and then we'll bring Granlund in.'

'No,' I say. 'Fredriksson. I think Granlund is a decoy.'

'John Grimberg,' Birck says. 'Jonathan Granlund. People who do this sort of thing need something to hold on to, something that stops their personality splitting and them going mad. They need something with a link to who they really are. Initials, for example.'

'I know that,' I say. 'And he knows it, too. I think he's thought of this kind of deduction.'

The line goes quiet, for a surprisingly long time.

'You're going to get so much shit for this, when it's over.'

'I don't give a fuck.'

'So you think it's Fredriksson?'

'Yes.'

Birck sighs again.

'Check Fredriksson then. My money's on Granlund. If we find him, we'll have found Grimberg's current alias. I'll try and get some extra resources in. We'll take Granlund. Ring when you get there.'

'That sounds almost like a job for a policeman in active service,' I say.

He hangs up without another word.

I GET OFF at Hammarbyhöjden, a couple of stations south of Södermalm. The sun is shining, white and warm, and the trees and bushes are rustling. As I look for the piece of paper with Fredriksson's address on it, my phone rings — a number I don't recognise.

'Is that Leo?' says a shaky voice.

'Who is this?'

'Yes, I'm, my name is Ricky. Is this Leo Junker?'

'Calm down. Yes, it's me.'

'I'm Sam's boyfriend. Sam Falk. You know her, right? I was supposed to call you if anything happened.'

'Eh? If what happened?'

'She ... she didn't come home last night. I thought she was working late, but ... when I woke up this morning, she wasn't there. So I thought maybe she'd slept at the studio, she does that sometimes, but I'm standing outside the studio now — it's empty, no lights on, all locked up. She's not here. I've tried calling her, and her phone's switched off; Sam's phone is never off. I think ... I'm afraid that something's happened.'

My head starts spinning. I lean against a wall for support. The surface is sharp and uneven against my palm. I close my eyes. He sounds smaller, weaker than I'd expected.

'Call the police. Say that you want to speak to Gabriel Birck.'

'Are you coming here?'

'Yes.' I start running back, back towards the underground. 'I'm coming.'

On the underground back towards Södermalm, I stand all the way; I can't sit down. People stare, but I don't care. My phone receives a text from Grim.

3 hours, leo

till what?

till you need to find me

And then he adds:

till she dies

XXVI

Södermalm police get there before me. Once I'm out of the underground and have sprinted across the road, I see the cars from a distance. Even though I know Sam isn't there, it's still as though one of my worst fears has been realised: blue lights striking the walls around s TATTOO, Sam lying there inside, motionless and pale. When I get to the studio I have to look in, just to reassure myself that it's not true.

No body. Instead, two police officers are inside, walking around carefully. A forensic technician in blue overalls and purple latex gloves, the same person responsible for the investigation on Chapmansgatan, arrives and screams at them to get out of his crime scene. Those words, hearing them and realising they're talking about Sam's studio — that alone is enough to set me off.

In the corner, a bit inside the cordon, a uniformed officer is standing talking to a short man with stubble for hair and an equally stubbly beard. He's pale and brown-eyed, with piercings in his eyebrow, nose, and bottom lip. This must be Ricky. When he sees me, he waves me over frantically, and the officer, a young woman I don't recognise, lets me through.

'Are you Leo?'

'Yes.'

'I thought I recognised you from the pictures,' he says, but I don't find out what pictures he's talking about.

Ricky is shaken, doesn't say much other than what he's told me on the phone. Inside me, the frustration grows: I was here just a few hours ago. I walked right past. I saw her then; everything was fine. She wasn't hurt. I stop and look around. Was he here then, waiting somewhere? I take another Serax.

The forensic technician wanders around in there, muttering to himself. A short time later, Birck arrives in an unmarked car. He doesn't seem surprised to see me.

'There are indications of a struggle, well inside the studio, in the office,' the technician says. 'My guess would be that she was in there, he came in through the door, and probably neutralised her somehow.'

'By neutralised, you mean that he hit her,' Birck says, glancing at me. 'Right?'

'More like electrocuted her. There's evidence to suggest that it happened very quickly. That's just a guess, of course,' he adds.

'Of course,' Birck says coolly, and turns to me. 'Sam Falk. You were t—'

'Yes.' I hold up my phone, show him the texts. 'Three hours. Or,' I say, feeling my pulse rise, 'more like two now.'

'Till what?'

'According to him, till he kills her.'

'But why?' Birck says, his eyes wide. 'I don't understand.'

I look at the phone in my hand, and show Birck the latest message again, as though that might explain something. He stares at it, bewildered.

'I'll put out a search for her,' he says, and gets his phone out. 'The more people who see this, the more difficult for him to keep her hidden away. The greater the chance we make ...' He turns away. 'Hello? This is Gabriel Birck.'

His voice zones out. I try to keep calm, but it's hard. For the first time in my life, I'm imagining myself physically injuring Grimberg, and the feeling this gives me is warm and pleasurable.

My phone vibrates:

keep the police out of it

I need to sit down, and I flop onto the bonnet of one of the police cars. The bonnet's warm, and I can hear the engine ticking underneath it. He can't be serious. This is a game. He can't be serious.

impossible, I write, *this is too big for that*

'Leo,' someone says, and I feel a hand on my shoulder. 'Leo.'

'Yes?'

I look up at Birck. He looks genuinely worried, which surprises me.

'Do you need anything?' he asks.

'I need to find Tobias Fredriksson.'

That's all I can think about right now. If I do, I'm one step closer to Grim. Birck puts his hands on his hips. His hair is ruthlessly slicked back, and his black tie is flapping about in the wind. He's trying to think. It looks painful.

'You take Fredriksson,' he says. 'We'll take Granlund. We didn't get there before ... well, before all this.'

'I need something to protect myself with.'

'You can go with someone.'

'That's not enough,' I attempt. 'And who am I going to go with? Everyone is busy here. Shall I go with an officer from Västberga or what?'

He looks away and shrugs his shoulders.

'I don't know.'

'I need something to protect myself with,' I try again.

'You'll have to manage without.'

'I can't. You know that as well as I do.'

'Come with me to the car.'

IT'S A SIMPLE WEAPON, a black Walther pistol. I imagine Birck hides his SIG Sauer somewhere else. I feel the weight of it in my hand, and how my fingers form around it. It makes me weak at the knees. When I rest my finger on the trigger and then squeeze it carefully, feel the resistance of the coil inside, my peripheral vision turns black and I get tunnel vision. I sink to the ground, and hear the sound of something scraping and scuffing, like furniture being dragged across a floor. It's the clouds, the clouds moving above my head, towards me.

'Leo,' Birck says.

It isn't the clouds scraping across the sky. The sound is my own breathing. I'm hyperventilating. It's the first time this has happened. The psychologist said that this is what the attacks would feel like when they did come.

'Take it,' I blurt out, and hold the gun out towards him, but I drop it and it falls to the ground. Birck calmly picks it up and places it on the driver's seat of his car, leans against the open door, and looks at me.

'Fuck that. You're not going. You're staying here. I'm sending a squad car instead.'

'It's okay. Just give me something other than a pistol.' My breathing is slowly returning to a rate that would allow me to stand again. I try and stand up. 'A knife.'

I slump against the bonnet, coughing.

'Not a chance,' says Birck.

'It's a kidnapping now,' says one of the uniformed officers, who has joined us beside the car. 'Right?'

'I suppose so,' Birck says.

'What do they want? If I may ask?' the policeman insists.

'Me,' I say, still shaking. 'He wants you kept out of it.'

'We don't even know where the bastard's holed up,' says Birck. 'Keep communicating with him.' He stretches out his arm. 'Give me the phone.'

'No.'

'I want to write something.'

'Say what you want to write, and I'll do it.' I add, sullenly. 'It's my phone.'

Birck sighs, quite understandably. I feel like a child.

'Ask him to send a picture. So we've got proof that she's still alive. And that he's really the one holding her.'

I write to Grim, asking for a picture. Birck goes inside the studio. I look up at the sky, the strong sun that's holding the clouds at a distance. Less than two hours left.

My phone vibrates, receiving the image. It's not a picture of Sam. It's a photo of her tattoos, a sort of Norse medicine wheel with detailed spokes, and a unique pattern on her shoulder. Sam's the only one with that tattoo.

EVENTUALLY, I GET HOLD of a uniformed inspector — Dansk, he says his name is — to call for a car for me. In the meantime, I'm allowed past the tape and into Sam's studio. I pass her chair, the sofa, and walk into her little office. It feels weird being here. Her smell is still lingering, as though she's just left the room for a moment and will be back any second. An invisible hand squeezes my heart.

I pull out one of the desk drawers, and there it is, just as I recalled: Sam's knife. It reminds me of the one I saw Karin holding yesterday — small, a flick-knife, but considerably cheaper. I stuff it in my pocket, and hope that no one's seen me.

Someone finally manages to get hold of a car, a boxy, wine-red Volvo, of the kind that twenty years ago earned the titles of World's Safest and World's Dullest. It arrives, rolling in from Södermalm Police, and Dansk waves me over. Dansk disappears, the car stops, and an officer climbs out and looks around inquisitively. I get into the car and leave Södermalm, head for Hammarbyhöjden alone, to pay Tobias Fredriksson a visit. Birck's already left to go to Telefonplan.

HAMMARBYHÖJDEN. A lone car, a white BMW, goes past at the crossroads. The journey has been nerve-racking. I'm even more out of practice than I thought. I wonder if I'm being followed, if Grim's got someone watching me. He might well have, but I'm not sure.

The building in Hammarbyhöjden is four storeys high and is right at the foot of the hill. The entrance door is black, the glass panes slightly tinted. CODE REQUIRED 9PM–6AM, a note on the door informs me. Fredriksson lives on the third floor. I call the lift, and it creaks into life somewhere up there, groaning as it slowly makes its way down. I haven't got time, so I take the stairs.

The door is brown, with FREDRIKSSON written in white on a black background across the letterbox. I try the door handle. Locked. There's less than an hour-and-a-half to go. The door to the flat is an old-fashioned one, and I convince myself that I can get through it. I start fiddling with the knife in the lock, but all I manage to do is scratch lines in the wood around it. I can't even get the point of the blade into the keyhole. Pathetic. From nowhere the panic arrives, and I start banging on the door. The noise echoes and bounces around me between the cold, hard walls of the stairwell.

I stop for a moment, and just breathe.

Behind me, one of the locks is turning. I turn around and see a door being opened, slowly and nervously. An old man's face peers out.

'Don't shoot,' he says.

'I'm unarmed.'

He looks at the knife in my hand. I carefully retract the blade and put it in my pocket, look at the door. MALMQVIST. The smell of cigarette smoke escapes from inside.

'I am a police officer,' I say as slowly as I can. 'And I need to get in here. Is your name Malmqvist?'

'Lars-Petter Malmqvist. What's going on?'

'Do you know who lives here?'

'He's never there, that fellow.'

'So you do know who lives here?'

'Fredriksson, Torbjörn, or something.' Lars-Petter Malmqvist is grasping the door handle tightly, as though it were the only thing stopping him falling to the ground. 'Tobias,' he says. 'Tobias Fredriksson.' His expression is stiff, his jaw clenched. He's scared. 'What has happened?'

'What else do you know about him?'

'He ... he lives alone.' He squints. 'Are you really a policeman?'

'I don't have my badge,' I say. 'But I've got my driving licence, and I can give you a number to call to confirm that I am a policeman.'

The man coughs — a deep wheeze.

'I was a squadron leader,' he says. 'Air Force. In my day, we learnt to tell who we could trust and who we couldn't.'

'I understand,' I say, distracted. I need something to force the door with. 'Do you have a crowbar?'

Malmqvist raises an eyebrow. That he doesn't do more than this, that he doesn't go back inside and slam and lock the door, is surprising. I wonder if I am as mad as I sound.

'No. But I've got a list.'

'A list?'

'These apartments are privately owned,' he says, as though I had insulted him. 'Fredriksson refuses to give any personal details. That has troubled the rest of us on the residents' committee. All we've got is an ID number and a telephone number. That's the bare minimum, you see. But the ID number is wrong, and we've left notes about it on many occasions. He must have made a mistake when he was filling in the forms or something.' He hesitates. 'Might you be able ...?'

'Do you have the phone number?'

'He never answers any calls,' the man says, and starts retreating into the flat.

I follow him, unsure what to do next.

'But you can have it, if I can just find that list.' He stops. 'He's a suspect, isn't he?'

'Yes.'

'I thought as much,' he mutters.

I stay in the hall, holding my phone in my hand. It rings. It's Ricky's number. I don't answer, because I know what it is he wants to know and I don't have an answer for him. Lars-Petter Malmqvist goes through the hall, and turns left; after a little while, he returns with a folder. He moves jerkily, as though he could really do with a stick but is too stubborn to admit it.

'Here,' he says, running his finger across the page inside the folder. 'O, seven, three, O, six, five, two, five, seven, three.'

I double-check the number before I save it in my phonebook.

'Thank you.'

'Ask him to contact me. I want the correct ID number.'

'I'll ask him to call,' I say, and head back out to the stairwell.

'And by the way, don't go around waving that about.' The old man looks at my jacket pocket. 'People might wonder.'

I manage a 'Thank you', and Lars-Petter Malmqvist closes the door without another word.

I call the number, hold my breath.

'The number you have dialled is not in use,' chimes an androgynous voice in my ear.

It is, of course, a diversion. The number is probably for a pay-as-you-go SIM that might well be no longer in use, which might never, even have been active.

Birck calls.

'Granlund is a smokescreen,' he says. 'We've got nothing.'

ONE HOUR LEFT. I'm standing outside the building where Tobias Fredriksson is officially resident. Fredriksson is a smokescreen, too. Grim has hidden himself too well. He is invisible. It's over. I'll never touch him, and I realise that this — powerlessness — is the whole point. It is devastating. His intention was never that I would find him, make it in time. His intention was, in fact, exactly this.

you win, I text.

what's that supposed to mean? comes the reply, as though he'd been waiting for me.

I'm not going to find you, I write.

what a shame

I close my eyes. Grim could be anywhere. He's not necessarily even in a flat; he might not even be above ground. He could have pulled Sam into one of Stockholm's countless tunnels. They run under the city, long, deep, and many — and Grim knows it. He's lived down there himself.

He could be underground. I open my eyes. Or high above it.

The water tower.

At that moment, my phone receives a message, a picture. A severed index finger. Sam's finger.

XXVII

It's somewhere down the motorway, just after Huddinge, that it pops into my head. SWEDEN MUST DIE, it said on one of Salem's tunnel walls when I was last there. I wonder if it's been removed yet. Tags and graffiti have always tended to survive for an unusually long time in Salem.

I'm driving too fast; the speedo's red needle hovers around one-forty, one-fifty. I daren't go any faster. The car would probably cope, but I wouldn't. I check my watch. More than twenty minutes left. I'm going to make it, and I try and slow down.

I drive through Rönninge, and before long Salem appears, the place where it all began. A minute or so later, the Triad's three blocks whizz past. They look untouched, unchanged. Time marches on, inevitably and incessantly, but certain places play tricks on us, make us think for a moment that nothing has changed. From the corner of my eye I spot the window that was once Julia's, which was opposite mine. I remember all those times I stood by the window just to catch a glimpse of her, how I ducked down when it was Grim and I didn't want him to suspect anything.

In the distance, the water tower looms dark grey against the pale sky. I try and spot anything unusual about the tower, but I can't see anything odd. For a second, I'm afraid I might have got it wrong, that he's taken her somewhere else entirely. But then, through the trees that encircle the base of the water tower, I catch sight of a dark-blue car, and that's how I know I've come to the right place. It's been parked outside my flat, waiting in the dark.

The car, a low-slung Volvo, is parked on the road and looks perfectly innocent. I park further up and walk over to it, peer in through the tinted windows. The car could be straight from the factory and waiting for an owner, considering the complete absence of any personal effects inside it. My phone rings. It's Birck.

'Hello?'

'Where are you now?'

'Salem, by the water tower. I think he's here.'

'Don't do anything until we get there.'

'Okay.'

'I'm serious, Leo. Wait till we arrive.'

'I said okay, didn't I?'

I hang up. I fish a Serax out of my inside pocket and swallow it, but the pill goes down wrong, gets stuck, forcing me to bend double and cough violently. The pill hits my tooth on the way out and lands on the tarmac in front of me, shiny with spit. I pick it up and feel its slippery surface between my fingers as I swallow it. Then I head for the water tower, one hand squeezing the knife in my jacket pocket.

The gravel surface around the tower is empty and quiet. I make my way from tree to tree, being careful not to be seen. The only sound is the hum of a fan, or something, on the back of the tower. It takes a while for me to hear it. I'm still used to that sound, which surprises me. I try to remember what the view is like from up there, what you can and can't see. I squint up towards the tower's two ledges, expecting to see Grim up there. He could be watching me right now. But the ledges are empty, and the sight makes my mouth dry: I got it wrong after all. The Volvo is a decoy, or maybe it's nothing to do with Grim. It could just be a coincidence. Grim and Sam are somewhere else. I squeeze the knife even tighter.

That's when I spot it: the rope.

It starts from the upper ledge, running outwards and upwards, first towards and then onto the overhanging roof of the tower, before disappearing out of sight. He must somehow have secured it to something up there. I wonder why. Instead of scouring the ledges, I'm now studying the mushroom-shaped tower's roof, looking for some kind of movement. It takes a little while before the shadowy silhouette — a head, shoulders — swishes past. One minute it's not there, the next minute it is, and then the next minute it's gone again. I start running towards the tower. When I get to it, I stop, lean against the body of the tower, and listen. Nothing.

I look at the spiral stairs that run up to the ledges. I remember how every step, no matter how careful, rattles and bangs through the whole ladder, up into the tower. No matter how I do it, I'm going to be heard.

With quick, light steps, I climb upwards. Halfway up, the exertion makes my thighs burn. I slow down, then stop completely and listen. No sound yet.

I take another few steps, and soon I'm up on the first of the two ledges. To get up onto the upper ledge I have to get out on the ladder and climb up the outside. If I lose my grip I'll fall to the ground. I'm now above the trees, and I remember how, when the clouds hung really low in the autumn, you could sometimes convince yourself that you could touch the sky. I take a step out and stand on the ledge's handrail, holding tightly onto the rungs of the ladder. I put one foot on the bottom rung, then the other, and I'm hanging on an old iron ladder on the outside of a water tower. Only after climbing a couple of rungs do I notice that I'm holding my breath, and breathe out. I haul myself up onto the second ledge, and then I am in exactly the same spot, the exact same pose, as I was that first time I met Grim. I now realise for the first time just how much braver I was when I was sixteen.

I stand up, take a look around, and go over to the rope that's hanging a bit away from the ledge. I lean out over the railing and get hold of it, give it a tug to test it. The rope is thin and black. I wonder if he forced Sam to climb up on her own. If he did it before he hurt her.

To get onto the roof of the tower I need to climb the rope, with nothing underneath me. I look at my hands, red from the cramp-like grip I had on the metal rungs. It might not take the weight. Grim might have cut the rope, so that it's just hanging by a few small threads. I tug the rope again. It doesn't give way. I take a deep breath and haul myself out, over the edge of the ledge.

The rope starts to creak, once, then another time, and again. I struggle to get my footing back on the railing on the ledge, but it's no good; I'm too far out. I can't reach and I close my eyes, prepare myself for the fall, and hope that I don't land face first.

I DON'T FALL. I don't think so. I open my eyes and notice that I'm being winched up, jolting up a bit at a time. Someone's pulling me up. Soon my face is level with the water tower's roof — the thick, rounded concrete disc. I'm being hauled up gradually, until I can swing one leg round and crawl up onto the roof. It's windier up here, and I can feel the cold wind on my cheek.

'It's not going to be that easy,' a voice above me says, and I feel his hand grabbing my hair, so hard that I'm sure his grip is going to pull clumps of hair from my scalp.

I have time to see someone lying a little way away, in a red pool. Right in front of my face are two legs, and a hand in my hair is pulling me upwards. *He's trying to help me stand up*, I think to myself. Far too quickly for me to react, he smashes my face back down into the concrete. Something cracks — my nose, maybe — and my eyes water. Everything starts spinning, and the darkness, when it arrives, is threatening and unnaturally black.

XXVIII

There's buzzing in my ear, like feedback. I'm blind, I think. My eyes are open, but I can't see a thing. I blink, but all that happens is a slashing sensation and vibration in my temples, as though someone were drilling into them. Maybe the pain makes me scream; I don't know, but I think so, because as it wanes slightly there's a scraping in my throat.

I'm not blind. Everything is a tunnel, and somewhere, far away, is an opening that is growing, pushing the black walls of the tunnel to the periphery. I don't know how much time has passed, but it can't be that long. It's light around me, light and blurry, but gradually it gets sharper. My eyes are stinging because I don't want to blink. In the end I have to, and it flashes in my head again, but not as violently.

Grim is standing a little way away and sucking hard on a cigarette, taking two steps, turning around, taking two steps back the other way, turning around, another few steps. Just behind him, Sam. She's no longer lying down; maybe she wasn't before either. Everything happened so fast, I'm just not sure. She's sitting holding her hand, a red lump. She's pale.

I manage to sit myself up, which makes him come over and stare down at me. He's holding a black pistol. His eyes dart back and forth.

'Where are your colleagues?' he asks.

I try to say something, but I don't think I succeed, because he grabs my shoulder and pushes the pistol to my temple, asks again, screaming this time, where they are. Spit flecks my forehead, and I think I'm shaking.

'They don't know where I am.'

He lets go, backs away. I move my head from side to side, try to establish if anything's broken. Something must be, but there's no pain in my neck. I follow the thin black snake of a rope that leads from me to a little hook, projecting from the roof like a bent finger. The rope is attached by an intricate knot. A bit away from the hook, I notice, there's only a thin slip of rope left. The rest has worn away. He must have been up here before, many times.

'So you did as you were told, at least.'

I shrug my shoulders; my fingers fumble across my coat, looking for the pocket.

'I'm here now. You got what you wanted.'

My hand finds the pocket, grasps for the knife. It's not there. Grim's stare follows me, but reveals nothing. He might have taken it off me. It might have fallen out; it might be lying on the ground down there. I can feel my phone in the other pocket.

Sam looks up from her hand to me. Her hair is a mess, up in a plait like she sometimes has it when she's working. The plait looks worn out. Grim has been pulling it; maybe he dragged her along by it. A little bit to the right is what must be Sam's finger, a little stump lying in a pool of dark, dark red. She avoids looking at it. I lift my hand to my face; I'm not sure if I'm bleeding. I am, from the forehead. My nose and throat feel swollen and raw. I wipe the blood onto my jeans.

'Put the finger in your pocket,' I tell Sam.

'Shut up,' Grim says.

He swings an open palm towards my cheek. The slap feels muffled, the pain remote. It's still flashing inside my forehead. I think I'm bleeding internally, too, somewhere. My head is swollen, throbbing.

'Let her go.'

'No.'

Grim is just as straw-coloured as he was this morning, but he's no longer dressed in black. Instead, he's wearing light-blue jeans and a dark-green hoodie. It's him, my friend, and yet it isn't. He's hollow, emptier. He sits down on his haunches by the hook and adjusts the rope, quickly undoing the knot and then tying it back on.

He takes a little tube out of his pocket. His hands are shaking violently, making the pills rattle around inside it. He flips off the lid, takes a tablet, puts the lid back on, and stuffs the tube back in his pocket. Only now do I notice how he's sweating, how hot he looks.

'I tried,' he says, smiling apologetically. 'I really did try, Leo. But it ...' He laughs, to himself, as though it were an absurd thought. His eyes have that insane glint that you only see in people going through a psychotic episode. 'It didn't work.'

'I understand.'

'Do you?'

'Yes. I got the diary,' I say.

A dark veil falls over his face, and I'm surprised at just how crazed he looks.

'It's as though something inside me is driving me to this,' he says. 'I can't explain it.'

'You can let go of it,' I attempt. 'You can drop all of this. I saw the car, the Volvo down there. You can just drive away. No one needs to know anything.'

'Stop. You know what happened. Do you think I wanted this? Do you see that I feel completely ... How completely fucked everything turned out? And it all started with you, getting to know you.'

I need to stall for time. Maybe Birck can get here. Behind Grim, Sam is looking at her finger. Then, with her eyes on his back, she starts carefully moving towards it. But Grim turns, beats her to it. From here, where I'm sitting, it looks weird, as though his hand has an extra finger for a moment, before he throws it over the edge. Sam gasps.

'Take it easy,' I manage to force out, and look at Sam. 'Everything is okay.'

Sam nods slowly.

'Everything is okay,' repeats Grim, and he turns towards me. The pistol is dangling loose in his hand. 'Everything is okay.'

He laughs, an empty laugh, and looks past me, out over Salem. I glance at Sam, who looks like she's about to pass out. Her eyelids are heavy, and she rocks back and forth every now and then, as though she were falling asleep.

'Can you understand,' he starts slowly, with an urgent look about him, 'can you at least *understand* me? Can you understand what you did to me? To us?'

'Yes. I've told you that I understand.'

'In that case, can you understand why I have to do this?'

'No.'

He waves the weapon towards me and pulls the trigger.

I scream, I think, and my heart is beating so fast that my hands are shaking. The shot rings out and seems to echo over Salem. The bullet bounces off the concrete next to me, so close that I can feel it cleave the air as it bounces past. Grim's eyes flash back and forth between me and the pistol. I think he regrets it, that he realises he shouldn't have fired.

'You're not listening to me,' he says, calmer.

'I am listening to you. But you're not really making any sense.'

I get my phone out, simultaneously swiping the screen to unlock the keypad.

'Put it away.'

'No.'

'Put it away, now.'

'Let her go, and I'll put the phone away.'

Grim laughs, blankly.

'You're not the one who gets to decide here.'

'I know that,' I say, and look down at the phone.

'What are you doing? Put the phone down.'

I put the keylock on again, and put the phone down next to me. I struggle to get up — first one knee, then the other, and eventually I'm standing on my feet. My head is spinning; it feels heavy. I look for a chance to get close enough to him to reach him, close enough to disarm him. He's only using one hand — the other one is stuck to the weapon — but those seconds where I could make an attempt are too short, too risky. I'm afraid of Sam being hurt.

Grim looks at the phone, unsure, and waves the pistol.

'Throw it over.'

'If you want it, you'll have to come and get it.'

He doesn't dare. He'd have to bend down.

'You really don't get it, do you?'

He goes over to Sam, takes a tight hold of her plait, and pulls her up. Sam says nothing. Instead she's breathing noisily and laboriously, as though fighting against the panic.

We're in the middle of the roof. He pushes her in front of him, towards the edge of the roof, and Sam struggles, but the grip on her plait is hard to resist. She's holding her injured hand to her chest and is gripping it tightly with the other one; she can't use them to fight back. A shiny film of sweat covers her face, and she avoids my stare. As they get closer to the edge, she shifts her centre of gravity, like she's scared of burning herself on an invisible flame.

He pushes her again, so close to the rim that the point of Sam's shoe is now sticking out over the edge. I stretch out my arm, as if to break her fall. Grim just stares at me, until I take it down. I can smell his aftershave.

'She's innocent,' I say. 'She's done nothing wrong.'

'Like that makes a difference? Do I get anything back because of the difference? Do I get my life back, my family? Myself? Eh?' He stares at me. 'Answer!'

'No. But this won't give you anything back either.'

'All that matters are the consequences. And the consequences are the same. We will both have lost something.'

'It's not fair,' I whisper.

'Fair?' Grim looks confused. 'Do you think the world is fair?' Holding onto her plait, he pushes Sam in the back, forcing her to lean over the edge. 'Get back,' he says, looking at me.

I take a step back.

And then he lets go of her plait.

TIME SLOWS TO A CRAWL, as though gasping for air in vain, and I see Sam fall forwards, outwards, as Grim backs away. I throw myself towards her and grab hold of her coat, pull her to one side, and we fall on top of each other, Sam beneath me. I'm lying on her injured hand, but the adrenalin seems to be blocking out the pain because she doesn't say anything. Instead she looks at me, surprised, and then starts retching.

Behind me, I hear Grim pulling the tube of pills out again; I can hear it rattling in his hands.

XXIX

'You're sick in the head,' Sam says after several deep breaths to control the retching.

'That's probably very true,' Grim says, and wipes the sweat from his forehead with the back of his hand. 'I think you would be, too.' He looks at me. 'And it's your fault.'

'Please, Grim …' I start.

'It will soon be over, Leo.'

He might let me live. Maybe I'm just supposed to see Sam die. Or perhaps he's going to let us both live. He might be about to kill himself. Or he's chosen this place to give himself an escape route: if something doesn't go according to plan, he can always throw himself off. That might be why we're here. I don't know; anything's possible, Grim seems so unpredictable.

'You are right,' I say. 'You've lost your mind.'

Grim looks at Sam, who's still lying on her back, staring back at him. As I turn towards the centre of Salem, to see it one last time — weird, I think to myself, that this seems like an important thing to see; maybe it meant more than I realised — there's a flash of blue. Then it's gone. I can almost see the block I grew up in.

'What's your name?' I ask.

He looks up.

'Eh?'

'Daniel Berggren, Tobias Fredriksson, Jonathan Granlund. That's as far as I got.'

'Ah-ha.' Grim furrows his forehead slightly, and in that instant

I see Julia's face, her expression in his. 'It's not possible to get far enough to find that out.'

'That's why I'm asking.'

He seems to be contemplating for a moment, before shaking his head.

'Were you trying to stitch me up?' I ask instead. 'For Rebecca's murder?'

'What do you mean?'

'I just don't get wh—' I begin, but I don't know where to go with it because I just don't understand. All I know is that I have to try and spin this out. 'You've followed me. You've sent me text messages. The necklace in her hand, which put me at the scene of the crime, was that ... you could have done things differently.'

'How do you mean?'

'I don't know, but something more ... watertight. I don't know. What you did was never going to be enough to get me convicted. And yet you seem to have planned it all so carefully. I just can't make sense of it. Were you just trying to fuck things up for me, or what? I just don't get it.'

'I have no answer,' Grim says and looks at me, his eyes darting about. 'I can't explain it. But it all makes sense to me.'

'But not to anyone else.'

'I don't give a shit — this isn't about anyone else.'

'No, that's what I'm starting to think.'

'What do you mean?'

I take a deep breath. My head is throbbing.

'Do you remember the party at the rec?' I say.

'Eh?'

'The weekend before she died, there was a party on the rec.'

'Oh. Yes.'

'Everything you said back then about Julia, or about all of you ... it scared me. I got so fucking scared, for some reason. I can't remember if I'd been scared of you before, but I don't think I had. I think that was the first time. That was what made me have a go at Tim on the way home. And that was what made Tim ... yeah. Do what he did. It would never have happened if you hadn't been so fucking overprotective, if you hadn't taken it upon yourself to try and keep it all together.' I have to make a real effort not to look away. 'It is your fault that she died. It is your fault that your life turned out the way it did. Not mine. If you are going to take anyone's life, it should be your own, just like you wrote.'

Grim looks at me with glassy eyes, and I wonder how much time is passing, wonder what he's thinking.

'You're wrong,' he says.

'I don't understand how you can take it this far, just to ... well, what? Just for the sake of doing something? I don't buy that. This isn't going to make anything right; you're just pushing yourself towards your own destruction. Everything you've built up, I don't know how extensive that is, but everything you've built up is going to be fucked by this. You're not going to have anything left.'

'Good,' Grim shouts. 'That's what I want. Don't you get it? I prefer nothing. None of this means anything. The only thing that meant anything to me, I lost a long time ago. My whole life has been changed by that.'

'Why did you bother killing Rebecca Salomonsson? Why didn't you just let her go to the police?'

'She deserved it.'

'I think you're actually doing this to hurt yourself, not to get at me. You know full well what it would mean, being guilty of conspiracy to murder. You would never get away with it. This isn't about her, or us. This is all about you — so that you won't have any other way out. You know that it's your fault that it turned out like this.'

'You are wrong!' he screams, and bends down to grab hold of Sam's plait.

In that movement, as he bends himself over her, reaching for the plait with one hand and holding the pistol in the other, I take a step to one side and throw myself at him. Grim tries to get the nose of the pistol up to her temple, but my shoulder cracks against his ribs and he stumbles backwards. We fall to the roof. Grim's body is hard and bony underneath me. The smell of his aftershave, again. I think it's the same aftershave he's always used. And sweat. I notice for the first time just how bad Grim smells.

Half lying underneath me, he grabs my hair while I try to prise the pistol out of his hand. He lets go and hits me in the side instead; the blows make me gasp for air. He writhes quickly and powerfully, he's much stronger than me, and I'm about to fall off him, and then, any second, I think to myself, the shot will come and I'm going to die.

It comes, unintentionally, when Grim touches the trigger and it passes me, up towards the sky. From the corner of my eye, beyond Grim, who I'm lying on top of, I see the coil of rope straighten to a taut line. Grim stops for a second before he cranes his neck. Someone else is on the way up.

IT ALL HAPPENS QUICKLY: a heavy, black shoe seeking purchase against the roof; I see the beginning of a leg, equally black. Someone is trying to haul himself up.

I'm thrown off Grim, and fall on my back. My neck jerks backwards, followed by a cracking sensation inside it, a shooting pain that reaches up towards my ears and down across my shoulders.

Grim is standing over me, the barrel of the pistol like a never-ending black tunnel, just darkness followed by darkness. I strain to keep my eyes open, not to blink.

The shot is like a heartbeat. It's a weird sound, not one but two, which are bound together and follow one another. For some reason, Grim misses. There's a great bang on the concrete right by my ear, searing pain, and then the world goes quiet. I'm deaf in one ear. Grim stiffens, and grabs his arm before his leg collapses underneath him to the sound of another explosive bang that seems weirdly disorientating because I only hear half of it.

Someone screams — I don't know who — and as he falls, Grim pushes off with his good leg and grabs my shoulder; his eyes are glossy and wide. I smell his odour, the sweat and the aftershave in a sharp, sour mix, and I don't understand what he's trying to do until I realise that he is falling and I'm being dragged outwards, towards nothing, only thin air. He releases the pistol mid-movement, and it flies past me, out over the edge.

THE EDGE OF THE ROOF is cutting into my ribcage. I'm lying flat, pressing against it. My arms are outstretched, one in his armpit and the other on his injured shoulder. He stares at me, hanging there, his face contorted and purple-red. Grim is holding on tight, and gravity is pulling my jacket tighter and tighter around my neck.

'Let go,' he hisses. 'Let go of me.'

But, as if he realises that he's lost, that I'm not going to fall, he lets go himself, and the only thing stopping him from falling is me. He is too heavy. I'm going to drop him.

'Let me go now,' he screams. 'Let me fall …'

I try to lift him, pull him back up, but it's impossible. I'm starting to get cramp in my hands, and I'm struggling to breathe. With his uninjured arm, he tries to make me let go. When it doesn't work, he throws his head forward and bites my wrist. A shadow appears in my peripheral vision and crouches down. Two arms reach out, and a voice tells me not to let go.

Grim's bite breaks the skin. I can't see the wound, but the area around his mouth is spattered with a shiny red colour which is smeared over his lips. I feel nothing, no pain. The two arms grab hold of Grim, start pulling him up.

'No,' he screams, and his voice cracks, sounds erratic, like he's a teenager again. And then: 'No. No,' until the noises coming from his throat become meaningless, just sounds.

On one of the dark-clothed arms I read the word POLICE, embroidered in gold capital letters.

XXX

The first unit to arrive at the scene by the water tower was made up of an unlikely and — considering the task in hand — unsuitable pair: Dan Larsson and Per Leifby. Larsson comes from Vetlanda, and was sent to Stockholm by his father, a retired superintendent. He couldn't stand having his waster of a son around Vetlanda, and Larsson has been in Stockholm ever since. As if that isn't enough, he's also scared of heights. His partner Per Leifby, who, unlike Larsson, actually comes from Stockholm, supports Hammarby and isn't racist, but has expressed concerns about immigration — something widely known throughout the force. In addition to that, he is also scared of using firearms.

The vertigo sufferer had wanted to stay on the ground by the water tower. The one who was scared of guns, on the other hand, was on his way up the spiral stairs when the first shot rang out, the one Grim had fired to scare me. The sound made him go stiff and pale, and he turned around and headed straight back down again. They decided they would wait for the next unit to arrive. The opportunity to intervene had been, they would later plead with Birck, unsafe. Not only that, but their bulletproof vests were still in the car, which was behind a badly parked Volvo a little way away.

Larsson and Leifby were beat officers in Huddinge, and were a bit lost in Rönninge after exiting at the wrong junction when the call came through. The officer raising the alarm was Gabriel Birck of the city police, who claimed there was a hostage situation at the water tower in Salem.

Car after car was sent, all under orders from Birck to drive with blue lights but no sirens, for fear of scaring the suspect. The SWAT team were preparing for deployment, although they were unlikely to get there in time. Larsson and Leifby were at the foot of the tower in less than two minutes, and there they remained.

The second unit to arrive was, in marked contrast to the first, made up of two robust, competent inspectors from Södertälje: Sandqvist and Rodriguez. Both have backgrounds in the Stockholm force. They'd just finished a shift at a Salem school, where they had been involved in a drug-and-crime-prevention day for the pupils. They reached the base of the structure three-and-a-half minutes after the call went out. Larsson and Leifby explained the situation, and Sandqvist and Rodriguez scaled the spiral steps with their weapons drawn. It was Rodriguez who reached the top first, and fired live ammunition at Grim. He might have made it sooner, if he hadn't had to test the rope to make sure it would take his weight. He was also the one who, along with me, pulled Grim back up. Rodriguez's shot caused Grim's to miss me and hit the concrete instead, because it was fired a fraction of a second earlier. Together they sounded like that heartbeat I'd heard. Birck himself was down on the ground, well placed to hear the shots being fired from up on the tower, but not knowing who was holding the weapon.

All this is information that I find out later, when Birck tells me about it. When I wake up, I just remember relaxing and rolling onto my back, how the pain returned to my head, and how a veil fell over my eyes.

I'M LYING IN A LARGE BED, wearing a white shirt that isn't mine, with a pale-orange blanket covering my feet and up to my thighs. Above me, the lights are off, but there is some light coming from somewhere. I turn my head, and the pain seizes my neck. A desk-lamp is on. I'm in a hospital. I turn my head and look out the window. Södertälje, I think. I haven't been here since Julia died.

Birck is sitting on a chair in the corner of the room, engrossed in a file full of notes.

'I …' My mouth is parched.

Birck lifts his head, and looks at me with surprise.

'Eh?'

Outside the window, the country lies in the ambivalent gloom of bluish darkness. It could be dawn, or it could be dusk.

'What time is it?'

'Half-four.'

'Morning?'

Birck nods. He puts the file down, stands up, and walks over to the table next to the bed. He pours water into a plastic cup and gives it to me.

'Serax,' I say, and Birck shakes his head.

'Afraid not. You've had morphine. You can't go mixing them.'

I drink from the plastic cup. The water feels clean and smooth.

'What day is it?' I ask, unsure.

'Relax. You've been asleep for a little over twelve hours. You're going to be all right, don't worry. In spite of your gross stupidity.'

Birck's voice is lacking its usual blunt bass. Instead it is unexpectedly soft and low. It could be my hearing playing tricks on me. I can hear on both sides again, but a thick lid covers one ear. I lift my hand, and the bandage feels rough and dry against my fingers.

'For your head injuries,' Birck says, and takes the cup off me. 'Why the hell didn't you wait?'

'I didn't have time,' I manage. 'Where's Sam?'

'In the next room. She's going to be okay. Physically, I mean. Apart from the finger. We found it, but by then it was too late. Far too late.'

'How long?'

Birck looks away.

'At least an hour. She's going to be okay, Leo, but … she's in

286

shock. So, mentally, it might well take a while. Her boyfriend is here somewhere, if you want to talk to him.'

Even though it really hurts, I turn my head away from Birck. I don't want to hear any more. Birck stands there next to me, as though he knows.

'And Grim?' I say, still facing away from him.

'He's not here.'

'Where?'

'Huddinge. Under constant supervision. I chose the officers myself, so they're good. He was operated on, and will be moved to Kronoberg Remand Centre as soon as he's discharged from hospital.' He clears his throat. 'Your family were here. They sat with you for a while. Levin came about eleven, and he's only just left. Everyone has been informed.'

'My ... my dad, too?'

'Him, too.'

I look at him, and wonder if he knows. If he's worked it out. Maybe.

'Your psychologist was here,' says Birck, tentatively. 'He was called in because his name was in your diary. I sent him away.'

'Thanks.'

One corner of his mouth is twitching, but he doesn't say anything.

'Tired,' I say, instead.

'You need more sleep.'

'No, you. You look tired.'

'I've had a few reporters to deal with. As well as the preliminary investigation to go through.'

'My phone.'

I want it for some reason. I don't really know what I plan to do with it, but I want it. I think I want to see the picture of Rebecca Salomonsson's face again.

'I can't give it to you yet, because Berggren, or Grimberg, or whoever the fuck he is, used it to communicate with you, and furthermore he had the good taste to record the injuries that he caused Sam. It's evidence now. And,' he adds, 'are you sure you don't want a new one?'

'Save the pictures,' is all I say.

'Carry on sleeping.' His eyes flicker, as though he is hesitating. 'Levin says he's going to try and get you back in the force. On my team.'

'With you?' I think I grimace. 'For fuck's sake.'

'I thought you might feel like that.'

He smiles slightly.

'Thanks,' I force out.

Birck leaves the room.

NEXT TIME I WAKE UP, it's lunchtime, I think. They move my drip out of the way, and I have a sandwich, drink some juice, go to the toilet. My footsteps are cautious but surprisingly steady. Later in the day, I get a visit from Pettersén, head of the preliminary investigation. He's a short, pear-shaped man who chews gum incessantly in order to distract himself from the fact that what he actually wants is a cigarette.

'I need to ask you a few questions,' he says quietly. 'If that's okay.'

'I want Birck to do it.'

'That's not possible. This is my job. And Gabriel needs to rest.'

He puts a dictaphone down between us. The few questions he poses multiply the more I tell him, and Pettersén excuses himself to go to the toilet, changes chewing gum once, then twice, and then three and four more times.

I GET DISCHARGED that evening. I'm able to put on my own clothes, which have been washed in the intervening twenty-four hours. In spite of this, just the sight of them makes me uneasy. The bandage around my head has been replaced with a big white plaster on my forehead and something similar over one ear. Apparently my nose

288

isn't broken; it's just a hairline fracture, an injury that will take care of itself. I get some morphine for the first few days. Then I ask if I can see Sam.

'She's asleep,' says the nurse.

'Is anyone else there?'

'She's alone. Her partner just went back to their place.'

Their place? They live together?

I am given permission to sit with her for a little while. Sam is lying in a bed identical to my own, with the same orange blanket over her legs, and she's wearing a white shirt that's the same as the one I had on. Her hair is down now; the plait is gone. Her breathing is deep and regular. The visitor's chair is placed right next to the bed, and I lower myself onto it.

A thick bandage is wrapped around the injured hand. Her good hand is lying open with her palm facing the ceiling, her fingers slightly bent. The sight of them makes everything start swaying, and I wonder why that should be, until I realise.

I did this. No matter how odd that seems, how far back the chain of events goes, and regardless of how many coincidences had to align themselves in a straight line to bring about the events of the last few days, it still started with me. With me destroying Tim Nordin, pushing him over the edge. With me pulling the wool over Grim's eyes. Maybe he was right; maybe I did make Julia fall for me. But she wasn't the only one who fell. I wasn't the only one to blame. If anyone fell, it was me.

I reach out my hand and lay it carefully in Sam's. She is warm. The touch seems to slowly bring her back to the surface, because before long she turns her head towards me.

'Ricky?' she asks, sluggishly, apprehensively, still asleep and her eyes still closed.

'No,' I say quietly. 'Leo.'

'Leo,' she repeats, as though testing how it feels in her mouth. I think she's smiling. She squeezes my hand carefully.

REBECCA SALOMONSSON'S PARENTS have once again been informed, and this time with the real reason for their daughter's death. Whoever robbed her near Kronoberg Park is still at large — most likely somewhere in Stockholm, maybe even on Kungsholmen. It's unusual for offenders to cover a lot of ground.

As far as I can tell, the media don't know the background to the bizarre events that took place on the roof of the water tower. That drama fills the front pages, but my involvement has been covered up. Despite this, I know that interest will soon turn to me again, unless something more interesting happens. Maybe the whole story, starting with my friendship with Grim and my relationship with Julia, will come out sooner or later. I don't know. Right now, I don't care. I think about Anja, the woman Grim had once loved. She died, just like so many others seem to.

I might one day come to understand the man who was once my friend, work out what it was he was actually trying to do. Maybe not. That's so often the way, with things that turn out to be crucial; we just don't understand.

ONCE I'VE BEEN DISCHARGED from the hospital in Södertälje, I head north using public transport. It feels good, to just be a lonely individual among thousands of other equally lonely people. I'm wearing a hat to hide the bandages. Nobody seems to notice. The only odd thing about my appearance is my swollen, red nose, but nobody looks in my direction. On the commuter train, I pass the tower blocks of the million-homes project. Somewhere close by, someone is throwing firecrackers on the platform. The sound scares me; I stiffen up, and I can feel my pulse racing. I'm under doctor's orders not to take Serax. They've given me Temazepam instead, for emergencies. I don't know if this is one, but it feels like it. I pull the packet out of my inside pocket and pop a tablet on my tongue. It dissolves by itself, fast.

Instead of getting the bus from Rönninge, I decide to walk it. I pass a poster featuring the prime minister's face. Using black spray-paint, someone has embellished it with a swastika.

I remember how, on my way back from trips into town when I was growing up, I would always look out for the water tower as a marker for how much of the journey was left. You see it from miles away. This time, I avoid it. I keep my eyes fixed on the ground, on my shoes, and wonder how many times I've walked this stretch. I wonder who still lives here, of all the people I used to know. It's probably not that many, but I don't know. People have a tendency to get stuck in places like this. People from concrete satellite towns like Tumba, Salem, and Alby. Either you make your way out and disappear, or something keeps you there.

Rebecca Salomonsson. I see her as Peter Koll must have seen her, above and from a slight angle, how she hobbles down the street, high as a kite and with her hand to her mouth, not knowing that she has only a few minutes left to live. Koll thought it was nausea, but perhaps she was crying about just having had her bag stolen.

I am going to have to see Grim, again. I know it, but at the moment I am trying hard to suppress any thoughts of him. I try to remember exactly what I was doing on this day, at this time, sixteen years ago, but it's impossible. I realise that I can no longer recollect what her face looked like when she laughed, but for a second I can almost feel it, Julia's skin against mine. My skin remembers.

In my inside pocket, I'm still carrying Grim's diary entries, and as I feel the envelope with my fingertips, I notice something else: a sheet of paper, stiff and folded in half. I know of only one person who communicates like this. Levin must somehow have sneaked it into my pocket during his visit to the hospital.

I'm glad I can sit at your bedside and hear your breathing. Hear that you're alive, just as I did after the events on Gotland. Events which, no matter how you look at it, can be traced back to me, not you.

I was given a memo. It instructed me to put you on our unit: someone who could be held to account if necessary. They'd done a search and considered you an eligible candidate. Everything was hypothetical, 'if', 'in the worst case', and 'in the event of one of our operations being compromised'.

It came from above, from the paranoid people, and I had no choice. They were threatening to leak details from my past. They still are. I can't say any more. Not now.

Forgive me, Leo.

Charles.

I TRY TO ESTABLISH what I'm feeling, now that I actually know. The knowledge ought to come with some relief; perhaps it does, but that means nothing right now. I feel nothing. Everyone betrays everyone, and everything falls down. I know surprisingly little about Levin's background, and I wonder what they've got on him, what made him obey.

I stand near the Triad, on the other side of the road. The blocks look like they did last time I was here, and the time before that, and the time before that. Time swooshes past inside my head, until I'm sixteen again and I'm standing in front of our block, on my way home from somewhere. It looks exactly like this. Certain things only change on the inside.

I take the lift up to the seventh floor, then walk the few steps up to the eighth and highest floor. I look at the door, at JUNKER, push the handle down, and carefully open the door.

'Hello?' I say, hearing my own voice, unsure.

The rug in the hall is a bit rumpled, but the hall looks otherwise untouched. The smell in here is the same, as though it were eternal. From the opening into the kitchen, my mum pops her head out. Her short hair is flecked with grey.

'Oh my God, Leo.'

She lets go of something, presumably crockery, and doesn't bother washing her hands. Instead she puts her arms around me and gives me a hug. I reciprocate carefully. I can't remember the last time I got a hug from either of my parents.

'I … we came to the hospital, but they said you were asleep. Oh goodness, is it … we talked to a policeman there, we got so …'

'It's okay, Mum.'

She looks at me. I've always thought I had my dad's eyes, but the older I get, the more I think that the ones I see in the mirror are, in fact, my mother's.

'Are you hungry?'

'No. How's Dad getting on?' I ask.

'Good,' she says. 'He's sitting in there.'

'Did he really go with you?'

She nods.

'Are you sure you're not hungry?'

'Yes.'

'You look a bit skinny. Come in.'

I sigh, frustrated that she can still make me feel like I'm twelve again, and I step out of my shoes, take my jacket off. She goes back into the kitchen. I go in to what was once my room. It's a sort of home office now, with a desk, computer, bookcases, and wardrobes. At the table, my father is hunching over something, in that way that only people capable of weirdly intense concentration do. He's wearing a checked shirt. His grey hair hasn't been combed, and he runs his hand through it.

'Damn thing,' he mumbles. 'Damn … where's it got to, where have I …'

'Dad,' I say, carefully putting my hand on his shoulder.

'Leo?' He looks up at me. His gaze is emotional, glossy, and medicated. 'Is that you?'

'Yes, it's me.'

'Leo,' he repeats, not sure what to do with the information.

'Your son,' I say.

His eyes look sad. He frowns, turns back to whatever's lying on the desk in front of him.

'I need help. I can't remember how to do this.'

It's a remote control, lying buttons-down on the desk. The battery compartment is open, and three batteries lie spread out around it.

'Do you really not remember, Dad?'

'It is ... it's there somewhere, right at the back.' He blinks over and over again, his stare fixed on the opening, the small coils sticking out inside it. 'I almost remember.' He looks up. The sadness is gone. He smiles. 'You hear that? I almost remember.'

'Shall I help you?'

'Let him do it himself,' my mother says, standing in the doorway. 'He remembers. He just needs to make the effort.'

I look at my parents — first one, then the other.

'Mum, I don't think he's going to manage it.'

'He will.'

A few years ago he started forgetting things: where he'd put the keys, what he'd had for dinner, when he'd last spoken to me or my brother on the phone. At first, we didn't react. Instead, we were irritated by him forgetting whether or not he'd made coffee. When he actually had made it, he'd forget whether or not he'd turned the coffee machine off. It went quickly: before long, someone called the police. They wanted to report a man sitting in his car outside a school, staring at the kids through the windscreen. The person making the complaint was worried about the children — as, presumably, was the unit that responded. They soon realised that he was telling the truth about having forgotten the way to work.

'Does he understand what has happened?'

'He understands that something has happened,' she says. 'He's about to have his medication; he'll be better once he's had it.'

I study his back. The front door opens. It's my brother, still wearing his work clothes. He gives me a long hug, and I think I respond to it.

'How are you?' he asks.

'I think I can't hear very well.'

'That's good.' He slaps me on the back. 'Then you don't have to listen to all the bullshit.'

For some reason, this makes me laugh. In the office, my father drops one of the batteries onto the floor, and it rolls off under one of the bookcases. My brother goes straight in to help him.

'Leo?' my father says, unsure, looking at him.

'Leo's in the hall, Dad,' my brother says, distracted, looking for the battery.

'Uh-huh.' He's looking out the window; his stare is uneasy, and his hands are tightly locked round the armrests of his chair, as though it were the only thing stopping his head from floating off. 'Leo is in the hall.' He smiles and turns his head, looks at me. 'Good.'

LATE THAT EVENING, I leave Salem. I step out into the cool air, and out of the corner of my eye I see the entrance that used to be theirs — see it there, waiting in the darkness. I don't want to leave yet, and I go and prowl outside their door, as I used to then. It's summer again, for a second, a summer from long ago.

And after a while: I leave. I walk towards the bus stop, to get into Rönninge and carry on further south. I want to sit with Sam, at the hospital. There's a fog moving in. I make my way through the place where I grew up, and it's a long way home, but tonight everything in Salem is unusually quiet. Stockholm's southern suburbs are all but silent.

Afterword

As authors, we take liberties. In this book, I have taken many: among other things, I have re-imagined a number of details surrounding the water tower, and its form. I've squeezed in a bar here, a homeless shelter there, rechristened a trio of high-rise blocks, and so on. Not to mention the great many lines of text I've taken the liberty of inserting!

There are a few people I need to thank. Mela, Mum, Dad, my little brother, Karl, Martin, Tobias, Jack, Lotta, Jerzy, Tove, Fredrik, and my wonderful Swedish publishers, Piratförlaget: one way or another, you have all contributed to making sure that Leo Junker and *The Invisible Man from Salem* actually saw the light of day.

It is never easy to write a story, but to be the partner, friend, parent, or colleague of the author in question is probably harder still. You are all fantastic.